I begin to wish the Wolfs did not live next door. They only came last year: before that it was nice, dull old Mr and Mrs Bloxham, who were ever so old and quiet. I believe Nanny is just a little frightened too, and even Mother is crosser than ordinary.

I told Nanny about meeting Mrs Wolf and Pa in the park, and about the birds and having to take Mrs Wolf home. Nanny sucked her teeth and tut-tutted a bit, pretending not to look worried. Then she said I mustn't laugh at Mrs Wolf (I wasn't laughing) and your father has too kind a heart for his own good, always has had. Now cut along, Miss Lally, do, and get your hands washed for tea.

But later, I heard her talking to Milne on the back stairs. 'The balloon's about to go up, Clarice' (that's Milne's Christian name, but only Nanny is allowed to call her it) 'you mark my words. And when it does, I want my girls out of it. Whatever can Master Ned be thinking of?'

'She's a beauty, Em, that's what he's thinking of, even though she may be missing a screw or two in the top storey. And Master Ned is Master Ned, as both of us have cause to know.'

About the Author

Virginia Budd was born into a large family and spent much of her childhood travelling, including visits to India and Malta. She has worked in several different jobs – PR, advertising, and insurance amongst others – and experience of these, together with her studies of local history, have combined to add authenticity and originality to her writing. She has lived in London and Bath and has now moved to Colchester.

VIRGINIA BUDD

FATHERS

CORONET BOOKS
Hodder and Stoughton

The CIP catalogue record for this book is available from the British Library

ISBN 0-340-56342-7

Printed and bound in Great Britain for Hodder and Stoughton Paperbacks, a division of Hodder and Stoughton Ltd., Mill Road, Dunton Green, Sevenoaks, Kent TN13 2YA (Editorial Office: 47 Bedford Square, London WC1B 3DP) by Clays Ltd., St Ives plc.

PART I

I have decided to be a famous author when I grow up. Mother's friend Mrs Fanshaw came to tea today, and her Aunt Maud is paid for writing things for the newspapers. Why cannot I? Mrs Fanshaw's Aunt Maud wrote a fairy story and the newspaper paid her 5s. I can tell fairy stories *easily*. But first I am going to write a diary for *ever and ever*, all through my life. Suki says I will not keep it up. Mother says I should go out more and play with my little friends. Little friends, my eye. Hilda and Muriel French aren't little and Bernard is huge and the Browns are horrid. Pa says I'm a rum little thing and a bit of a pickle and why shouldn't I write fairy stories if I want to? I do love Pa. Miss Beastly Brownlow says The child must learn to concentrate, and if she can't learn her tables now she is twelve, when can she? I say Never, they are stupid and silly and give me a headache, so there. It is snowing quite hard now. I have just got out of bed to find a new nib for my pen (there's a blot of ink on the sheet, who cares). While I was out of bed I drew back the curtain and looked out into the square. The trees are white and the poor cab horses on the rank on the corner are covered in snow. Noisy, smokey old London is all quiet in its white blanket. The bars on the window are white too. The fire is nearly out, so I cannot write any more even with the new nib, my hands are too cold. But I will, I'll go on writing my diary every day for ever and ever (perhaps not every day).

2nd January   Nanny is fussing about the ink blot on my sheet. What will madam say? That sheet has only just been turned and money is running short. Nanny does talk nonsense.

Suki and Bob and me went sliding in the park today, it was such ripping fun. Suki fell down and hurt her knee. She blubbed so much Nanny had to take her home. Bob and me stayed on and came back with Mrs Wolf and Julian. Mrs Wolf is beautiful and sad and wears lovely clothes. Bob says Julian is a milksop, but I don't think he is, he can climb better than any of us and he does make some awfully funny faces. Today he pretended to be the Queen sitting on the lavatory. Mrs Wolf cried, 'Oh dearest boy, please stop. Whatever would your father say?' But Julian did it even more and made rude

3

noises as well. Bob laughed so much he fell over, and that made poor Mrs Wolf sadder than ever. She was wearing a grey fur hat with violets tucked into the brim and she carried a matching muff. Her hair is dark and curly and never quite tidy, but ever so pretty.

Julian has asked us to his birthday party next Wednesday, he will be fourteen. There is to be a conjurer, he says. When we told Nanny she made her clicking noise and said she didn't know, she would have to ask madam. What is wrong with Mrs Wolf and why doesn't Mother like her? Bob says it's because she is married to Mr Wolf, who is a Jew and awful. Our Lord was a Jew so what is wrong with being one? But Mr Wolf is horrid. He is small with a yellow, cross face. He wears a coat with a fur collar and his hat is too big for his head. He looks rather wicked. Why did poor Mrs Wolf marry him? Pa likes Mrs Wolf. I have seen them walking together in the square and once Mrs Wolf was smiling. I do hope Mother will let us go to Julian's party. I want to see inside their house and Julian says there will be a band and dancing as well as a conjurer. This is the second entry in my diary. Who says now I cannot keep it up?

3rd January We are to be allowed to go to Julian Wolf's party. Hurray! Mother didn't want us to, but Pa came back from the office while she was telling us. 'We cannot be rude, Elvira,' he said, 'they are, after all, our neighbours. I give you Mr W. is not quite what the doctor ordered, but Mrs W. is a fine woman and much put upon from what I hear.' Mother went red and pulled at the buttons on her blouse. She always does this when she is cross. 'If you say so, Ned, but it is not what I hear. I confess I am not very good with the *nouveaux riches* and the Wolfs are Israelites to boot.' Pa made his snorting noise and tossed back his hair. That's what *he* does when he is angry. 'For the Lord's sake, Elvira, move with the times. This is the twentieth century and all this talk of *nouveaux riches* and Israelites is out of date. We've reached the new millenium; all such old fashioned, nonsensical prejudice will soon be swept away and the old class system gone for ever. Besides, to talk of *nouveaux riches* is surely not quite right; my own grandfather, when all is said and done, was a mere country saddle-maker, and yours, if I remember rightly, a jumped-up attorney in a small provincial town.' 'Upstairs, children!' Mother looked as if she was going to cry. 'You may go to the party, and your pocket money this week can be spent on buying the Wolf boy a birthday present.'

It's funny how Mother always manages to have the last word.

5th January   Bob stole this diary and read it, the bully. He says it's not a proper diary 'cos I don't tell who I am. I say there is no need to tell that 'cos I know who I am and I am the only person who will ever read it 'cos diaries are secret. 'Yours isn't now,' he shouted, dancing round the nursery holding the diary above his head. I tried to get it from him and he fell backwards into Dobbin and hit his head. I snatched the diary, but tripped over the rug and knocked Nanny's little china lighthouse from Margate off the shelf by the fire and it smashed in the grate. Then Bob and I made it up and hid the pieces, and if Nanny asks where it is, we're going to say Polly broke the lighthouse when she was dusting. It's wrong to lie, I know, but sometimes you have to, and besides Polly is always breaking things. Bob is going away to school next September. I am glad, I think. He's so rough and rude now, and never wants to play our special games any more, he says they are sissy. But perhaps he is right and I should say who I am. It would make my diary more interesting, especially if I am to become a famous author.

My name is Alice Mary Morgan, but I am always called Lally. Pa says its 'cos Bob could say Ally (short for Alice). But Pa says Lally seemed the right name anyway, it suits a little girl with freckles and red hair, so there I am. Mother calls me Alice when she's angry, but no one else does. I am twelve years old, but will be thirteen in September. I live at No 6 St Wilfred's Square, Kensington, in a tall, thin, red house with bars on the top-floor windows, a green front door with a lion's-head door knocker, and a plane tree in the garden. The plane tree has a squirrel living in it, and once we saw a woodpecker. You can hear the underground trains from our house, and Pa says if we get much more traffic in the square, the houses will fall down and what is the place coming to?

Pa's name is Ned (short for Edward, but no one calls him that) Morgan. He is a book publisher and sometimes writes for the newspapers. The books he publishes are pretty dull, actually. Dictionaries and sermons and things about engines. He says they are our bread and butter, as people will always want dictionaries and books about engines, no matter what. He also publishes French and German novels with orange paper covers and small, smudgy print. Mother says she'll not have these in the house, but Pa brings them home all the same. I'm going to learn French as soon as I can so that I may read them. Mother is called Elvira Elizabeth Morgan. She has yellow hair and is tall and thin. She's quite pretty, but not as pretty as Mrs Wolf next door. I have one brother called Bob, who is nearly fourteen, and one sister, Suki, who is nine. So I am in the middle. I am the cleverest of the family. Just as well, says Mother, 'cos she'll never be a beauty with that hair and complexion; where she gets it from I cannot imagine, it certainly does not come from my side. But I don't care what Mother says. Polly says I've got eyes that will drive the boys wild, and that's all that matters really, isn't it, to have plenty of chaps to choose from?

We have a cook called Mrs Jessop, who is always angry and smells of mothballs, and a kitchen maid called Annie. Annie has only just come, the one before was called Nokes and ran away one night with the butcher's boy and the joint for Sunday's dinner. Then there is Milne, our parlour maid, who looks like a waxwork and never smiles. Polly, who is ever so nice, and my friend, helps her. And Nanny, who is a hundred years old and looked after Pa when he was little. Nanny wears a widow's cap like the Queen and has a mole with whiskers growing out of it on her chin. I think I love Nanny – it's hard to tell when you've never not known a person. We have a dog called Pincher, the colour of marmalade, and woolly all over with white tips to his paws. We have had Pincher since he was a tiny puppy, Pa found him in a paper bag on the floor of a hansom. The cabby said his last fare must have left him behind and he certainly didn't want him, so Pa brought him home and we all love him, except Mother and Mrs Jessop don't.

The person I have left until last is Miss Beastly Brownlow, who is our governess. That is, she is Suki and mine and Hilda and Muriel French's, who live at No 10. She comes every

6

morning and gives us lessons in the study. She is the horridest person I know. She is fat and squidgy, with tiny eyes like buttons and a bun like a mouse on top of her head. We don't think that she ever changes her clothes and she smells of sweat. She keeps a switch in the pocket of her skirt to hit us with. Her voice is whiny and very quiet, and she creeps up behind you and suddenly shouts in your ear. When Bob goes to Eton, Pa says I can go to St Christopher's School and give up Miss Beastly. How I long for that day.

There now, I've told everything. Except that every summer we go to Granny Morgan's for a month and it is lovely, and every Christmas we go to Granny Lloyd's, which is not very nice and where it is always cold and there is not enough to eat.

Only three more days before Julian Wolf's party. I am to wear my green velveteen, and we have bought him a cricket bat for the summer. I hope he likes it, it was very expensive and took all our pocket money.

9th January   I must tell about Julian Wolf's party. It is the most important experience of my life. I will never feel the same after meeting Rupert Eagon. I think that yesterday I grew up.

I am writing in bed as I have been sent upstairs for cheeking Miss Beastly again. This morning in history she said Oliver Cromwell was a good man who did his best. I said he wasn't and he didn't. She said not to be impertinent and I was a Miss Clever-Stick who must be taught a lesson. I said I thought that was what she was supposed to be there for, and Pa didn't like Cromwell either. She smacked my hand with her switch (the hardest she's ever done, I nearly blubbed) and said she would tell Mother. I don't care. I stole a candle from the pantry cupboard so I can write my diary, and I wasn't hungry anyway.

I do not think Julian was very pleased with his cricket bat (it was Mother's idea). He said he doesn't play many games, actually, but it was the thought that counted, and he could see it would be a ripping present for most fellows.

I wore my green velveteen dress, a green hair ribbon and my seed pearl necklace I had as a present for being a bridesmaid at Aunty Dollie's wedding last year, Suki wore her blue and a blue bow in her hair, and Bob wore his new suit and a

7

stick-up collar. He looked ever so grown up. Quite the little toff, Nanny said. Mother said he was her darling boy and not to get jelly down his waistcoat like he did at the Browns' party before Christmas.

The Wolfs have a butler *and* a footman. Their front door looks just like ours does, but their inside is not like our inside at all. First of all the house is so warm – hot, really, like the orchid house at Kew. Everywhere is covered with thick carpets so your feet sink right in. There are hundreds of pictures on the walls and a full-size statue of a nearly naked lady carrying a torch in the hall. There is a funny smell everywhere (Nanny says this is incense; 'That stuff them Romans have in their churches'; but surely the Wolfs aren't Romans?) The footman – who winked at me when Nanny wasn't looking – took us upstairs to take our cloaks off. Such a bedroom! All pink satin stuff and velvet, with lovely bows. White lace curtains round the bed and pretty, frilly pillowcases. When you lie on the bed you can see yourself in a great big mirror on the wall opposite – I know, I tried it. 'Get off there at once, Miss Lally,' Nanny shouted, 'or it's home to bed for you!' But I didn't, it was so lovely just lying there feeling beautiful and rich and wiggling my toes on the satin quilt. Then Nanny had to stop Bob, who had put on some lady's cloak and was pretending to be a Prussian cavalry officer, so she forgot about me.

Then the footman came back – he winked at me again – and took us downstairs to the drawing-room, which is ever so big and has glass doors leading on to a conservatory. We don't have a conservatory in our house, I wish we did. The drawing-room is the grandest room I have ever seen – grander even than Hampton Court. All the furniture is golden and the walls are covered in rose-pink brocade. Over the fireplace there is a picture of Mrs Wolf, not looking sad, wearing a green riding habit. She's holding the bridle of a black horse and seems to be in the middle of a sort of forest. There are lots of other pictures too, but I only remember the one of Mrs Wolf. An orchestra was playing in a little room that led off the drawing-room, but the doors were folded back so you could hear quite easily. The floor was polished and covered with bright-coloured rugs with strange birds and flowers on them, except where there was a space cleared for dancing.

There were quite a lot of children there, but they weren't talking much, just giggling. I saw one boy with spots, fiddling with a sort of brass chain that hung down from a lamp above his head, and it came off (the chain, I mean, not the boy's head). He put it in his pocket and looked round to see if anyone had noticed. When he saw me looking at him, he stuck out his tongue, the rude thing.

'How lovely to see you, my dears,' Mrs Wolf said. She was wearing a white, lacy dress with a pink sash and had little gold combs in her hair. She looked like a beautiful, sad swan. 'Julian is *so* pleased that you have come.' That was when Julian said he didn't want a cricket bat.

'Pretty boring show, this,' he whispered to Bob, 'but it pleases the Mater.' I was beginning to think it pretty boring myself. The conjurer was the same one they had at the Browns' party, so we knew all his tricks and they weren't very good ones anyway. One boy shouted he'd seen a lady behind the curtain with the rabbit in a basket, so it couldn't be a magic one. The conjurer looked quite cross and told him not to spoil the fun for the other boys and girls.

After the conjurer we had dancing, but no one danced. The music played and played and all the children just sat round giggling and fighting, and Mrs Wolf stood about looking as if she wanted to cry. Then suddenly the drawing-room door opened and there was Mr Wolf. He looked like the Demon King in the pantomime at Drury Lane on Boxing Day, and all the children suddenly stopped giggling and the orchestra stopped playing.

'What, no dancing?' Mr Wolf has a funny, hoarse, foreign sort of voice. 'And I hire a band especially? But this I cannot have. Come, my dear, let us show them how it is done.' And he put out his arms to Mrs Wolf. She walked across the floor towards him as though she were fastened to a chain and he was pulling, her white dress trailing on the shining floor and her little gold combs glinting in the lamplight. 'A waltz, my friends, I think,' Mr Wolf shouted to the leader of the orchestra, and as the music started he took Mrs Wolf in his arms so roughly that she gave a little cry. But still none of the children moved, it was as though Mr Wolf had cast a spell over us all.

Then suddenly a boy was standing in front of me (Suki and I

9

were sitting together, Nanny was in the parlour with the other nannies). 'May I have the honour of this dance, we can't leave it all to our host and hostess, don't you agree? You do waltz, I take it?' For a moment I couldn't believe the boy was talking to me, he looked so grown-up and handsome.

'Oh yes,' I said at last, 'I practised with my father at Christmas and we go to Miss Mentoni's every Thursday afternoon.'

The boy smiled – such a lovely smile. 'We should be well suited, then. I learned last half at school, our housemaster's wife is keen on that sort of thing, and I practise with m'sisters. Can you reverse?'

And I can too. Oh praise be for dearest Pa!

My legs were a little wobbly at the start, and when we came to a corner I nearly stumbled and fell. 'Steady up,' the boy said, as though I were a horse, and then I was all right. Soon other couples were dancing, and the music went faster and faster until we were flying round the floor. I shut my eyes and I seemed to be floating through the sky with the waltz music in a great cloud all around me. Faster, faster, faster . . .

Then suddenly the music stopped and I opened my eyes. The boy was looking at me. 'You're a great little goer,' he said, 'and I don't even know your name.'

'Lally,' I said, 'Lally Morgan. I live next door at No 6.'

'Hullo, Eagon, you frightful tick, what are you doing with my sister?' Bob barged up (one of his collar studs had come out and his hair was sticking up on end, he won't let Nanny put stuff on it, he says it's not manly). 'I didn't know you knew each other. Look here, young Wolf says some fellows have a game going in the billiard room – coming?' How I hate Bob sometimes.

'How could anyone as ghastly as you, Morgan, have a sister like this,' Rupert (that's his name) said. 'It's not possible. I always thought you crawled out from under a stone.'

'Well, I always thought you were born in the monkey house at the zoo, you old lump of cat meat,' Bob said, and then they were on the floor punching each other and behaving like stupid babies.

'Boys, *please* – one must not fight in the ballroom, and it is time for tea.' Mrs Wolf swayed beside us. She had a screwed-up handkerchief in one hand and bits of her hair had started to come down. Rupert jumped to his feet, pulling Bob with him. 'I'm ever so sorry, Mrs Wolf. We're a pair of absolute oafs. Can you ever forgive us? Actually, I was just about to escort Miss Morgan here to the dining-room when we were, er, interrupted.'

Mrs Wolf smiled; just a tiny smile, as though she thought she might get slapped if she smiled too much. She was looking at Rupert as if he were a grown-up. 'Were you really, dear, how charming. I saw you dancing together – so pretty. Bob, dear, your collar stud, it seems to have come out. I wonder if Nanny . . .' She floated away.

Rupert took my arm – he's ever so tall for a boy, and had to bend down. 'I may look in at the billiard room later,' he said to Bob, 'if young Wolf's governor ain't there, that is. Young Wolf's a good un, but his Pater . . . Meanwhile, Miss Lally Morgan and yours truly are about to partake of jellies and ice cream.'

Such a spread in the dining-room! Tables and tables of it. All the usual things you have at parties and lots of other things as well – funny, spicy bits of chicken and queer little cakes. Rupert said they were special food for Jews. 'But Mrs Wolf can't be a proper Jew,' I said, 'she goes to church on Sunday.'

'She ain't, poor thing,' Rupert said, 'my Pater says that's part of the trouble.' Then we forgot about Mrs Wolf, and Rupert told me about school and how he's a dry bob. At Eton, he says, there are wet and dry bobs; wet ones are rowing men and dry ones play cricket. His people live in Onslow Square, he said, but they also have a place in Devonshire. He was at the same private school as Bob and captain of the first eleven. 'Your bro's a damned good bat,' he said (Pa says so too). 'He should do well at Eton.'

Then, just as I was trying a funny, puffy pastry thing filled with fish, Nanny came worrying up. 'Wherever have you been, Miss Lally? You shouldn't go off and leave your sister on her own like that. Madam found her crying, and not a sign of you or Master Bob anywhere.' I wanted to hit her, I felt so ashamed and babyish still having a Nanny.

'My fault, I'm afraid.' Rupert shook Nanny's hand (she was looking at him just like Mrs Wolf had). 'I kidnapped Miss

11

Lally. We were waltzing together, you see, and after that the least I could do was escort her in to tea. Am I forgiven? My name, by the way, is Rupert Eagon, and for a brief period I shared the same educational establishment as Master Bob. I gather he will shortly be joining me at an even larger establishment of similar ilk.'

Nanny made her gobbling turkey noise. 'That's as may be, sir,' she said, 'but you weren't to know Miss Lally's little sister was with her, and Miss Lally did. Look after your own first, I always say, and the world can take care of itself.'

'How right you are, how very right.' I could see Rupert was trying not to laugh and I wanted to sink through the floor. 'All that is left for me to do,' Rupert went on, 'is to make myself scarce and join Miss Lally's reprobate brother in the billiard room. Goodbye, Miss Morgan, I hope we meet again soon.' And then he left us. I wanted to kill Nanny.

'That young gent's too big for his boots by half,' she said, re-tying Suki's bow, 'he talks like a book. Where they get it from nowadays I can't imagine; you would think he was thirty years old, not fourteen. Now, come along, you two, there's musical chairs starting upstairs.'

But after Rupert had gone the party was just like any other boring old party: I could not even be bothered to try in musical chairs, and Hilda French won (she always does anyway, she cheats). I did not see Rupert again. Bob said his Pater had collected him, 'cos he'd seen Mr Eagon in the smoking-room talking to Mr Wolf.

One more thing that happened. Nanny sent me upstairs to tidy my hair and go to the lav. While I was in the lav (more like a throne-room in a palace than a lav, with little blue tiles on the walls with pictures of Chinese people doing things on them, and a washbasin with gold taps and a hot rail to hang towels on, and you had to go up steps to the lav). Well, I was sitting on the seat when I heard Mr Wolf's voice. He must have been in the room next door and he was shouting quite loudly. 'You are useless, woman, do you hear me, useless; no good to man or beast. Look at you! With your hair coming down, your dress torn – can you do nothing – nothing? "Isaac, Isaac," you come whining to me, "please let us have a party for our boy; let his friends come to our house. I can manage, they will be no trouble."' (Mr Wolf said this last bit in a silly, whiny voice). 'I come home from my day's work, and what do I find? All these so-called little ladies and gentlemen sitting round my drawing-room gawping like freaks in a sideshow, picking their noses and pinching each other, while the band I have hired at great expense and trouble plays to an empty floor. And what is my dear wife doing about this state of affairs? She is standing there bleating like a sheep in a thunderstorm wetting herself.'

'Please, Isaac, please don't be so cruel. I cannot bear it.' It was Mrs Wolf's voice, but not like her usual voice; it was wild and strange. 'The party is a success, I swear it. The children loved Mr Salvador, the conjurer, they laughed like anything. Why, Mrs Sief said – '

Then there was a noise as though Mr Wolf was hitting her, and she gave a little cry, like poor Pincher did when he caught his paw in the mousetrap Nanny put out in the nursery. It was awful. I pulled the lavatory flush (although I hadn't finished) just to drown their awful voices. As I was pulling up my drawers, I heard Mr Wolf come out of the room and bang the door shut behind him. I couldn't hear his step in the passage outside because of the carpet. I waited for a moment, then peeped out and he had gone. I listened outside Mrs Wolf's door, but could not hear anything, not even crying.

Nanny and Suki were waiting in the hall. 'What have you been up to now, Miss Lally? We thought you'd taken a trip down the plug hole.' I love Nanny really, though she makes me cross when she treats me like a baby; she feels so safe. I don't think I want to go next door again, though I do like Julian. I've not told anyone what I heard, not even Bob, I don't know why. Oh *please*, God, let me see Rupert Eagon again.

14th January   Nothing has happened, so nothing to write in my diary – until now, that is. It rains every day and I have a sore throat and Suki has a cough. 'A poultice for you, my bird,' Nanny says to Suki, 'or we shall have you in bed with a chest.' Why does she *fuss* Suki so? My throat was so sore yesterday I couldn't talk. Nanny just said that would be a rest for us all. But I was excused lessons (Hurray) and read my book instead.

Pa has asked me about Rupert Eagon. 'You're growing up then, imp.' We were walking back from church on Sunday. 'I hear you have a young man. Quite the dandy, Nanny says.' I felt myself go red, and Mother, who was in front with Suki, turned round and looked. 'Not a young man, Pa, just a boy called Rupert Eagon. He's at Eton now, but he was at Belvedere's with Bob. He asked me to dance. None of the others were dancing, you see, and poor Mrs Wolf had to, all by herself with Mr Wolf.'

'A harsh fate indeed.' Pa gave one of his snorts, and Mother looked round again and then told Suki off for not picking her feet up properly.

'After we danced he took me down to tea, that's all,' I said (I do wish it wasn't, but I couldn't say that).

'I know young Eagon's father,' Pa said. 'A pretty warm man, by all accounts. Made his pile out of cheap brandy. Not a bad old stick, though. Met him once or twice in the City Club. Always writing to the papers about omnibuses using Onslow Square; he says the place will fall down if it goes on. Besides, he don't like coves gawping in at him in his study from the tops of the damn things. He wanted to get up a petition about it last year, but nothing came of it, of course. Apathy, that's what's wrong with this country, apathy.' The trouble with Pa is, he does go on so. 'Have you met Mrs Eagon?' I interrupted. You have to interrupt with Pa, he won't stop otherwise. Mother says I'm the same, but I don't think I am.) Pa squeezed my hand and laughed his special laugh. 'No, my pet, I have not. A beauty once, I'm told. Comes from an Anglo-Irish family, one of the Galways, I think, and much younger than old Eagon. A bit of a step down for her, I shouldn't wonder, marrying into the drink trade. Deuced haughty lot, those Anglo-Irish families. Two boys at Eton and a couple of girls. Now then, who says her old Pa don't know everything?'

'You do, Pa, you do'. *And* he does.

That was the day we met Mrs Wolf. We were just turning into our front door, Mother and Suki already in the house, when Mrs Wolf walks past; her head was bent and she was hurrying as though she didn't want to be stopped. 'Good morning, ma'am,' Pa called. 'Will this rain ever cease, I wonder. You should have shared our brolly.' Mrs Wolf stopped then, she had to, really, but you could see she didn't want to. 'Good morning, Mr Morgan, Lally. It is indeed wet. I have been visiting a sick friend in Church Street and came out without my umbrella – so silly.' She turned to look at Pa and a gust of wind blew her veil up from her face. Pa and I both gasped at what we saw. Mrs Wolf's poor face was bruised and black-looking all up one side, with one eye half-closed and puffy. Then the veil blew down again and hid it.

'Edith, my dear, in God's name what's happened? Your face!' Pa dropped my hand and took a step towards Mrs Wolf. I have never seen him look like that before.

'It's nothing, please don't – '

'Go inside, Lally,' Pa ordered, 'don't stand there getting wet. I'll be in directly.' And he pushed me through the front door and motioned to Milne, who was standing watching, to shut it behind me.

Later, when I asked Pa if Mrs Wolf had had an accident, he said yes, she had tripped and fallen down the stairs. But I know better; I'm certain Mr Wolf did it. If I were Mrs Wolf I should run away.

I cannot think of anything else to write. Rupert Eagon must be back at school now and I won't see him until the Easter holidays (perhaps not even then). It's not fair, is it, to meet someone and have them taken away so quickly? Better not to have met them at all.

30th January   In bed with quinsy. My eyes ache, my throat hurts and I wish I were dead. There's a pea-souper outside, Pa says it's the worst he can remember. Fog is creeping through the window even though it's shut, and floating about, all ghostly, over the room. Polly says, 'If I dusted all day, with this dratted fog it wouldn't make no difference, and I was going up West tonight with Arnold.' Arnold is a trooper from Knightsbridge Barracks and Polly says he's ever so handsome in his regimentals and knows how to give a girl a good time. Nanny is cross too, and Suki has earache and whines all day.

Some more has happened with Mr and Mrs Wolf. One day last week I was in our garden teaching Pincher to shake a paw (he's not much good at tricks really, but never mind that) when I heard someone crying. It wasn't like ordinary crying,

15

it was horrible and a bit frightening, and I was certain it was Mrs Wolf. I crept up to the wall between the Wolfs' garden and ours, and climbed on to the old rainwater butt – from the top you can look straight into the Wolfs' conservatory, and even though there are lots of plants and coloured-glass windows, you can see quite a bit. When I got to the top (you can kneel on the water-butt cover although you have to be careful as it's all green and slimy) I could just see Mrs Wolf through the branches of a big, feathery fern thing. She was wearing a pale blue silk afternoon dress with leg-of-mutton sleeves and a frill round the neck, and she had her back to me. The sun shone through the coloured glass above her head, covering her in a red glow that made her hair look as though it were alight. I couldn't see Mr Wolf properly, only his boots and the smoke from his cigar; but I could hear quite clearly what he said.

'Tomorrow he goes to Hamburg and that is that. The boy's a milksop and a mother's pet, it's time he grew up and learned which side his bread is buttered.'

'He didn't mean to make you angry, Isaac, it was only a boy's silly fun. Please, please . . .' And Mrs Wolf went down on her knees and seemed to be trying to hold on to Mr Wolf's legs. Suddenly his arm shot out, and bending down, he pressed his lighted cigar into her arm. She cried out in such pain I felt sick and nearly fell off the water butt. Then I heard Nanny calling (I was glad really). 'Come down off that there tank at once, Miss Lally, and you know what happens to little girls with long ears.' But Nanny had heard the crying too, I could tell by her face, and she pushed me in front of her into the house so fast I nearly fell over.

The very next day Bob came home from school and said Julian had not come in, and old Trumpers, Bob's form master, had told them Wolf had been sent to live in Hamburg with his uncle and was to go to school there, as his Mater was not well. 'A rum go, all the same,' Bob said. 'Wolf was to be Henry V in the school play next term, and he told Jones major last week his Mater was taking him to Paris in the Easter hols.'

'Now don't make a mountain out of a molehill, Master Bob,' Nanny said, 'and eat up your tea. Mr and Mrs Wolf know what's best, I'm sure. That young man's a saucebox if

16

ever I saw one; cheeks his poor Ma no end. I expect they've sent him away to give her a rest, poor thing.'

'But, Nan . . .'

'No more, I said, and when she says no more, Nanny means no more.' And she does too.

But I asked Polly when she came in with my tea this afternoon – Mrs Jessop has made a special jelly for my throat; she's not a bad old stick . . . Where was I? Oh yes, I asked Polly if she had heard Mrs Wolf crying, and she said no, she hadn't, and it wasn't her place to listen at what goes on next door anyway. Besides, those Jews aren't the same as us Christians and she was brought up Chapel and what could you expect of heathens?

'So you have heard something, Polly, you have, and if you don't tell me, I'll tell about you having Arnold in to nursery tea on Nanny's day off.'

'You wouldn't, Miss Lally!' Polly went pink and puffed out her cheeks. 'I'd lose me place. It's all-right for the likes of you, but my dad's chest is playing up again and Mum's got her legs and can't go charring no more.' I felt awful then, and said I was sorry, but do, please tell (I could see she wanted to really).

'Well,' she said, sitting down on the edge of the bed, 'and don't you tell no one, mind. It was on me evening off last week. Me and Arnold were strolling home from the Brewers Arms, proper little sing-song they have down there of a Thursday night. And Arnold's got a fine voice; his Ma was Welsh, you see, makes all the difference being Welsh.

'Oh Pol, *do* get on with it.' I was on pins, Nanny would be in at any minute with my medicine. 'I am getting on with it, but I've got to tell it proper, haven't I? Anyways, we'd just stopped under the lamp outside No 2 to have a bit of a kiss and a cuddle – we always stops there; down our area, that Mrs Jessop can hear a pin drop twenty miles off, and she don't half create, stupid old cow – when this hansom drives up outside No 4. Out gets Mrs Wolf, all bent over like, as if she'd a pain in her belly, followed by your Pa. I saw Mrs W.'s face under the lamp; it were that pale, with bits of hair coming down over her eyes. Your Pa leads her by the arm, like he were her dad, and I hear him say: "I'm coming in, Edith, I don't care what.

Things have gone too far." And up the steps he goes and lifts the knocker, dragging her behind him. I couldn't catch what Mrs W. was saying, but she were pulling away from your Pa and they were having a bit of a scuffle, when suddenly the front door bursts open and out comes Mr Wolf.

'Like the devil himself, he looks, standing there with the light from the hallway shining on him. He's got this silver-topped cane and he's waving it about above his head. "Get off my doorstep, Morgan," he shouts, "and leave my wife alone – " his voice don't half give you the creeps " – or I cannot answer for the consequences." Then your Pa, as cool as you please, but firm, mind, says, "Don't be so damned melodramatic, Wolf, we're not on the stage at the Lyceum. Your wife's ill, she should see a doctor. I was on my way home from a meeting when I saw her in the High Street, running away from some roughs who had accosted her. Naturally I called a cab and brought her home. What can you be doing to allow her to be out unaccompanied at this hour?"

'Then Mr W. smiles, showing his gold fillings, and shoves his cane under his arm as though he'd never meant to use it (which he had, if you ask me). "I must apologise, Morgan," he says, "for jumping to conclusions. It is, as you say, late, and I was worried for my wife's safety. I thought she had retired early, but later I found her room empty. Her fool of a maid told me she'd gone out for some air; as a matter of fact I was about to call the police." Then Mr W. snatches Mrs W.'s arm and shoves her behind him through the door, while your Pa just stands there looking like he wanted to follow her.

'"I see," he says, all cool-like, "but all the same, I would suggest you consult a doctor. I myself can recommend Sir Giles Stevens, a first-class man for nervous disorders. Forgive my interference, but it is plain your wife needs help."

'Old Wolf smiles even wider.

'"Much appreciated, my dear fellow, and I am most grateful for your concern. However, I think perhaps I am better acquainted with my wife than yourself; we have, after all, been married these past fifteen years. As a matter of fact, she is a little upset; she is missing our son, Julian. I should have sent the boy away to school long before now – lately he has become quite out-of-hand – but she begged me not to, and

18

you know how persuasive the fair sex can be. Now, pleasant though it is to chat with you on my doorstep like this, I really must go in and look to my wife. Goodnight to you." With that he slams the door in your Pa's face. Your Pa stands there looking up at the house as though he were lost, then shrugs his shoulders, bangs his hat back on his head and makes off down the street; he didn't even notice Arn and me though he passed right by us.'

Polly is good at telling stories and she's a really good mimic; she tells us ghost stories sometimes, when Nanny is out. But this is different, this is actually happening and I wish that it wasn't. What does it all mean? I asked Pol if she thinks Mrs Wolf is mad – like Mr Rochester's wife in *Jane Eyre* – and Mr Wolf has to hit her sometimes to keep her under control. Polly made a rude noise. 'She ain't mad,' she said, picking up my tray, 'she happens to be married to a bloke who gets his fun by knocking her about, that's all.'

'All! But that's dreadful. I mean, how can you get a laugh by knocking someone about? It's impossible.'

'I don't mean that sort of a laugh, dearie, you ain't old enough to understand yet. But that's how men are. It's because Mr Wolf's gentry you can't believe he likes knocking his wife about.' And suddenly Pol's voice sounded different somehow, not like a servant's voice at all. 'You seen working women being beaten up by their blokes before now. What about that time we lost our way down Battersea Park? We was meeting Nanny and took a wrong turn and found us in Inkerman Street. That poor cow lying in the gutter covered in bruises, with her old man lamming into her with his boot and no one taking a blind bit of notice.' I did remember, too, and the sound of the poor woman's cries; I had nightmares for weeks after. But that was not the same as Mr and Mrs Wolf, surely. Was it?

'Whatever on earth is going on in here? Off with you, girl, and see to nursery tea, it's gone four o'clock,' storms Nanny, coming in in a rush. And that was the finish of that.

But when I shut my eyes I can hear Mrs Wolf's scream as the lighted cigar butt presses into her arm. Is Pa trying to save her? I think I shall speak to Pa. Horrid things like that don't happen to our sort of people. We are different from the working class, whatever Polly may say.

19

3rd February   Allowed up after lunch today, and the fog has gone. Dr Spencer says I can go out tomorrow if the weather holds.

Pa sat with me last evening by the nursery fire, it was so cosy and nice. Nanny had taken Bob and Suki to the Magic Lantern Show in aid of the missionaries in China. I don't mind missing the Magic Lantern. Last time we went it was ever so boring. The Rev. Phipps kept putting the pictures in the machine the wrong way up and shouting Sorry! every time, and the hall was freezing. Much better to sit on the arm of Pa's chair watching fire-castles in the grate, like we did when I was little.

I wanted to ask Pa about Mrs Wolf, but didn't know how to start. But I can always talk to Pa, why not now? In the end, I just said it must be sad for Mrs Wolf now Julian has been sent away to Hamburg. Pa was filling his pipe and didn't answer for ages. Then he said it was best for the boy; boys must go away to school in order to learn to become men and make their way in the world; it was different for girls. 'Why, Pa, why is it different for girls?' Pa smiled, but his eyes weren't smiling. I wanted to put my arms round him and somehow push happiness into him. 'Girls must learn too, surely? Lots of them have to work just as hard as boys and have babies as well. Annie drags sacks of potatoes up from the cellar, and coal, and gets up at half past five each morning and – '

'We are not discussing kitchen maids,' Pa said (quite crossly for him), 'we're discussing girls and boys of the same class as you and young Julian. A gently nurtured girl, when she grows up, will fall in love and marry some decent chap who will protect and love her. For this she must, of course, learn many things: how to run a household, to entertain guests and dress prettily, to take care of her children and servants. But all these things can be learned – indeed, should be learned – at home, under the care of parents who love her. For a boy it is different. A boy must leave home and go away to school because only in this way can he learn to stand on his own feet; to deal with the world as it is, and take on the role of breadwinner and head of a family. All this applies in the case of young Wolf, as it does to any other young man past his fourteenth birthday.'

Suddenly, and for the first time I can remember, I knew that Pa was wrong. Wrong about everything. Julian was being sent away not to learn about life, but because Mr Wolf hated him and wanted to torture Mrs Wolf. What's more, kitchen maids and young ladies *are* the same underneath. They all have their monthlies (mine has just started and Nanny says not to complain about having a pain, I should be proud it has come, and to thank Jesus 'cos it means I am a normal, healthy young woman). The only difference is that young ladies can lie on sofas when they get a tummy-ache and kitchen maids have to carry sacks of potatoes upstairs.

'Pa,' I said, ever so quiet, 'I saw Mr Wolf press his lighted cigar into poor Mrs Wolf's arm.' Then I wished I'd kept quiet. Pa leapt up from the chair (not caring about treading on poor Pincher, or dropping his pipe on the floor and scattering the tobacco) and walked over to the window. Then he just stood there looking out at the square, not saying anything. I wanted to cry; suddenly I was in a place I didn't understand; nothing was as it ought to be; everything was different. Then at last he turned and put out his arms. 'Come here,' and I ran into them. 'Lally, my little love, there are things grown-ups do sometimes that you cannot, at your age, understand. Pray God you may never have to learn: suffice it to say that they are done, and they are wrong. Cruelty will always be punished, make no mistake, always. It may take a long time, but in the end judgment will come.'

'But now. What about now? What about Mrs Wolf now? Mr Wolf should go to prison, he should – '

'No more!' Pa shouted. 'No more, I say! It's wrong to interfere between a man and his wife; they've been joined together by God and – '

'Mr and Mrs Wolf haven't been joined by God, Mr Wolf is a Jew, and besides, I remember how you knocked Smith down in the stable-yard that time at Granny Morgan's when you saw him hitting *his* wife. Bob and me were watching out of the billiard room window. You said a man should be put in the stocks for hitting a woman . . .' Then I stopped 'cos Pa was smiling. 'Out of the mouths of babes,' he said softly, as if he was talking to himself. 'You infernal imp, why in Hades are you always right?' And he looked like my own special Pa again. I was just about to ask him what he meant, when there was a knock on the door. Pol, in her black with the cap with lace streamers ('Arn don't half fancy me in this rig-out,' she says).

'Please, sir, madam says to come down, the guests will be arriving any minute.'

'Tell her I'll be down directly, there's a good girl.' After Pol had gone, Pa took my hand and smoothed each finger, as he used to when I was small. 'Have you spoken to anyone about what you saw?' I shook my head. Its true, I haven't told a soul, not even Polly or Bob, only my diary. 'We'll keep it a secret between us, then, shall we? Now, I can't promise I can help Mrs Wolf, but although not exactly the sort of cove who'd fit nicely into a suit of armour let alone dash about on a charger, I'll do my damndest to help her. Now, to bed with you, you look like Banquo's ghost.'

How I do love Pa. But what will he do about Mrs Wolf? I couldn't bear him to be hurt; I'd rather Mrs Wolf was, than Pa. *14th February* St Valentine's Day *and* I had a card! Such a topping one, too. A big pink heart with two arrows through it and lace round the edge. 'Now who do we know who lives in Slough,' Nanny says at breakfast when Polly brought up the post. 'How absolutely putrid!' shouts Bob, snatching my envelope out of Nanny's hand. 'Don't tell me that ass Eagon has sent my snub-nosed sis a Valentine.' That boy makes me so cross sometimes I could murder him. In the end I had to fight him to get the envelope, knocking over my cup of tea in the process. Luckily the tea spilt over the carpet, not on my beautiful Valentine. Nanny got cross and shouted that any more nonsense and she would tell Mother, and she spooned out the porridge so fast, she dropped a blob on the tablecloth (and that made her crosser than ever).

'Anyway,' I asked Bob when we had settled down again, 'how do you know it's from Rupert Eagon? It could be from anyone.'

'Because Slough is joined on to Eton, you ninny, don't you even know that?' No, I didn't know that, and even though Bob is a rude boor I have to admit he can be useful at times. Now I wish I had sent Rupert a Valentine, but of course I never thought of it.

22

Nothing much else happened. Just lessons and walks in the park and dull things like that. Mrs Wolf has gone away for a rest, to stay with friends at a place called Menton. Suki and me watched her go. We waved and waved out of the nursery window, but she never looked round, just hurried into the cab with her veil hiding her face. Mr Wolf was not there to see her off. I suppose he was working in his office. I'm quite glad she's gone, I was getting tired of worrying about her.

15th February I heard Polly and Milne talking about Mr Wolf this morning. They were making the beds and didn't know I was outside the door. Milne was saying Mr Betteridge (that's the Wolf's butler who's quite friendly with Milne) had told her he was looking for another place. 'Don't let this go any further, girl, or it'll be the worse for you,' Milne said, 'but Jonas' (Mr B.) 'intimated' (Milne always talks like that) 'everything at No 4 is not quite as it should be.'

'I could have told him that,' Polly interrupted.

'Don't be pert, girl. If you aren't interested, say so.'

'Oh I am, Miss Milne, really I am.' Pol puffed up Mother's pillows. 'Please go on.' And you could tell Milne wanted to really. 'Well . . . Jonas says that Mr W. has some very rum parties indeed. Even before Mrs W. went away, but now! He says the servants have to be upstairs by ten o'clock on party nights – just put drinks and a cold supper out in the library before they go up. Some very rum guests too, he says. Young men and girls of a certain sort, real riff-raff, and the Lord knows what goes on between 'em. The noise they make is something chronic. One night last week he had to come downstairs for something, quite late it was, he thought they were all safely in the library, and there was this young man, not a stitch on, doing things to that statue in the hall – he'd never seen the like, and he's seen a good bit in his time, has Jonas. He told me he won't let the other staff into the library to clean until he's been round himself first. Never do to let young servants see some of the things that are lying about. Things like . . .' I couldn't hear, because Milne whispered what the things were, but I heard Pol gasp, so it must have been something awful. 'It will be a police job before long, Jonas says, and he wants to be out of it by then. As to that poor woman, she's black and blue all over, she . . .'

23

Then Nanny comes upstairs and asks me what I'm doing dawdling about when I should be downstairs at lessons. But what fun if the police come and take Mr Wolf away.

25th February (Monday)   I saw Pa and Mrs Wolf in the park today. They were sitting on a seat by the Round Pond. It must have been ever so cold, no one else was sitting down.

I was looking for Pincher when I saw them. The devil had run after a little black-and-white mongrel we sometimes see on our walks. I called and called, but he took no notice, so I was forced to run after him. He and the other dog were going quite fast and I had a job to keep up with them. I could just see Pincher's orange feather tail bouncing ahead of me over the frosty grass. Then, when I was beginning to fear I should lose him all together, he suddenly swerved away from the other dog and trotted towards the Round Pond in the direction of the only occupied seat on all that side of the pond. It wasn't until I caught up with him, I discovered that the two people sitting on the seat were Pa and Mrs Wolf. They were sitting quite close, Mrs Wolf wearing her fur hat with the violets. Pa had his hand on her arm.

'Pincher, what in Hades . . . ?' Pa jumped up and grasped Pincher's collar, then he saw me. Did I imagine that he wasn't pleased? I must have, Pa is always pleased to see me. It's funny, though, I was about to ask him why he wasn't at his office, when suddenly I knew that it would be wrong to do so.

'Hullo, imp, has that cur been misbehaving again? I was just having a quick constitutional before coming home to tea, when I bumped into Mrs Wolf.'

'Good afternoon, Mrs Wolf,' I said, 'did you enjoy your stay in Menton?' Mrs Wolf tried to push a strand of hair back under her hat (you could see the hairpin sticking into her collar). 'Yes, dear, very much. Such a lovely climate, and the most charming people. One would almost have liked to stay a little longer, but . . .' Her voice trailed away and she began pulling at her gloves. Pa didn't say anything (not like Pa), just stood fondling Pincher's ears, while Pincher kept jumping up at him.

So I asked how Julian was getting on in Hamburg and if she had heard from him recently. This was not a good idea. Pa shut his eyes, as if he thought something dreadful was about to happen, and Mrs Wolf jumped up from the seat and said she must go home immediately; some friends of Isaac were dining and she must not on any account be late. She looked quite wild, with her big, brown, beautiful eyes wide open and two red spots on her cheeks. Another hairpin fell out, and she dropped the paper bag of bread she always carries with her when walking in the park, for the ducks. Seeing the bread, the ducks came quacking and flapping out of the water to gather tightly round Mrs Wolf, pecking at the crumbs and treading on her feet. There were sparrows too, and crows, and one old, frowsy pigeon even jumped up on her shoulder. Usually she loves the birds to gather like this, that's why she carries a bag of bread, but this time they seemed to frighten her. She hit out at them with her muff, begging them to go away, as if they were people, not birds. Then Pincher started barking, and somehow it was awful, not funny at all, as you might think it would be. Pa pushed his hat on to the back of his head and looked at me. 'Take an arm, imp, and I'll take the other, we must get her home.' So Pa and me walked back across the park with Mrs Wolf supported between us and Pincher dancing along in front.

'So sorry, so very sorry,' she kept repeating, 'to be such a silly nuisance.' And as she stumbled along, her lovely, blue-black hair, strand by strand, escaped from under her hat, leaving a little trail of hairpins on the path behind her.

Pa and me were hot and harassed by the time we delivered Mrs Wolf at No 4. Mr Betteridge opened the front door and his eyebrows went up at the sight of Mrs Wolf's tumbled hair and red face. 'I hope we haven't met with an accident, madam?'

'No, no, of course not, man.' Pa sounded cross. 'Your mistress was feeding the ducks and one of those damned pigeons jumped on her shoulder. I'm afraid it gave her a bit of a fright.'

'I see, sir,' Betteridge said (but you could see he didn't). 'I'll fetch Madam's maid at once.'

'Mrs Wolf isn't better after her holiday, is she?' I asked Pa as we went up the steps to our house. But Pa didn't answer, he just shook his head as though he had bees in his ears, and tossing his hat and stick on the hall table, he hurried into his study and shut the door.

I begin to wish the Wolfs did not live next door. They only came last year: before that it was nice, dull old Mr and Mrs Bloxham, who were ever so old and quiet. Then poor Mr Bloxham died one afternoon, sitting on a seat in the square garden, and Mrs Bloxham went to live with her married daughter in Twickenham. I believe Nanny is just a little frightened too, and even Mother is crosser than ordinary.

I told Nanny about meeting Mrs Wolf and Pa in the park, and about the birds and having to take Mrs Wolf home. Nanny sucked her teeth and tut-tutted a bit, pretending not to look worried. Then she said I mustn't laugh at Mrs Wolf (I wasn't laughing) and your father has too kind a heart for his own good, always has had. Now cut along, Miss Lally, do, and get your hands washed for tea.

But later, I heard her talking to Milne on the back stairs. 'The balloon's about to go up, Clarice' (that's Milne's Christian name, but only Nanny is allowed to call her it) 'you mark my words. And when it does, I want my girls out of it. Whatever can Master Ned be thinking of?'

'She's a beauty, Em, that's what he's thinking of, even though she may be missing a screw or two in the top storey. And Master Ned is Master Ned, as both of us have cause to know.'

'Walls have ears,' hisses Nanny. 'I'll join you for a pot of tea after bedtime, Clarice, if I may, and we can try those fancy biscuits I bought at Mr Peter's. All the rage, he says, let's hope he's right, they were dear enough.'

Tomorrow we go skating at Queen's with the Frenches. Bernard is coming too (oh dear). Last time he came he would keep holding on to me; he says he's a better skater than me, which he isn't, and he can guide me. Also, you can go faster and it's more fun two together. He managed to pull me over last time and it really hurt. He and the others just laughed, and when I got angry, he said it was all good fun and not to be a cry-baby. How I hate the Frenches. I like skating, though. How ripping it would be if Rupert were coming, not Bernard.

2nd March   I'm so cold, but how could I possibly sleep? So I sit by the nursery window with a shawl round my shoulders, watching and watching the square. St Wilfred's church clock has just struck ten, but I don't feel tired. All I can think of is what is happening inside No 4. Two policemen guard the door now, and outside on the flagway the ambulance horses are getting impatient. Dr Green's brougham is still there, and two men wearing ulsters and bowler hats have just arrived in a hansom and are looking up at the house. The fog that earlier was so thick has almost gone now, and you can see the houses on the other side of the square and the hoar frost glinting on the branches of the plane trees in the square garden. A black cat has just jumped over the railings, and over by the cab rank a little crowd has gathered: the flower lady, who sits outside the underground station, the hot-chestnut man, and others I don't know.

What hours it seems since we arrived home from skating. I am going to write what has happened this evening to help pass the time while I wait. And I must wait for Pa, I must. Let him be alive, please God, let him be still alive. Suki is in Nanny's bed: she was crying, so Nanny took her there and sat with her until she slept. But Nanny is downstairs waiting with everyone else, only me alone upstairs waiting. Lucky Bob, he's spending the night with a schoolfriend and does not know what has happened, but he will know tomorrow and that might be worse. Now I must tell what I know.

It was past 6 o'clock when we left Queen's after skating. We stayed for tea and cream cakes as it is Hilda French's birthday today. (Bernard stuffed so much cream bun into his mouth, he choked, and Miss Pritchard, the Frenches' governess, was forced to bang him on the back so hard he fell off his chair.) It was cold and foggy when we came out, so Nanny and Miss Pritchard said we would go home by cab, not wait about for a bus. We all piled into a four-wheeler, laughing like anything because we were squeezed in so tight. (Bernard tried to take my hand, but I pinched his leg and he said I was a spiteful little cat.)

When we turned into the square you could hardly see the houses, the fog was so thick, and once the poor cab horse stumbled on to the pavement and nearly fell. First we stopped at No 10 to let the Frenches off (Nanny and Miss Pritchard had an argument over who was to pay the fare) then went on.

'Quick, children,' Nanny said when we reached our house,

'inside with you before the fog gets into your chests.' So Suki and me ran up the steps with our shawls over our mouths, while Nanny paid the cabby. I had to stand on tiptoe to reach our knocker, and nearly slipped on the slime the fog makes on the steps.

Suki had just said, 'Hurry up, Lally, do, I'm freezing,' when the front door burst open, and there were Pa and Mr Wolf. Mr Wolf rushed past me down the steps, pushing Suki and Nanny out of the way with his cane. At the bottom, he turned and shouted up at Pa, 'In future you'll leave my wife alone, Morgan, d'you hear me, or I swear I'll not answer for the consequences.' Then he hit the railing really hard with his cane, as if he hoped he was hitting a person, ran up the steps to his own house and crashed the door behind him. Then Suki was crying and everyone talking at once. I heard Pa's voice. 'The fellow's mad, I tell you, Elvira, mad. You've seen what he's like tonight, you surely cannot believe such nonsense.'

I do not think Pa saw us at first, we were cowering back from the front door – even Nanny. 'Pa,' I shouted, 'what's happening, what have you done?'

'Be quiet, Miss Lally, can't you see your Pa's upset? Upstairs with you.' But I took no notice and rushed sobbing into Pa's arms. He held me so tightly it hurt, and I could feel him trembling all over. 'Hush, darling, hush,' he whispered, 'it's only the wicked ogre getting his deserts, that's all.' Then it was Mother, her face white and her eyes angrier than I've ever seen. 'Lally, you're twelve years old and no longer a baby; do not behave like one, and go upstairs to the nursery with Nanny at once. Do you hear me, at once!'

Pa let go of me and took a step backwards; he look dazed. Nanny held my hand and squeezed it. 'Come on, dearie, upstairs with you and I'll make you both a nice, warm drink'. I didn't want to leave Pa, but he had turned away from me, so what could I do? As we went up the stairs, I heard Mother call him from the drawing-room. 'For God's sake, Edward, come in and shut the door, do you wish every gawping servant in the place to know our business?' But Pa took no notice, he just stood there in the middle of the hall with his hands in his pockets and did not move at all.

Nanny has been ever so kind and nice to us all evening, like

28

when we were small. She brushed my hair after my bath and kissed and cuddled Suki. 'Don't fret about that horrid old Mr Wolf, my lovelies,' she said, 'your Pa can deal with him all right and tight, and if he can't the police soon will.' I wanted to ask about Mrs Wolf, but somehow I couldn't. But all the time Nanny was talking and laughing and bustling about, I could see her eyes weren't laughing, and the little pulse was beating at the corner of her mouth, which means she's worried. It was there when Suki caught diptheria, and when Pa was knocked down by a runaway cab horse in Kensington Church Street and they brought him home in an ambulance. Every now and again she would go to the window and twitch back the curtain, as if she were just making sure that everything was all right.

At half past eight Nanny went downstairs to the servants' hall for her tea and biscuits with Milne and Mrs Jessop. She always does this on nights when there are no guests; Mother and Pa dine early then, and Milne has finished serving soon after eight. On nights when there are guests, Nanny brings her tray up and has her tea in the nursery. Tonight Nanny let me sit up a bit and read by the nursery fire, after Suki had gone to bed. She does sometimes when she's in a good mood. Usually it's a lovely time, especially in winter, like now. I curl up on the rug by the fire in my dressing-gown, with the lamp turned down and Pincher at my feet, and imagine I am all alone on a tiny, cosy island, the shadowy nursery a dark sea around me. I am reading *Treasure Island* again, it doesn't frighten me now, not much anyway, though sometimes I hear blind Pew's stick tapping outside in the square, especially when I'm in bed.

But tonight, after Nanny had gone – 'Nine o'clock and into bed with you, Miss Lally, if I'm not back' – I couldn't read, even though I'd come to the exciting bit. I just lay stroking Pincher, feeling this horrible, churny feeling in my tummy. Why, why had Mr Wolf come to our house? What had Pa *done*? Why was everything so wrong? Suddenly I could sit there no longer, I had to find out what was happening.

I pinned a shawl over my dressing-gown – it was freezing cold away from the fire – and crept out on to the landing and down the flight of stairs that leads to the bathroom. Our bathroom faces on to the back garden and from the window you can see into the Wolf's garden and a bit of their conservatory. I shut the bathroom door behind me and opened the window. It was ever so stiff and heavy and made a tremendous noise, but no one heard, they were all downstairs. Then I knelt on the bathroom floor with my elbow on the sill, and listened.

At first, all I could hear were the ordinary London noises: rattles and bangs, horses' hoofs and hooters, the rumbling of the underground trains – but everything muffled, as though I had a blanket over my head. The fog was clearing a little and I could see the lights of the houses in Blenheim Road, and a crescent moon flickered now and again through the smoky haze that billowed over the tops of the trees in the park. I could see too the lights from the Wolfs' conservatory shining on their garden; they lit up Nelson crouching on the wall by the water butt. Nelson belongs to Mr Wilson, who runs the livery stables in the mews. Mr Wilson calls him Nelson 'cos he only has one eye, the other was lost in a fight with a bulldog, but he's a good mouser all the same. After a minute or two of watching, my teeth were chattering and the fog was making me cough, but I didn't stop, it was as though I knew something was going to happen. Then it did.

I heard a scream, more a squeal really, like the sound of a rabbit in a trap, only much, much louder. Nelson jumped off the wall and I felt sick. A second later there was a crash of breaking glass and Mrs Wolf, her hair down over her shoulders, with no cloak on, came out into the garden. She was moaning and crying, and she stumbled over to the wall where Nelson had been sitting, and started to climb it, clawing at the bricks like an animal trying to escape from a cage, but each time getting caught up by the long trailing skirt of her white evening dress, and slipping back down again. I wanted to help her, I knew she would never manage to get over the wall by herself. I shouted down at her with all my might. 'Don't worry, Mrs Wolf, we'll save you, only hold on and I'll fetch help.' Then I saw Mr Wolf behind her, and before I had finished calling out, he had grasped her ankles and was dragging her through the creeper that grows on that part of the wall. She looked up once to see where the voice came from, then her poor head fell back and she collapsed on to the flagstone path at the foot of the wall, and Mr Wolf picked her up and carried her into the house.

I wanted to scream out, but I couldn't; it was like those nightmares where you know something absolutely awful has happened, but you cannot move or speak, or do anything at all about it. Then I knew I must get Pa. I had promised to save Mrs Wolf, so that was what I must do.

I ran out of the bathroom, not bothering to shut the window and not caring who heard me; slithering and sliding down the stairs so fast I nearly fell. When I reached the hall, Polly was coming out of the dining-room with a loaded tray. She shouted something, then I was past her and opening the door into the drawing-room. They were having coffee by the fire; Pa in his green leather chair, Mother on the sofa. For an instant I saw Mother's face, it was frozen in shock like a waxwork lady's. She was wearing the red velvet dinner frock that doesn't suit her, and one hand clutched the jade necklace Pa bought her for her birthday last year.

'Quick, Pa, quick, we must save Mrs Wolf, she was trying to escape over the garden wall, but Mr Wolf pulled her back. He's going to kill her, I know he is. Please, Pa, *please*'. Then everyone was shouting, even me, and Pa had rushed out into the hall with Mother after him.

'Don't be a damned fool, Ned. If what the child says is true, it's a matter for the police, what in God's name can you do?' Mother was pulling at Pa, trying to drag him back, but he shook her off quite roughly and she fell against the wall. 'That swine's been systematically torturing his wife for months, do you really want me to sit back and let him kill her? I must get there before it's too late.' Then he was gone, and Mother and me and Polly were standing there looking at the empty space where he had been.

'Polly, go round to the police station in Blenheim Road and tell them to go at once to No 4, and for God's sake make haste.' Mother's voice sounded harsh and odd. But Polly still hovered. 'I'll just nip downstairs, ma'am, and fetch a cloak – '

'Go now!' Mother screamed. 'Or it will be too late. You can take this,' and she threw Polly the silk shawl she was wearing

31

round her shoulders. Polly took it and fled through the front door, left open by Pa, and you could hear her footsteps tapping along the pavement outside, then silence. Mother closed the door, then just stood quite still, one hand still clutching her beads.

'Is anything the matter, madam?' Nanny and Milne together on the back stairs. 'There was shouting and . . .' Then Nanny saw me. 'Lord above, Miss Lally, what ever on earth . . . ?' More shouting, then Mother's voice, calm now, although she was shivering with cold without her shawl. 'Please don't all talk at once. There has been an upset at No 4, and I have sent Polly to fetch the police. The Master, however, has elected to go there himself before the police arrive; a gesture I consider to be both foolhardy and ill-judged. All we can do now is wait.'

And that is what we did – wait. Mother went back into the drawing-room and closed the door behind her, and I went down to the servants hall with Nanny and Milne. 'Give the child a nip of brandy,' Mrs Jessop said, 'she looks as if she needs it.' So we sat round the table with the red plush cloth on it, and I sipped my brandy and told what I had seen.

'I always say there should be at least one male servant in a house, what good is a load of women at a time like this, with Master Ned in danger of his life?' Milne said when I'd finished. Nanny gave her a look. 'It won't come to that, I'm sure. Master Ned will know what to do . . .'

But Nanny was wrong, because Pa didn't know what to do, he didn't know at all.

It seemed hours and hours after that before we heard the front door knocker go. We raced upstairs, even Annie who was still doing the washing-up in the scullery. Mother was already in the hall.

'Mrs Morgan,' the policeman said, 'would you mind coming with me, ma'am? I'm afraid your husband has sustained an injury.' Mother just nodded, as if she knew what was going to happen, and waited for Milne to fetch her cloak. 'Prepare the Master's bed – hot water and bandages – and send for Dr Greene,' she said as she took the policeman's arm. Did I see him shake his head, or did I dream it? Perhaps it is all a dream, and I will wake in my bed and it will be morning.

After Mother had gone, Nanny drew back the hall curtain and looked out. A police van was drawn up outside No 4, and all the lights were blazing inside the house. 'Where *is* that dratted girl – never there when you want her, and who's to go for the doctor?' Milne said she would go. 'It's only a step, I'll be all right'. Then Polly came, white-faced, breathless, crying a bit, Ma's shawl slipping off her shoulders.

'She's stabbed the Master,' she said, 'that Mrs Wolf, and there he was, trying to save her – '

'Don't talk nonsense, girl,' Nanny's voice was sharp and shrill with fear. 'You have it wrong, as usual; if anyone has been stabbed it's that devil, Wolf, and if he has, I'm sure he deserves it.'

'Be quiet, Em, let the girl speak, she must know more than us – '

'The sergeant gave me a lift from the police station in their van, and I followed him up the steps of No 4. Mr Betteridge said he'd already sent the footman for the police, he looked quite wild, poor old devil, and there was blood on his shirt front. He told the sergeant a gentleman had been stabbed and to hurry before it were too late. Then they all rushed into the house and slammed the door. But I waited on the steps for a minute, just to see what had really happened like – '

'You should have come straight home, girl, not pried into matters that don't concern you.'

'Let her speak, Em, let her speak, we want to know, don't we?' But Nanny had sat herself down on the stairs and was crying and crying and wouldn't stop.

'Pol, tell me, please, before they send me away,' I whispered while Milne and Mrs Jessop were trying to calm Nanny. 'Tell me what happened.'

'All I know, dearie,' Pol said, 'is a constable was sent to fetch your Ma. He told me Mrs Wolf had gone at her old man with a knife and your Pa had got between 'em and copped it instead, while that useless old fidget, Betteridge, just stands in the doorway watching and flapping his arms about. If your Ma hadn't sent for the police – '

'Then Pa's not dead, he – '

'Not yet, he ain't,' Pol put her arms round me. 'Not when I left.'

And that's the last thing that happened. Mother has not come back, and we just wait and wait and wait . . .

5 o'clock It's nearly morning now. I can hear the carts rumbling in along the High Street and the factory hooters have gone.

I shan't write this diary ever again, not now my Pa is dead. Yes, he's dead: I saw them bring his body out of No 4 on a stretcher; it was covered with a white sheet, and they laid him in the back of the police van, while Mother and Dr Greene stood under the lamp and watched. I saw Mr Wolf too, but he was alive, not dead like Pa. He came out bare-headed, a constable on either side of him. His coat was open and he looked straight in front, as though he didn't care about anything. He stumbled a little as they pushed him in the van with Pa, someone in the crowd laughed.

After the police van drove away with Pa and Mr Wolf in it, Mother still waited under the lamp, Dr Greene holding her arm. Then, just as I was beginning to wonder why she didn't come home, they brought out Mrs Wolf. They had dressed her in one of those back-to-front coats they make lunatics wear, and a nurse held one arm and a policeman the other. The three of them waited on the pavement while the ambulance men put the steps down, but when they tried to make Mrs Wolf climb up them into the ambulance, she refused to go and struggled and kicked and threw herself about. They got her in at last, though, after the nurse had cuffed her quite hard on the side of her face, but the constable had to carry her up, and even then she fought so hard he nearly lost his balance and fell, and in the scuffle one of Mrs Wolf's white satin evening slippers came off and rolled in the gutter.

After the ambulance had gone, the little crowd that had been there all evening slowly began to disperse, and Betteridge closed the front door of No 4 and switched the lights out one by one, until the house was quite dark. But Mother still stood there under the lamp and I still went on watching, although now my body was ice-cold as though I were dead like Pa. Then I saw Mother bend down and pick up Mrs Wolf's slipper where it still lay in the gutter, and turning, bury her face in Dr Greene's chest.

PART II

It was one of those days in early March when you suddenly feel there's hope for the human race. The feeling, illogical and ephemeral as it is, persists in spite of increasing evidence to the contrary, and only serves to show that no matter how small the microchip or how fast the feedback, we remain at heart creatures inexorably linked to the earth that spawned us. On this particular day the almond tree outside my office window floated in a pinkish haze of bursting buds, the sky was a brilliant blue dotted with high, white, scurrying clouds, and I was almost certain that above the roar of traffic I could hear a blackbird singing.

Heaven knew, there was little in my life to cheer me up. As a result of my senior partner's meanness, coupled with his obsession for purchasing the latest piece of labour-saving office gadgetry without the smallest understanding of whether the wretched thing was of any use to our particular firm, we were in our usual state of being chronically over-worked and under-staffed; I had an incipient head cold, and that very morning I'd had a letter from my son, Marcus, in America, announcing – albeit in such convoluted language that I had to read the thing three times before I understood it – that he and his wife, Barbie, were splitting up. And, unless I was mistaken in my interpretation of his closing paragraph – i.e. paranoia had taken over at last – he was blaming me for what had happened.

Nevertheless, and bravely ignoring all my difficulties, I was dictating away without any great hope of having the stuff typed back in under a week, when my phone rang. Phoebe, our current receptionist: 'Mr Wolf, Peter Davenport's gone home with 'flu, he said would you mind awfully nipping in to see a Mrs Flynn on your way home, to draw up a Will?'

'Oh God, Phoebe, must I? I've got a lot on this evening.' (I hadn't, actually.) 'Surely it can wait?'

'Peter says Mrs Flynn's in her nineties; her great-granddaughter, or that's who Peter thinks she is, says Mrs Flynn had a turn last night and wants to make a new Will. She might pop off at any minute. It's not far out of your way, Mr Wolf, I've looked it up. Palmer's Building, Shot Street – down by the river.' I knew Shot Street, and a pretty rough area it was too, a far cry from the flower-decked, newly

37

scrubbed gentility of tourist Bath. 'Oh, all right then, get me out the file, will you, I'll be leaving at five.'

'No file, Mr Wolf, it's a new matter, only a few notes Peter made over the phone . . .'

The wind was quite nippy as I turned the corner into Shot Street. Crisp bags blew gently along the cracked pavement, and a gaggle of small boys played a hazardous game of football in and out amongst the densely parked cars and piles of builder's debris; a broken-down warehouse loomed at the end of the street, blocking the view of the river.

Palmer's Building consisted of two immensely tall eighteenth-century tenements, whose walls, black from the pollution of two centuries, stood out like decayed teeth in an otherwise perfect set of dentures. Quite a sizable slice of Shot Street, it appeared, had already been 'reclaimed' since my last visit a couple of years back – 'reclaimed', in this context, being a euphemism for pushing the indigenous inhabitants out to jerry-built estates in the surrounding countryside and selling the place off, floor by floor, as luxury flats to the highest bidder.

A swirl of builder's dust blew in my eyes as I optimistically pressed the bell to No 8. Absolutely nothing happened; the house, a lifeless rookery that had no right to exist in our poverty-conscious age, reared blindly above me.

'Push the door open, my love,' came a woman's voice behind me. 'Those bells haven't worked in years. Is it Mrs Flynn you want?' Surprised, I said it was, and that I believed she lived in No 8. The woman nodded. 'Has done for years, my love. Such a wonderful old lady. It's a crying shame, the state the place is in. The council won't help, of course, but they play their own rules, so my husband says, just make them up as they go along. You a solicitor?' Not wanting to become involved, I nodded vaguely and pushed open the heavy front door. The smell of damp was almost tangible, and the sheer chill of the place clamped down on me like a soaking wet overcoat.

'Second floor, my love, ask for Kevin or Amanda – they see to Mrs Flynn.' I trod gingerly up the gracefully spiralling staircase which, patched and rotten though it was, still retained a vestige of its original style and purity of line. Below

me in the hall, the woman watched my progress, her pat-
terned headscarf flapping in the chill breeze that shivered
through the open front door. As I approached the second
floor I heard the raucous beat of pop music, the kind that to
my untutored ears appears to consist of someone chanting the
same few words over and over again to the accompaniment of
the aimless banging of drums and a twang or two from an
electric guitar.

'Mr Davenport?' A rather beautiful red-headed girl of
around twenty stood on the landing above me. She was
wearing jeans and a baggy green T-shirt with the words 'Back
to Somerset' emblazoned across the front.

'Wolf, actually. Mr Davenport has 'flu.'

'Oh, poor him, there's a fearful lot around. Do come in.
Sorry about the mess. I'm studying, and the lodger works
nights, so its rather a job to get organised.'

I was wafted into an enormous, monstrously untidy sitting
room with as much ceremony as though I'd arrived to pay a
formal call at Buckingham Palace. 'Lally's just woken up, so
you couldn't have chosen a better time to call.' The girl gave
me a blinding smile that, like the almond tree and the
blackbird, made my almost extinguished middle-aged soul
turn over, sit up and even scratch itself. I smiled too, and
shouted above the music that I understood Mrs Flynn wished
to make her Will.

'She says all her others are out of date, everyone in them is
dead. She'll be ninety-nine in September.'

Good God! The oldest person I'd ever come across was my
great-uncle Roger, and you couldn't count him really, he'd
been little more than a vegetable for years.

'Mrs Flynn retains her faculties, then?'

'Heavens yes, she's fantastic.' To my great relief, the girl
suddenly became aware of the noise and switched it off. 'By
the way, I'm Amanda Fenton-Langly, I'm Lally's great-
granddaughter. Hang on a minute and I'll tell her you're
here.'

I looked around me; the room had once been beautiful, and
under the dust, old newspapers, electronic equipment, dirty
coffee cups and assorted underclothing, there were some
beautiful things in it. (I have, though I say it myself, quite a

sound knowledge of antiques.) But the house was surely no place for a frail ninety-nine-year-old? Ms Fenton-Langly appeared in the doorway. 'And if you're thinking Lally should be taken into care, forget it.' I jumped guiltily and shuffled the papers in my briefcase. 'I'm only here to carry out my client's instructions.' I said, slipping effortlessly into my solicitor's patter, 'but the place does feel a little on the damp side, and what about the stairs? I mean, shouldn't the council be involved, or even Age Concern? I know a Mrs Bell – '

'I said, forget it. Lally's lived for damned near a century; I doubt whether houses in the 1880s were any dryer than this.'

'But that's not the point, is it?' I found myself being drawn into an argument as silly as it was irrelevant. 'Your great-grandmother was a hundred years younger then, and there-fore better able to sustain the cold and damp. I only thought – '

'I know what you thought.' Amanda's eyes were as blue as the wild spring sky outside. 'But every case should be judged on its own merits, surely? And Lally's OK. Besides, Mrs Creed sees to her when we're out and she makes her laugh, which is more than you can say for most of those dreary people from the Welfare.'

'You speak from experience?' I snapped. I felt myself getting annoyed and hurt at the same time. I was only doing my duty as a citizen, wasn't I? Were not our masters conti-nually exhorting us to keep an eye on the aged, make sure they did not die of cold, or damp, or neglect? And here was this child with all the wisdom of the ages in her eyes, telling me to mind my own business . . .

'Manda, what in hell's name are you up to? I thought you said the solicitor had arrived. They charge the earth for one letter, you know. If you keep him hanging about much longer, I won't have anything left anyway, it will all have gone on paying his bill.' The voice was surprisingly robust for anyone so old; I felt a frisson of excitement. The red-headed girl, the chaotic room, the sharp spring sunlight slanting through the grimy Georgian windows – suddenly I was glad that Peter Davenport had caught the 'flu.

'Let's go.' Amanda led the way through into a much smaller room – once, perhaps, in palmier days, a dressing room. It faced on to the street, was stiflingly hot, rather dark, and crammed with furniture. A convector heater blazed away in a corner, and yellowing net curtains were tightly drawn across the window. On one side an enormous television set, mercifully switched off, jostled uneasily with a Chippendale commode and a rather beautiful early nineteenth-century French armoire – both extremely dusty.

My first reaction to Lally Flynn was amazement that anyone so small and frail should possess so overwhelming a presence. She was seated in a blue velvet armchair by her bed, the latter a highly ornate affair, its carved wooden head alive with dragons, pagodas and sundry other assorted chinoiserie. Drawn up in front of her chair was a small trolley loaded with medicine bottles, books, newspapers and a large box of tissues. In the general chaos, Lally Flynn herself looked extremely neat; like the eye of the storm, within her orbit all was peace and order, and there was a delicate, dancing fastidiousness about her that was quite entrancing. There could be no doubt that Mrs Creed, or Amanda, or even the elusive Kevin, looked after her all right. Her silky white hair was cropped and set in little curls all over her head, pearl earrings glinted in her ears, and she was wearing a smart navy blue dress with touches of white at the collar and cuffs. But it was her green eyes that were the most remarkable thing about her. Enormous, triangular; sunken now, the skin around them mottled and stretched taut over the fine bones of the face, they nevertheless held in them such sharp intelligence, such humour coupled with that I can only describe as an innate buoyancy of spirit, as to make them more truly a window on the soul than any eyes I have ever seen. I doubt whether she'd ever been a beauty, her mouth was too large and her jaw too strong, but my goodness me, she must always have been *someone*.

'So good of you to come, Mr Davenport. Do sit down.'

'The name's Wolf, actually, Mrs Flynn. My colleague, Peter Davenport, unfortunately succumbed to the 'flu.' Something flashed between us that had nothing whatsoever to do with mundane pleasantries. Why?

'I'm so sorry. Manda said Mr Davenport was most helpful when she rang him this morning. But how odd your name is

41

Wolf. You are not, I take it, a native of Bath?' I shook my head. 'Er, no, London really, if anywhere.' Mrs Flynn smiled. 'So am I, and I still miss it sometimes. We found your firm in the yellow pages – one of the more useful adjuncts to modern life, don't you agree?'

'Slow down, Lally, you're being overwhelming, and I don't suppose Mr Wolf has ever met anyone as old as you before.'

'I don't suppose he has.' The snort of laughter was wholly delightful. 'Go and make us some tea, girl, and you'd better use the Rockingham, Mr Wolf looks as if he might appreciate the Rockingham.' Bemused, I nodded my agreement.

'OK, but it'll be a bit of time, the electric kettle's kaput, and the water takes hours in a saucepan.' Amanda disappeared, and a moment later the music started up again. Mrs Flynn made a tiny grimace. 'I'm afraid my appreciation of popular music stuck at Benny Goodman; perhaps there is a limit to the amount of changes one can take in a single lifetime.'

'Quite possibly,' I said, raising my voice above the beat. 'I stuck at Elvis Presley, though I'm a classics man at heart. Now, Mrs Flynn, if you could give me a rough idea of what you want to do, I'll just make a few notes.'

'Poor young man, you must be dying to get home. I do go on a bit, don't I? Always have, actually, it's not just old age.' I found myself blushing like the boy she obviously considered me to be. 'Not at all, it's just that perhaps we ought to get the business out of the way before we start on the tea – especially if it comes in Rockingham.' What was the matter with me? I never talk like this to clients.

'Well, it won't take long, dear, there's not much left to leave. But all there is I want to go to Manda.'

She was right, it didn't take long. By the time we'd finished, Amanda had appeared with our tea. The cups were Rockingham and, so far as I could see, not a crack or chip among them; the biscuits were stale, though, and the tea itself distinctly odd. Mrs Flynn took a sip. 'A most beautiful girl, my great-granddaughter, but no damned good at making tea,' she said. Not liking to agree too openly, I smiled in what I hoped was an encouraging manner and boldly took another sip. Lally Flynn lit a cigarette. 'I'm sure you don't smoke, Mr Wolf, you look much too sensible.'

'I used to,' I said, feeling defiant. Was she laughing at me, and why did she always hesitate over my name in that odd way? 'I stopped about ten years ago, it was giving me sinus headaches and – '

'Do you know, I do believe I haven't made a Will since 1950.' Plainly my erstwhile smoking habits held little interest. 'I think I left everything to my son. Not that he deserved anything, pompous ass – he had plenty anyway – but one felt one should. He's dead now, of course, and so is my grand-daughter, Amanda's mother.'

'I see . . . and, er, Mr Flynn?' She gave one of her snorts of laughter. 'Tommy Flynn? Heavens, he died years and years ago. He was run over by a train in the Paris Metro while under the influence.'

'How absolutely frightful. I mean . . .' Suddenly and quite inexcusably, we were both roaring with laughter – what about, I've no idea, but I don't think it was the unfortunate demise of Tommy Flynn.

'Who was your father, Mr Wolf?' Lally peered at me through a haze of cigarette smoke. 'Forgive me, but you have a look of someone I used to know, and you bear the same name.'

'My father's name was Sidney. He was, amongst other things, a stockbroker. Not a very good one, I'm afraid; in fact he thought he'd made such a mess of things that he shot himself.' Suddenly I became aware of an almost unbearable tension in the stuffy little room. I wanted to open the window, shout, tear off my jacket. Instead, of course, I simply sat there, sweat trickling down my neck, waiting for something to happen. Nothing did, and slowly the tension between us cleared.

'The person I knew was a Julian Wolf,' Lally said carefully, looking at her small mottled hands. 'He was for a time on the stage.'

'My grandfather,' I said. 'How very odd you should have known him.'

For an instant someone else was sitting in the blue velvet chair; someone in pain; someone who wanted more than anything else in the world to communicate. Then she was gone. 'Life', said the old lady before me, 'is filled with such coincidences, especially if you have lived for as many years as I have. Now, young man, how long must I wait before my Will is ready? Not too long, I hope. One lives from day to day, d'you see.' I was dismissed.

Hastily I rose to my feet. 'Would Monday be all right? There's the weekend ahead, otherwise it could be tomorrow. With word processing, engrossing a Will is not the trauma it used to be. Perhaps someone could bring it round for you to execute on Monday afternoon – say about three o'clock?'

'That would be admirable. Let us hope I shall survive the weekend. And thank you so much for coming at such short notice. Such a bore on a Friday evening. You have children?'

'One son, grown up now and lives in America. I live on my own, apart from a dog.'

'How nice! I've always considered children to be rather over-rated; grandchildren are much more satisfactory and great-grandchildren the best of all. Now, off with you, and don't forget your briefcase.' Suddenly, absurdly, I wanted to kiss her goodbye. I compromised (as usual) by shaking her hand. 'Goodbye, Mrs Flynn, nice to have met you, and we'll have the Will ready by Monday.'

Next door, Amanda uncoiled herself from the floor where she appeared to be practising yoga. 'Bye, Mr Wolf, and don't go sending a load of snoopers round to see about the drains – OK? Lally wants to die here, not in some God-awful council home.'

'Of course I won't. It's none of my business.' Who did she think I was? 'Someone will be round with Mrs Flynn's Will at three o'clock on Monday. Perhaps you would see she reads it through carefully before she signs it.'

'So you won't be coming?'

'I doubt it, I'm rather busy. One of our clerks probably.'

'Shame. Lally fancied you, I could see. She and I have the same taste in men, she – '

'Look, I really must be going, I – '

'It's OK,' she said, looking me up and down in a manner I found both disconcerting and exciting at the same time. 'I've no intention of trying to rape you.' Honestly, I could have strangled the stupid chit. Instead I smiled weakly. 'Well, er, goodnight,' was all I could produce in the way of cutting repartee as, head bent, I hurried down the stairs.

In the hall the lady who had let me in was standing by the unemptied rubbish bins. 'All right, was it?'

'Yes, thank you. Someone will be round on Monday.'

'I'll keep an eye open . . .' I was sure she would.

Now, the odd thing about all this is that normally, from the moment I got back into my car and drove away from Shot Street, I would have put Lally Flynn out of my mind. I wouldn't forget her exactly – all the information would be there, neatly docketed in a compartment of my mind – but I would cease to think about her, at least until such time as it became professionally necessary to do so; in her case, on Monday morning. If, as a member of the legal profession – or any other profession that serves that hydra-headed monster, the public – one did not compartmentalise in this way, one would simply collapse like an overloaded donkey under the sheer weight of human egotism. You cannot go to bed at night worrying about the fact that Mrs Bloggs' husband will only have sex with her under the kitchen table, or wake up in the morning wondering whether Mr Smith can be persuaded to make it up with his neighbour, whose offspring have thrown a firework into his garden and ruined his best rose bush. This way lies madness. After being in the business for as long as I have (too long, actually, nearly thirty years) this switching-off process is second nature and requires no effort of will whatever.

But to my surprise, as I negotiated the car through the customary rush-hour traffic black spots, Lally and her rude, beautiful great-granddaughter simply refused to go away; indeed, at times I almost felt their presence in the car beside me.

I was on my own most of the weekend; my lodger, Warren, a bumptious but kindly young American who works at the university, was away on some course. I'd had a lodger ever since my wife, Amy, moved out three years previously. It was company, it paid the rates, and, I felt, it acted as a deterrent to any marauding female who might show signs of wanting to move in.

Anyway, this particular weekend I pottered about cheerfully enough, shopping at the supermarket, taking my labrador, Merry, for walks, sowing my first batch of broad beans, and generally enjoying having the freedom of the house for a change. There was just one thing, however. Whatever I was doing, wherever I was, I found myself thinking of Lally Flynn. Not worrying about her; not that at all; just wondering, and seeing her face in my mind's eye.

How well had she known my grandfather? Why, having discovered that he was my grandfather, had she so abruptly changed the subject? One would have thought such a discovery might be the cue for a whole string of reminiscences. Most old people . . . But Lally Flynn wasn't really an old person, was she, she was a young person imprisoned in an old person's body. 'For heaven's sake, David, don't drivel. Are you incapable of thinking in anything but clichés?' I heard my mother's voice, as of old, burst into my maundering. I was chopping shallots for tonight's chicken chasseur. I liked cooking, and if I was in, I usually tried to do something a bit special on Saturday nights. Warren seemed to enjoy my efforts, and usually contributed a bottle of wine to the proceedings.

As the weekend wore on, I even began to rather wish I had said I would deliver the Will at Palmer's Buildings myself, but being a senior member of the firm, it wasn't really my place to do so; besides, I'd named Peter Davenport as Executor. Anyway, I'd soon forget all about Lally Flynn, wouldn't I? Perhaps in a month or so I would read an account of her birthday celebrations in the local rag – or, more likely, of her death. Suddenly I thought of 'poor Tommy Flynn' under the influence in the Paris Metro and, God knows why, laughed out loud.

Then I went upstairs to the box-room.

Somewhere up there amongst the family photographs, I knew there was a photo of my grandfather, Julian Wolf. Amy had always relegated such things to the box-room. Like my mother, she mistrusted the past, claiming too much interest in it to be unhealthy; the present and the future, she maintained, were the important things, with the emphasis on the future.

I found the album I was looking for, a heavy, red leather affair with 'For Your Snapshots' in gold lettering across one corner. As I picked it up, a shower of photographs of the minute, yellowing variety fell out on the floor. Callously, I let them lie; Amy was right, they were of no interest now to anyone. But somewhere there was a picture of Grandfather Wolf, I knew there was. I remembered it from years back – one of those theatrical portraits, with 'Sincerely Yours, Julian Wolf' written in violet-coloured ink underneath. If I remembered aright, he was wearing a boater and smoking a cigarette in a long holder. I had never known my grandfather Wolf, he left my grandmother when Dad was little more than a baby, and was rarely spoken of in the family. Apart from leaving my grandmother in the lurch, the only other information I had about him was that he had been some sort of entertainer, and had died in Cairo some time in the 1920s.

My grandmother had married again, a young man by the name of Bobby Henshaw whom she met while nursing in the First World War, and it was he who, to all intents and purposes, became my paternal grandfather. After the war, Grandpa Henshaw set up as a solicitor in the small town of Coltswood, near Chelmsford in Essex, just when the whole area was beginning to emerge as an ideal spot for London commuters – the 'daily breaders', as Grandpa Hen always called them. He and Granny produced five children – my youngest Henshaw uncle being only three years older than I was – and were always said to be very happy. They certainly prospered. When Grandpa died a few years after World War Two, he was by all accounts what he himself would have described as a 'pretty warm man'. There's even a street in Coltswood named after him – an honour, let's face it, not given to many.

My father, ten years older than his eldest half-brother, part Jewish and with a temperament as alien to the little Henshaws as a giraffe to a pack of donkeys, hated the lot of them, and escaped from the stifling atmosphere of what he termed 'middle-class suburbia of the meat-and-two-veg variety', as soon as he decently could. Grandpa Hen, no doubt glad to be rid of him, managed to get him articled with a firm of accountants in the City, and luckily for Dad – 'luckily' is what I was always led to believe, but sometimes now I have my doubts – he met and married my mother, who just happened to be the daughter of the senior partner. So all seemed set fair for a rosy future. But alas, although for a brief time in the thirties my parents were genuinely quite rich, this bright promise was not fulfilled, and by the time war broke out, Dad's innate ability for backing a loser had brought him to the verge of bankruptcy.

Actually, the war not only saved him from bankruptcy but also did him some good. Someone, somehow, managed to wangle him a commission at the very beginning, and he came out at the end unscathed, a major, and with a DSO and bar to his credit. He never, however, recovered from those heady days; the return to civvy street was more than he could cope with. He started up a number of business ventures, all of which failed disastrously, and tired out with the unequal battle, he blew his brains out in the New Year of 1969.

Mercifully, Mother still had the house in St Wilfred's Square, Kensington, which she thriftily (she was a thrifty and sensible woman) converted into six bedsitters, herself living in a flat in the basement. By this means she managed to maintain herself in considerable comfort – she was in fact much better off than when Dad was alive – until she died in 1973. No 4 St Wilfred's Square was one of the few pieces of luck that came Dad's way. He inherited it from a great-aunt on his father's side, of whom, until her death in 1947, he had never heard. Left to himself, Dad would no doubt have sold the place as quickly as possible, but Grandpa Hen's advice had been to hang on. 'Bricks and mortar, m'boy – come up trumps one day – stands to reason – after all this bombing – people have to live somewhere.' And of course the old devil was right. In the years since Mother's death, converted now into four flats, No 4 has continued to produce me a very reasonable income, enabling my son, Marcus, to have a public school education (probably a mistake), and after we separated, allowing Amy to continue living in the manner to which she had become accustomed while we were married.

Dad and I were close, in our own, odd sort of way; much closer than my son is to me, despite the fact that Marcus and I tended always to try and 'talk things through' and Dad and I did not. As a child, he would play with me; wild, romping games that almost always ended in something getting broken and both of us becoming engulfed in Mother's wrath. In the end, like one of Pavlov's dogs, I would back away nervously as soon as I heard the loved, hesitant voice: 'Well then, young Dave, how about a rumpus in the garden? I'll be a dinosaur and you can be a brontosaurus, and bags I start first – '

'I've got my train set, actually, Dad, if you don't mind. I want to get those signals fixed . . .' And Dad would scrape his fingers through his hair and smile brightly. 'Of course, old man, of course, you get on with your trains. I say, you haven't seen my gaspers anywhere about, have you? They seem to have vanished into thin air.' And I would smile too, not daring to meet his eyes. I never could, not even when I grew up, face the sadness and hurt I knew I'd find in them.

As I knelt uncomfortably on the box-room floor, suddenly, without warning, I remembered our last meeting, Dad's and mine. I seldom thought about it; for years after his death I couldn't bear to, and after that – like the episode in a soap opera that contains within it the stuff of both tragedy and drama, but which, by the time it's considered fit for consumption by the masses, has been so cleansed and disinfected as to be almost meaningless – by some subconscious act of censorship on my part, that last meeting and Dad's subsequent death had become just another experience, all poison drawn. It seemed no longer part of 'real' life; an episode in a novel, perhaps, or a joke in rather poor taste.

Christmas had been pretty tiresome that year. I can't remember the ins and outs of it, but Amy had retired in tears halfway through Christmas dinner, and somehow Marcus, then aged eight, had ended up with three identical chess sets. Dad rang up, drunk, from a call box on Boxing night. We were having a few friends in for drinks, and the last thing I wanted was a long, incoherent conversation with Dad. These conversations had increased considerably of late – the world, I suppose, was closing its ranks on the poor sod; but I didn't see it like that at the time. Instead of being pleased, flattered even, that one of the few people I loved continued to use me as a lifeline when all else failed, I regarded his calls as an intolerable invasion of privacy and a damned nuisance. It was only the old, familiar sense of guilt that kept me standing there on the end of the phone, making soothing noises, taking the number of the call box ('Don't seem to have any more change, old man, would you oblige . . . ?'), ringing back.

'Look, Dad, go home, for heaven's sake, Mother will be worried – '

'Worried – her? You are joking, aren't you? That woman's never worried a tinker's fart about me since the day we were married, and I can tell you this now, Dave, I couldn't before, you see – '

'Look, Dad, I must go, we've people in and Amy's a bit upset – '

'Amy's always upset. Why the devil you married her I have never understood, I – '

'Dad, I *must* go – '

'OK, OK. I'm being a bore, you've made that quite clear. You've got your life to lead, old man, I know that. But surely you can spare a moment or two to talk to your old Dad? Look here, what about dinner next week – celebrate the festive season and all that. There's a damned good new eatery opened in Ken Church Street. On the trendy side, bits and pieces of Victoriana and dark as the inside of a cow, but the food's sound.'

'OK Dad, that would be nice.' I had to give in, he'd never let it rest if I didn't. 'How about next Wednesday. But I'll have to catch the last train home, I'm in court in the morning.'

'Hunky-dory, old man, Wednesday it is. My treat, by the way – I haven't had time to get you a Christmas present yet.' My heart sank. I'd pay, of course, but it wasn't that; it was, well – Dad. And yet, God help me, I loved him.

We met in the pub next door to his 'eatery'. Dad had already had a few: it was snowing outside. 'And that was the last we saw of the catering manager . . .' I heard his voice before I saw him, then the usual laughter. It was an old story, he'd told it a hundred times, but he was a good story-teller, I'll give him that. 'David, David, my son.' He put on his mock Jewish voice, the one that always made me cringe. 'What are you having, my boy?' Then in my ear, 'Lend me a fiver, will you, old man, I'm temporarily out of funds; Christmas, you know . . .'

He looked haggard and ill despite the gaiety, his thick black hair streaked with grey, dark lines under the sad, desperate brown eyes. But his smile still held the old spontaneous warmth, and while we were waiting for my drink he made some remark about Mother and Christmas that convulsed me. He looked sideways at me and gave his nervous grin; a comedian, doubtful of his audience, acknowledging the applause.

It was at dinner that things went wrong. We stayed too long in the pub and missed our table at the restaurant. When we finally got one, the service was bad and the food no better. Dad had a row with the proprietor, and they kept us waiting hours for the first course. We'd reached the coffee stage when Dad broached his idea. An old army chum had suggested they went into partnership together, he said, making a business of lighting his umpteenth cigarette; the venture, a travel company that catered solely for people interested in touring battlefields. 'Any battlefield, old man – Hastings, El Alamein – you name it. Can't go wrong, people love war, at least, they love reading about it. What d'you think?' He smiled brilliantly, a conjurer exhibiting his latest trick. I suppose I'd had too much to drink, I was certainly suffering from the Christmas blues. I don't know. But something in me snapped, and I just refused to go along with him. 'It sounds bloody daft to me,' I said. 'Has your friend any experience of the travel business? Who is he, by the way, do I know him?'

'Old Jimmy Farrar,' he said, not looking at me. 'I know you and your mother never liked him, but he's a damned good chap for all that. If I hadn't had him with me in the desert – '

'Fuck the desert, Dad, it's now you've got to think about.' And I went on from there. In my arrogance I thought I knew it all. This is a common complaint amongst newly fledged solicitors. All life is there, it seems, for them to direct. They know the law, don't they, and that, after all, is what matters. And Dad just sat there and took it. Once or twice he mumbled something about 'No right to speak to your father like that, old man, no right . . .' but mostly he took it. Eventually I ran out of steam and just sat there looking at him. There was a long pause, while a surly waiter ostentatiously flicked crumbs off the neighbouring table.

At last Dad spoke. 'It was my treat, you know,' he said with dignity, and for the first time I ever remember, looked at me without love. I felt both naked and ashamed.

'No hard feelings, Dad,' I said idiotically, 'I'll get the bill, then see you back to St Wilfred's Square. I've an hour before my train goes.' Dad got up from the table so suddenly he upset his glass of wine. I remember looking owlishly down at the red liquid as it slowly soaked into the white tablecloth; drunk as I was, I knew something dreadful was happening.

'You thought I couldn't pay for the dinner, didn't you? You even thought that, you arrogant, conceited young bastard. Well, I can, and I can see myself home, I don't want your help ever again. Go back to your safe job and your boring, self-centered wife, and I hope they bloody well kill you.' And he pulled a crumpled £10 note – obviously saved for the occasion – out of a side-pocket in his jacket, slapped it down on the table in front of me and walked out of the restaurant without a backward glance.

I remember resisting an enormous desire to burst into tears, and feeling more completely alone than ever before in my life; I wanted to cry out, run after Dad, say I was sorry, I didn't mean any of it. But of course I didn't; I was a big boy now, wasn't I? Calmly, I told myself that what had happened was the drink talking in both of us; better let him go. I'd give him a ring in the morning.

I never did, though – give him a ring, I mean. By the morning Dad was dead. He'd gone straight home, shut himself in his little study in the basement, then, after drinking a glass of 'Irish', his favourite tipple, he shot himself with the old service revolver he kept illegally in a drawer in his desk.

That was that, really. Except that they found beside him an unfinished note addressed to me. 'Sorry about this evening, old man,' he'd written, 'but things are . . .' That was all. But enough, when you come to think of it, to be going on with.

Suddenly a soft, impatient nose thrust itself into my back: Merry, indicating it was time to make a move. I realised I had cramp in my knee and that I was cold; cold in a way one is at times, that has nothing to do with the temperature. Painfully I got to my feet, the photograph album under my arm, and it was only then I realised I had been crying.

That evening, a Beethoven quartet weaving its intricate magic in the background, Merry snoring at my feet, I began looking through the photograph album, searching for something, I didn't know what; a clue to Lally Flynn, perhaps, and why my meeting with her had seemed so oddly catalystic.

It was hard going, and, I have to admit, rather boring. Page upon page of fuzzy 'snaps' depicting endless variations of the Henshaw family in toto; on beaches, in front of bandstands, standing about in gardens, and one rather racy one of (I think) Uncle Arnie, Grandpa Hen's brother, all goggles and leather, manfully astride a motorbike of vast proportions, with an extremely pretty (despite the hat) blonde crouched beside him in the side-car. Underneath was written 'Atta Boy!! Brighton 1925'. Stirring stuff, but not what I was looking for. The album must have been Dad's; it was certainly his surprisingly bold hand that had written what captions there were.

By the time I had reached 1937 and seen myself aged three scowling into the camera ('Mollie and Davie, Paignton 1937') I'd had enough. There was nothing for me here. This pictorial record of a rather dull middle-class family between the wars held no echoes of that other past – Tommy Flynn dying under a train in the Paris Metro, Lally Flynn with her wonderful eyes and her air of mystery, my grandfather Julian Wolf, who 'was for a time on the stage'. I'd pour myself another drink and see what rubbish TV had to offer. Warren and I usually strolled down the hill to our local about this time, but somehow it wasn't the same on one's own.

Then, as I got out of my chair, with the sudden movement the photo album, balanced precariously on the arm, slid to the floor, spilling out not only more yellowing snaps but a large brown envelope. The latter, postmarked sometime in the twenties – impossible to decipher which year – was addressed to 'Master Sydney Wolf, 18 Foxglove Avenue, Coltswood, Essex' in an unknown hand. On the back Dad had written, 'My Father, Julian Wolf, 1888–1926'. I stood quite still, turning the envelope this way and that, trying to deduce its contents, and became aware that my heart was beating uncomfortably fast and my hands were shaking. Ashamed of such emotion, I tried to think why I'd never seen the envelope before, then realised the answer to that was simple; I'd never bothered to look. I'd had all Dad's papers ever since Mother died in 1973. 'You sort them out, David,' she'd said that last time I saw her in hospital, 'you're the solicitor, I've never had the time.' But I didn't sort them out, I simply chucked them into a couple of tea-chests and had them shipped down to Bath with the rest of the furniture that wasn't sold, and they'd remained in the box-room ever since.

I poured myself yet another drink, and with fingers that were still trembling a little, carefully shook out the contents of the envelope.

It came to me then that I had never really wanted to know about my antecedents: if there were any guilty secrets, I preferred to remain in ignorance of them. As a background for a solid, middle-of-the-road, provincial solicitor (was that really what I thought of myself?) the dull, old Henshaws and Mother's family (the Potters had been doctors and accountants in South London for four generations; if they possessed any family skeletons, these had been decently interred long since beneath the bedrock of Potter respect-ability) suited me admirably. Dad, on his own was quite enough to be going on with. But now, suddenly, I knew I had been wrong. I should have wondered, asked more questions, when those who might have known were still around to answer them. Now it was too late – or was it?

I laid out the contents of the envelope on the sofa table; a photograph and a yellowing newspaper cutting; pitifully little if this was all that remained of my grandfather. I have to admit, I had hoped for more.

The photograph I recognised immediately; it was the one I had been looking for. I must have seen another copy. I remembered now, it used to be in a leather frame in Dad's bedroom when I was a child. It couldn't have survived the war; perhaps he took it overseas and it got lost in transit somewhere. The face under the stylised period trappings were oddly attrac-tive. Surprised, I realised it bore a strong resemblance to Marcus. It was certainly neither weak nor raffish, terms in my mind synonymous – God knows why – with my grandfather. Had I, perhaps, been the unconscious recipient of Henshaw propaganda? The photograph bore the date 1911 – a year after Dad's birth. For a moment I tried to envisage the Granny Henshaw I remembered as wife to the face before me; defeated, I turned to the newspaper cutting. This was frail and slightly blurred, as though it had at some time been soaked in water. On the back was an advertisement for corsets.

Mr Julian Wolfe – 'An Evening's Entertainment' at the Companions Theatre

Unlike my fellow hacks, who walked out after twenty minutes (they had, no doubt, better things to do with their time) I stayed to the end of Mr Julian Wolf's bizarre, marvellously talented and brilliantly funny entertainment at the newly opened Companions Theatre on Thursday evening.

Glad indeed am I that I did so. From the moment the curtain rose to reveal Mr Wolf – a tall, gangling young man with red hair, wearing a perfectly ordinary tweed suit of the kind young men wear – standing quite still in the centre of an empty stage, to its descent an hour later when, weak from laughing, I tottered from the theatre, I was conscious of that ineffable tingling of the nerve-ends experienced, perhaps, only two or three times in a critic's life, when he knows without any doubt that he is in the presence of a very rare talent indeed.

I have to add, however, that by no means all the audience shared my view. Expecting, no doubt, the usual red-nosed comedian to enter stage right amidst a cacophonous roll of drums and a barrage of comic patter, the sight of Mr Wolf's still and silent figure occasioned, from the very outset, a rumble of protest from those of the groundlings who preferred their humour to be, as it were, of the boiled-beef-and-carrots variety. Indeed, a large lady in the gallery, who had been exhibiting every sign of impatience at Mr Wolf's continued silence, at last felt compelled to shout in a voice the resonance and power of which could surely out-match any costermonger in the land: ''urry h'up, young fella, we ain't got all day. Do yer – tricks or get off the blinkin' stage'.

Whatever the good lady expected as a result of these instructions, I am perfectly sure she never envisaged what followed. It was as though her words released some hidden spring within the young man on the stage. For he simply disappeared; to be replaced by the only too familiar figure of our esteemed Chancellor of the Exchequer, the Rt Hon David Lloyd George. Gravely, the latter reprimanded the lady for her lack of patience, and went on to tell us, in startling detail, of a scheme he had in mind for the compulsory training of all young women in basket work. It will, he told us with some passion, serve to keep them off the streets, or from tying themselves up to railings, or even, indeed, from having babies. 'There are, my friends,' he told us, 'far too many babies, they must be stopped.' At this point someone shouted 'Shame!' to be quickly answered by a female voice from the gallery: ''E's right, though, ain't 'e – there are too many b---g babies. I've 'ad eight myself.' Further cries of 'Shame' and 'Fella's a Socialist, get him off', and it was plain a full-scale political discussion was about to ensue – except that the Rt Hon Gentleman had disappeared, and in his place stood Mrs Patrick Campbell. Did I mention that Mr Wolf has no props of any kind, not even a piano, to help him with his effects? He has nothing but his supremely talented self, and the gallery of painfully vivid, painfully alive characters he creates.

I do not think Mr Julian Wolf is a Socialist; I do not even think that he is preaching to us. He is, I suspect, simply giving us, in the only way he knows how, his joyously iconoclastic view of our Masters, using his inimitable wit as the surgeon does his knife, to expose their hypocrisy and their altogether too human frailty.

I also suspect that Mr Wolf is a young man born before his time. His humour is too sharp, too raw, perhaps too near the bone for present-day audiences. But his time will come, my friends. Make no mistake.

Meanwhile, I recommend those of my readers with an open mind and a strong sense of the ridiculous, to make haste to the Companions Theatre and see Mr Wolf for themselves before it is too late.

Christ! Why had no one told me? Had he really been as good as this? Why hadn't Dad . . . ?

Too many questions and too few answers.

But a talent encountered 'only two or three times in a critic's life'! And I'd always seen him as a sort of 'gentleman' comic' down on his luck, telling a few tired jokes at the end of some lost, Edwardian pier. There had been hints that though a 'bad hat', Grandfather Wolf came from a slightly higher stratum of the middle class than the Henshaws. Dad, old snob that he was, certainly believed this.

Frustrated at the lack of any further information, I carefully replaced the photograph and the cutting in the envelope. It was then that I discovered there was something else inside it; something hard, wedged in a corner. Childlishly excited, I shook the envelope until whatever it was became dislodged and rolled out on to the hearthrug.

The thing wasn't even silver. It was just a cheap-looking 'lucky' cat with a grinning mask, green glass eyes, and a tail cocked up to form a horseshoe. Oddly enough, though, even then I knew it was important. I also knew I must see Lally Flynn again.

Saturday morning, squally showers and wind, winter on its way back. This time the lady with the headscarf wasn't there; the entrance to Palmer's Building was deserted, except for a grey and white cat ranging round the dustbin in the entrance hall. Didn't they ever empty the rubbish in this part of Bath?

I'd made no appointment to see Mrs Flynn. Her flat was without a phone, and there was always the possibility that if I wrote she might refuse to see me; rightly or wrongly, I also felt that an unannounced evening visit might be unacceptable. I wasn't going on legal business, you see. Peter Davenport, recovered in record time from his bout of 'flu, had taken Mrs Flynn's Will round on Monday afternoon, and had reported her in sparkling form. Amanda Fenton-Langly had not been there, her place taken by Kevin Rogers, a bouncer at a local night club whose spare time was spent studying for a degree with the Open University. Mr Rogers told Peter he lodged at the flat at a reduced rent, in return for helping out with Mrs Flynn. 'A bit of a weirdo' was Peter's comment, but he went on to say that weirdo or not, he was obviously very fond of Mrs Flynn and appeared extremely capable.

'But the place itself, David, it's nothing but a tip. Of course I've been on to the Council about it. Honestly, if this damned Government stays in much longer . . .'

Peter and I were lunching in our usual pub. I sometimes wished we didn't have to do this, but it had become a routine that was difficult to break. 'You can't blame everything on the government', I said. 'Besides, Miss Fenton-Langly told me she didn't want the Council to interfere in case they put pressure on Mrs Flynn to go into a Home. In fact I promised not to.'

'You promised not to!' A nest of crumbs obstinately adhered to Peter's chin; I longed for him to wipe them off. 'With respect, David, I can't agree. In my opinion the Council should be told. It's a question of values – the place is a disgrace, they shouldn't be allowed to get away with it.'

'It suits Mrs Flynn,' I said. 'Did you know she's nearly a hundred?'

'No, but quite frankly, David, that's not the point, is it? I mean – '

'I must go,' I said, 'I've an appointment at two.' As I made my escape, I realised I hadn't told him of our possible connection – Lally Flynn's and mine. Still, that could wait. Perhaps it wasn't worth telling anyway.

The stairs at Palmer's Building seemed steeper than at my last visit. Perhaps it was because I had this odd constriction in my chest and my hands were sweating. An old man passed me on his way down, carrying a tattered shopping bag full of empty milk bottles. 'Got to put these out,' he whispered as he brushed against me, 'they'll have you if you don't.'

There was no reply when I knocked on the flat door; no music either, they must all be out. The door, however, was unlocked. Suddenly bold, I let myself in. A strong smell of curry, not unpleasant, filled the chaotic room. Wind rattled the windows and moaned down the boarded-up chimney, somewhere a washing-machine whirred.

'Anyone at home?'

'I have a loaded stick beside me. If you come any nearer I shall not hesitate to use it.' Lally Flynn's voice from the next room; pretty strong, really, for someone of her years, but tapering off a little at the end. I felt a sudden, shocked compassion. 'Mrs Flynn, it's me, David Wolf. The front door was unlocked. I wanted to see you – I found something about my grandfather – ' There was an explosion of laughter, followed by a prolonged bout of coughing. I waited until it was over. 'Mrs Flynn, may I come in for a moment?'

'You can make some tea first. The kitchen's through the

door on the left, the tea's all laid out ready. And shut the door when you've done, will you, I can't stand the smell of curry.' Obediently, I found my way round the kitchen – messy, but despite the antique equipment, a place one could work in.

'How very kind, Mr Wolf, and how delightful. I must apologise for threatening to murder you, but my young insist upon it. They tell me it is a common pastime nowadays to attack the aged or infirm. I find this hard to believe, but all things are possible, I suppose, and I promised.'

'It does happen, I'm afraid, all too frequently.' I cleared away the clutter from the trolley by her chair. 'Young thugs with nothing better to do, even girls sometimes – this country's not what it was.' Lally Flynn looked at me through a cloud of cigarette smoke, her green eyes mocking. 'And what was it, my dear,' she said, 'what was it?' I felt like a schoolboy being reprimanded for stupidity. 'I'm sorry, I'm afraid I tend to talk in clichés when I'm nervous. Do you have sugar in your tea?'

'Of course not,' she said, 'and I like the milk in first. Now, Mr Wolf, what's brought you here again so soon? Is there something wrong with my Will? It seemed such a splendid document. All done on a machine that types at five hundred words a minute, so your Mr Davenport tells me. I, for my sins, once worked as a typist, but I never achieved more than thirty words a minute, and even then I made lots of mistakes. I often – '

'I've come about my grandfather.' (She knew I had; she was playing with me.) 'I've found an old newspaper cutting – a write-up of a performance of his in London in 1911. They seemed to think he was practically a genius. I also found this.' And I held out the lucky cat. 'I don't quite know why, but I wondered if you had ever seen it before.'

A JCB ground noisily into the paving-stones at the end of the street; somewhere an ambulance siren whinnied; a radio droned traffic news from the next-door flat. I heard all these things, but still the silence in the little room was oppressive. We sat, Lally Flynn and I, two cut-out figures from a child's picture book, looking at one another; I with one hand thrust out in front of me, the tiny cat resting on the palm. A sudden shaft of sun caught the green glass chips that formed the creature's eyes, and made them twinkle.

At last the old lady spoke. Her voice, for a moment, was the voice of a girl. 'Despite the smile, he's not a lucky cat. They say cats always find their way home – what a very long time this one has taken.' She held out her hand, and I dropped the thing into it.

'I left my first husband for your grandfather – did you know? I loved him, for a time, more than life itself. He was a great artist – but of course you know that.'

'I know nothing; nothing whatsoever about him. Everyone forgot him, you see. No one told me anything . . . anything . . .' I heard my voice shaking with an incomprehensible passion. 'I didn't forget,' Lally said, 'but then I suppose I wouldn't. But that others should . . .' There was silence again while she turned the charm this way and that to reflect the light. 'So Florrie must have been your grandmother – what a lark!'

'Yes.' I stiffened slightly, prepared – I've no idea why – to defend my grandmother. 'I often stayed with her when I was a child. She's dead now, of course.'

'Of course.'

'I'm sorry, Mrs Flynn, I didn't mean . . .' I tried to make amends. Lally ignored my clumsiness. 'Poor little Florrie, she had a hard time, especially when the baby came. Sitting about in draughty dressing-rooms waiting for Ju can't have been much fun. He used to call her his little passport to respectability, the ass.'

'I've brought the cutting too,' I said, 'I thought you might like to see it.'

'How very kind. I shall enjoy that.' Damn her, she'd got away from me again. I had a sudden violent urge to break the complacency of age – a small boy deliberately peeing into his mother's best hat, poking his finger in her eye. 'My father rarely spoke of his father,' I said, 'except to say that he had died comparatively young. I always felt that perhaps his had been a tragic life.' I hadn't felt this at all, I'd never thought about it, I was just fishing. Lally, however, refused to rise to my bait.

'Would it be a frightful bore if you got rid of this tea and poured me another cup? This one is stone cold, you can tip it out of the window.' Angrily, I did as I was told. Below, a dog about to lift its leg against my car looked up surprised at the rain of liquid coming from above, and trotted huffily up the street. I turned back into the room and saw, for a fleeting second, such a look of anguish on the old lady's face as to make me ashamed; ashamed at what I had done, with my lucky charms and newspaper cuttings wrenched from her past. Was it she who had ruined my grandfather's life, or had he ruined hers? Lally Flynn was surely indestructible, but my grandfather? Carefully, I poured her out another cup of tea. 'How kind.' Her smile must once have been – indeed, still was – gorgeous. I noticed that the lucky cat had disappeared.

'In spite of your grandfather's end, Mr Wolf, you must not think of him as a tragic character; he had too much laughter in him for that. He lived in the wrong time and perhaps that was his tragedy. It happens sometimes, especially with people who are endowed with great gifts as Julian was.' She sipped her tea delicately, then lit another cigarette. 'Are you a gardener, Mr Wolf?'

'As a matter of fact, I am.'

'Good, then you will understand my analogy. Think of a plant grown in a part of the garden where the soil and conditions of light and shade are unsuited to its needs. What will happen? Its growth will remain stunted, and soon, preyed on by insects and encroached upon by weeds, it will disappear altogether. Yet that same plant, in the right part of the self-same garden, would grow and flourish to become the garden's pride and glory. So with Julian. If he were a young man now, he would be what they call a 'megastar', but because he lived when he did, he is forgotten by everyone – even, it seems, by his own grandson.

'You don't think that perhaps there was a tendency to self-destruction there?' I said. 'My father had a streak of it, I'm sure. His choice of the wrong thing, the wrong person, even the wrong time, often seemed to me to be deliberately perverse. In an odd way, I always had the feeling he gravitated naturally towards the dark. I don't mean he was an evil man – far from it – but, to continue your analogy, he disliked the sun.' (What was the matter with me, I never talked like this. Perhaps I used to talk like this a long time ago? I couldn't remember.)

'Self-destructive? Possibly. Your grandfather, in his way, was certainly a giver, and sometimes such people find they've handed out so much of themselves that there's nothing left to do but die. That might have been so with Julian. You know, I didn't see him in his last years.' She stubbed out her half-finished cigarette in the overflowing ashtray beside her, and carefully smoothed the neat navy blue dress over her knees; her fingernails were manicured, and painted a faint bluish-pink. Suddenly she looked tired and very old, and for the first time since I had met her, her eyes had lost their sharp intelligence; she was not, after all, indestructible.

'I'm sorry, Mrs Flynn, I've tired you out.'

'I am a little tired now. But I'm glad you came, Mr Wolf, so very glad. I don't get many visitors from outside, and you brought the cat back, and that was rather important.' She shut her eyes, then opened them again and smiled. 'Leave me the cutting, I will see it's returned.' She held out her hand but, ignoring it, I bent down and on impulse kissed her on the lips; it was like kissing a ghost. 'Take the tray with you, dear,' she said, 'I think I'll have a nap.' By the time I had reached the door she was asleep.

Late that evening, the phone rang. Philippa and I had been to *The Merchant of Venice* at the Theatre Royal and she'd come back afterwards for a coffee. Untypically, though it had happened once or twice before, the evening ended in bed. Actually not in bed; to be exact, we'd made love on the sitting-room floor – even more untypical. 'Has something happened that I don't know about?' Philippa said while we were dressing afterwards. 'It's not like you, David, to take a girl by surprise . . .' Anyway, the mini-cab came for her, and it had just driven away, and I was standing waiting for Merry to complete her interminable late-night ablutions, when the phone rang.

'David Wolf?' A man's voice, traces of cockney; ringing from a call-box. 'Yes, who – ?'

'Kevin Rogers, Mr Wolf. Lally wants to see you. She's dying.'

'Now?'

'Yes, if you don't mind. The doc says she can't last long – OK?'

'I'll be there. And Mr Rogers – tell her to hold on.'

She held on, but only just. I drove like a bat out of hell and of course at that time of night there was no traffic.

When I arrived at Palmer's Building all the lights in the place were on. An ambulance waited outside and a small crowd had gathered in the hall, even overflowing out on to the steps. It was like the passing of royalty. 'That's the solicitor,' a woman hissed as, head bent, I hurried through the throng and up the stairs. At the top a young man waited. He was wearing a combat jacket and dark glasses; he had obviously been posted there to look out for me. 'Mr Rogers?'

'No, Kev had to go back to the club, they only let him out for half an hour, the bastards. I'm Dwight. Manda and the doc are in with Lally.'

The curtains were drawn in the little room. Lally, her eyes closed, lay in the bed propped up by pillows. The doctor sat awkwardly – he was a large man and the chair was small – at the pretty French writing-desk, scribbling something. The death certificate? Amanda knelt on the floor by the bed, holding Lally's hand.

'I hope you realise this is your fault?' she hissed at me, one eye on the doctor. 'What in hell did you say to her this morning?' Without waiting for an answer, she pulled me down beside her. 'Darling, Mr Wolf's here.' Lally opened her eyes. 'Julian?'

'David, actually, Mrs Flynn. It's David, Julian's grandson. You wanted to see me.'

'David?' She half turned her face towards me, her eyes searching for something. Kneeling beside her, feeling more inadequate than I've ever done in my entire life – and that's saying something – I tried to get through to her. It was like trying to get a last-minute message to someone in a train that's already pulling out of the station; the train moves faster and faster, you shout louder and louder above the roar of the diesel, mouthing your words and gesticulating, until at last the train disappears from view and you never know whether your friend got the message.

I was beginning to get cramp and the sweat was trickling down the back of my neck, when at last Lally recognised me. She whispered something I couldn't catch, but her eyes were focusing on mine. I leant over the bed, my face close to hers. 'Mr Wolf. I want you to take my diaries and destroy them. Do you understand?' I nodded. 'So many . . . some lost . . . I don't . . .'

'Of course I'll take them, don't worry. Anything . . .'

'One more thing.' The eyes were a little desperate now. Slowly and with a fearful effort – the tide by then was coming in fast – she dragged her hand from where it rested, a limp, pink starfish on the quilt, and plucked at the blue ribbon round her neck. 'The cat, take him. Your son . . .' Gently, under Amanda's disapproving eye, I removed the fluttering hand and untied the ribbon. The little cat, satyr-like, grinned up at me.

'I have him safe, darling,' I said, 'you can go in peace now.' And once again I kissed her on the lips.

'Julian?' she said, quite loudly, and died.

I finally got to bed at four in the morning; to dream peaceless, harried dreams in which Dad and Amy seemed to be laughing at me, and a man called Julian, with a red beard, kept shouting instructions that none of us understood.

I woke, feeling rather ill, to the sound of church bells and the newspaper boy scraping his trolley on the gravel outside. It was ten o'clock, and Merry was frantic to be let out. Head pounding, I dragged myself out of bed and drew back the curtains. Ragged black and grey clouds chased each other over the sky, the road beyond the gate was wet with rain. I felt as though I were floating alone on a vast and oily sea of despair, with no land in sight anywhere. Quite suddenly I had become aware – and so overwhelmingly that I wanted to stick my head in the nearest gas oven – of all the missed opportunities in my life. With appalling clarity I saw the wasted years stretching useless behind me. What in hell had I got to show for them? When I died, would there be such signs of woe as I had witnessed last night at Palmer's Building? Like hell there would. Even my only son had chosen to live so far away from me as possible, and Amy for a long time now had regarded me as nothing more than a sort of glorified bank clerk.

God knows how long I stood there in front of the window, gazing out at the flat-topped hill across the valley. I was rescued at last by a soft but determined pressure on my knee. My God, Merry – I still hadn't let her out. (I've always maintained, despite ever-increasing, ever more shrill lobbying from the 'filthy, vicious, fouling-the-pavement, spreading-disease' brigade, that the presence of a dog in his life does more to keep the average person sane than all the pills and professional comforters put together, but that's by the way).

Later, feeling more ordered, having shaved, eaten breakfast and taken a brisk walk, I sat down to read the Sunday papers. But it was no good, today's disasters meant nothing; my eyes dutifully followed the lines of print, my mind got nowhere near it. Instead, I found myself thinking for the first time of Julian, Dad and myself as links in one continuous chain. Had we, when all was said and done, anything whatsoever in common? On the face of it, no. Julian, it now seemed, had been some kind of genius; Dad, I suppose, had possessed a certain spark, mishandled perhaps, but a spark for all that; I didn't even possess a spark. But there was one thing, wasn't there, one all-important thing? We none of us seemed capable of accepting love; it seemed that we were afraid of it. Like the boy in Hans Anderson's 'Snow Queen', we each of us had a splinter of glass wedged in our hearts.

I shivered. The silence in the house was, all of a sudden, oppressive – just a thin sigh of wind down the chimney and now and again the hum of the fridge from the kitchen. But this was how I liked it – surely?

When the phone rang I nearly cried with relief.

'It's Amanda Fenton-Langly. Lally's funeral – Thursday – two-thirty at St Botolph's, Whitesgreen. That is, if you want to come.'

'Whitesgreen. Isn't that rather a long way?' Whitesgreen is a small village in the downs near the Westbury White Horse, about twenty miles from Bath.

'I promised. Lally lived there years ago. She made us have the vicar of Whitesgreen to tea here the other day, so we could make the arrangements. Lally was pretty efficient, you know.'

'I can imagine.'

'Look, can you organise Peter Davenport? I'd like him to do whatever needs to be done over the Will.'

'Yes, of course.' Why Whitesgreen?

'By the way, Lally told me about the Wolf connection the day she died. By all accounts you're not much like your grandfather.'

'No,' I said, letting it pass. 'When shall I collect the diaries?'

'As soon as possible. We want to clear Lally's room. Dwight says he'll do the decorating, then we can have another lodger. We're staying on, you see, until the Council kicks us out – we might even try a squat.'

'The furniture,' I said, entering into the spirit of the thing, 'is worth a good bit. With the proceeds you could put a down payment on a house – '

'Quite the little man of business, aren't we?'

'It does happen to be my profession. Look, can I collect the diaries this afternoon?'

'Great. I probably won't be there, but someone will. Lally's at the undertaker's, so you don't have to worry about her.'

'I wasn't, actually,' I said, 'and there's no necessity to be rude.' The phone clicked; she'd rung off. I didn't care. I'd got the cat, hadn't I?

Back at Palmer's Building, I'd never seen the sitting-room so tidy. They must have been working all night. Someone had even cleaned the windows. An ancient Gladstone bag stood open on the floor in front of the unlit gas fire.

'Anyone at home?'

'God, you can't keep away, can you?' Amanda uncurled herself from the divan. She'd pinned her hair in a knot on top of her head; she looked manic. 'For heaven's sake,' I said, 'I've come to collect the diaries, I thought you said you'd be out.'

'Well, I'm not, am I?' We eyed one another. I became aware suddenly that I wanted very much to make love to her.

'The diaries are in that bag.' She pointed to the Gladstone bag. 'Would you like a drink before you go?'

'It's three o'clock in the afternoon – '

'So?'

'Thanks very much,' I said. In silence she loped into the kitchen, returning a moment later with two half-filled tumblers (Waterford). 'No ice, I'm afraid, the fridge's on the blink.'

'I don't like ice.' I gasped as the raw spirit burned my throat; it was Irish, not Scotch, and neat.

'Cheers!' She clinked her glass against mine.

'To life.'

Carefully she placed her glass on the table. 'Make love to me . . .'

Light years later (it was only a couple of hours, actually) I opened my eyes. Amanda, naked, lay spreadeagled beside me on the divan, her face pressed into the cushions. The room was cold now, and nearly dark; rain rattled on the window. I longed for a cigarette, something I hadn't done in years. I didn't feel too bad, as it happened; somewhere, I felt sure, Lally's ghost was laughing at us.

Carefully, so as not to disturb Amanda, I crawled off the divan and groped around for my clothes. Dressed at last, I lit the gas fire, and drew the curtains. Where on earth were the others? Ought I to write a note? But we had said all there was to say, Amanda and I, hadn't we? We'd honoured Lally's death in the only way possible – with life.

I picked up the Gladstone bag, then bent down and kissed the nape of Amanda's neck. She murmured a little in her sleep. Earlier, she had wept, but it had been the right sort of weeping for the right sort of reason.

Quietly, I let myself out.

Lally Flynn's funeral was a small affair: only Amanda (looking beautiful in a wide-brimmed garden-party hat of green straw), Kevin (in a black beret and dark glasses) and Dwight (in his camouflage jacket), plus a mini-bus full of elderly inmates of Palmer's Building and driven by the local RC priest, myself, and a distinguished, silver-haired gentleman wearing a very expensive-looking suit and an Old Etonian tie. The latter looked as though he thought he'd come to the wrong funeral, but had decided he'd better stick it out all the same.

'Who's he?' I asked Amanda as we waited by the lychgate for the hearse to arrive. 'Cousin Jeremy Eagon', she said. 'He's come to sniff out some of the Eagon stuff, I expect. His father claimed that their branch of the family should have had it, not Lally. Cousin Jeremy's father, James, was Lally's first husband's – my great-grandfather's – younger brother. That's why Lally wanted to make a new Will; to make sure the stuff went to me.'

A chilly wind swept round the corner, tugging at the brim of Amanda's unsuitable hat and flattening the daffodils growing along the stone path leading to the church porch. A foolhardy bee buzzed about in the ivy on the crumbling grey stone wall bordering the lane, and somewhere above us a lark was singing. Beyond the squat, square church tower, green downs climbed towards the sky. It was a lovely spot; I could see why Lally wanted to be buried there. Squabbles about family furniture seemed out of place.

'Sorry we're a little late, Miss Fenton-Langly. The driver missed the turning and there was a herd of sheep. Perhaps you would like to lead the way?' The professionals had arrived at last.

The coffin, a single wreath of white roses upon its polished surface, was unloaded with the expertise of long practice from its niche in the rear of the hearse on to the shoulders of four black-suited, black-tied young men, whose carefully oiled hair, polished shoes and gleaming white collars bore witness to the fact that Lally Flynn's funeral was not going to be a cheap one.

The procession slowly moved off, Cousin Jeremy and I falling in behind the chief mourners, followed by Dwight and the contingent from Palmer's Building. We were halfway along the path to where the vicar of St Botolph's, his surplice blowing in the wind, awaited us in the porch, when suddenly, shatteringly, the joyful, decadent sounds of ragtime, played on the organ, came belting out through the open church door. Cousin Jeremy's eyes closed as though in pain. The chief undertaker's shoulders quivered, and he turned a respectful profile to Amanda. 'Mrs Flynn wanted it,' she shouted above the din. 'We got someone special from the university, doesn't it sound super?' Swaying slightly, the cortège proceeded on its way. What was it one used to dance to this – the bunny hug? The church doors closed behind us.

Tea and champagne was arranged afterwards in the local pub. I must say, it was all very well organised. Some of the Palmer's Building crowd got pretty merry, and I saw the old man with the milk bottles, whom I'd bumped into on the stairs, regaling a rapt audience of students – friends of Amanda's who hadn't attended the funeral but decided to come to the do afterwards – with his experiences on the Somme in 1916.

'Quite a do! My name's Eagon, by the way; nephew by marriage to the deceased. My Uncle Rupert was Lally Flynn's first husband. You are . . . ?' Cousin Jeremy approached, a glass of champagne in one hand, a cigar in the other.

'David Wolf. I'm the solicitor, actually – '

'Good God, you're not going to read the Will, are you? I thought they only did that in Agatha Christie novels.'

'No, no, of course not,' I said huffily. Why do men like Cousin Jeremy always make me feel so aggressive? 'I'm just here as a friend.' Then suddenly I felt an overwhelming compulsion to shake the man's upper-crust complacency. He couldn't be here to snoop around for a few dusty antiques, he was much too well-heeled for that. Why, then, had he come? I threw a stone in the pool. 'My grandfather was a great friend of Mrs Flynn's, actually – Julian Wolf.'

'Not *the* Julian Wolf! Good Lord. Of course, how stupid of me – your name's Wolf too, isn't it. Well, this is really rather exciting.'

It was not the response I had expected. 'Really? I mean why? I don't see – '

'My daughter, Fiona Maplethorpe – you may have heard of her, she's one of these TV people – she happens to be doing a programme on your grandfather. Forgotten genius, master of black comedy, pre-dated the goons by fifty years – all that sort of thing. Julian Wolf's "in" at the moment, didn't you know? We like to think he has a sort of family connection with the Eagons, even though on the wrong side of the blanket as t'were. Fiona will be absolutely thrilled to hear I've met you.' Oh God, where was this all going to end? Absent-mindedly, I put my hand in my jacket pocket and pulled out the lucky cat. He was, it seemed, laughing harder than ever.

Meanwhile Cousin Jeremy had whipped out his address book. 'Look, can I have your number? You simply must meet Flea. How about you and your wife – ?'

'I haven't got a wife,' I interrupted rudely, 'she left me

years ago.' I was beginning to feel hunted. But Cousin Jeremy continued to burble on. 'They have J.W. on tape, did you know? And some scraps of film. Poor quality, of course, but even an old fuddy-duddy like me can see what he must have been like. Other stuff too, I believe; poems and so on he'd written, found in a collection of books belonging to some chap who taught at the University of Cairo in the twenties and knew Wolf in his last years.'

I took a gulp of champagne. 'I was with Lally at the end,' I said. 'She spoke his name as she died.' Cousin Jeremy looked solemn. 'Great romance, I believe. Shook the family rigid at the time. She was married to my Uncle Rupert, you know, when she ran off with Wolf. The family never forgave her. Long before my time, of course – my Pa, James Eagon, didn't marry until he was well over forty – but I can remember my aunt talking about it. The woman must have been some sort of femme fatale, if you ask me. She ditched your grandfather too – did you know that? Left him for some drunken Irish poet, then *he* came to a sticky end. God knows what happened after that . . .'

I dropped the cat back in my pocket. Poor Tommy Flynn! Lally stood beside me and she too was laughing. But it wasn't funny, was it, it couldn't possibly have been funny.

'Lally Flynn would never have ditched anybody . . .' How did I know that? I'd only met her three times, and on the face of it, it certainly looked as if Cousin Jeremy was right. 'Anyway, she's left me her diaries.' As soon as I'd said it I knew I had made a mistake. I could see the pound signs flashing on and off in his rather bulbous blue eyes.

'Did you say diaries?'

'One or two,' I mumbled. 'She wanted me to destroy them.' He winced. 'But Fiona – '

'Look, I'm sorry, I really must be going. I've been longer away from the office than I should – frightfully busy at the moment.'

'Your phone number, you haven't – '

'A remarkable old lady, Mrs Flynn. I only had the privilege of meeting her once, but . . .' Thank God. The vicar, waiting patiently for a word, had insinuated himself into the vacant space in front of Cousin Jeremy. The place seemed to be filling up; I saw a man I knew from the local rag.

Amanda was standing by the window in the sun; she had taken off the green hat and her blue eyes were bright with tears. I put my arms round her and kissed her. 'Great party – and I loved the music.'

'Did you find out what Cousin Jeremy wants?' I nodded. 'Your furniture's safe. It's stuff about my grandfather he's after, and like a fool, I told him I'd got Lally's diaries. He lit up like a lighthouse when he heard that. His daughter's doing a programme – Julian Wolf's "in", didn't you know?' I kissed her again. I have to admit it was rather enjoyable, and I'm not used to champagne at three o'clock in the afternoon. 'Promise you won't give Cousin Jeremy my phone number.'

'If you promise you won't get in touch with the Council about the flat, or let Mr Davenport poke his nose in.'

'I promise.' Amanda smiled, her red hair glinting in the shaft of sun. Lally must have looked like that long ago . . .

But I didn't go back to the office. I drove home, took Merry for her walk, and after a simple supper of pork chop and peas from the freezer, began my investigation of the Gladstone bag. As I did so, I experienced that stomach-churning, slightly breathless excitement so unfamiliar to me before my meeting with Lally Flynn, but which, in the last ten days I had known increasingly often.

The bag contained five exercise books of the fat, shiny variety. Each one – apart from the earliest, which was only half-filled – was not merely a diary but a general compendium of Lally's day to day living; it disclosed a veritable magpie's hoard of the trivial and the not-so-trivial – personal and household accounts, shopping lists, newspaper cuttings, letters and picture postcards. Otherwise the bag contained a broken comb, two ancient lipsticks, and sundry hairpins entangled inextricably with several perished rubber bands. Everything was lightly dusted with face powder from a half-open box – purchased, I noticed, at a shop in the rue de Rivoli in Paris – and redolent of some highly evocative and faintly musky perfume.

The first diary was easy to read, the twelve-year-old Lally's writing bold and clear; Miss 'Beastly' Brownlow had obviously done a good job. What came as a shock, one of the many, was the discovery that they had all lived in St Wilfred's

71

Square; that the house Dad had died in, that now provided my divorced wife's income and had paid for Marcus to go to his snob school – that was currently inhabited by yuppies from the home counties, plus an Arab or two – was the house in which my unfortunate great-grandmother had endured such horrendous suffering, and Lally's father, despite his claim that he was not the sort of cove who'd fit easily into a suit of armour, had met his end saving the live of another. The fact that in saving my great-grandfather's life he was, by all accounts, doing the human race a great disservice, in no way diminished Mr Morgan's act of valour. Would I have been able to do the same? I very much doubted it. How could I destroy this? It was part of history – not just Lally's part, but mine too, or at least my family's. As I think I've said before, I've never been much of a history man, preferring to take life as it comes; but somehow this was different. I poured myself a drink and then read the whole thing over again. It didn't take long. After Mr Morgan's death there were no more entries.

I'd have to let Marcus know about all this. . . . What on earth would he make of it? As a matter of fact, I'd never been too sure what Marcus made of anything. Actually, he knew No 4 St Wilfred's Square better than I did. My parents hadn't moved into it until after I was grown up and had left home – about 1955, when it was de-requisitioned by the Council; during the war the place had been used to house bombed-out families. But Marcus used to stay there with his grandparents quite a bit; as a little boy he'd been devoted to Dad.

Suddenly I remembered something. It was just after my mother died in 1973, when we were clearing up before the builders moved in. What I remembered was coming into the back room downstairs with a sackful of rubbish, and seeing Marcus's twelve-year-old face pressed forlornly against the dirty windowpane, looking out on the tangled, overgrown garden. He was chanting quietly to himself. 'Poor, old house. Poor, poor, old house, no one to love you any more.' Funny I'd never thought of that before, yet remembered it now. At the time I probably just considered it yet one more manifestation of the boy's 'oddness'.

Come to think of it, I owed Marcus a letter. He'd written, hadn't he, the day I met Lally Flynn. He and Barbie had broken up. God, that seemed a lifetime ago, yet it was only a couple of weeks.

On second thoughts, I'd read a bit more of the diaries first.

PART III

I *am* going to write a diary again – so there!

It's six years now since that dreadful time. Sometimes I can hardly believe it ever happened. And yet darling Pa is always with me, making me laugh, giving advice. Often, so often, I hear his dear voice: 'Come on, imp, use that brain-box of yours.'

Last night I made myself read that other diary; I've not been able to before. I cried, but the bitterness and rage have gone. I still hate Mr Wolf, and will do him down if ever I get the chance.

How odd I should have forgotten all about Rupert Eagon! I never heard from him again after he sent me the Valentine. Of course, I was only a child then and horrid old Bigbury is miles and miles from Kensington.

We moved to Bigbury after Pa's death. We couldn't afford to go on living in the house in St Wilfred's Square; anyway, Mother said she couldn't face the scandal. I suppose Rupert Eagon's people couldn't face it either. Poor old Bob never went to Eton, there wasn't enough money, but he says he's had just as much fun at St David's, so who cares. Mother says Bob's been a Trojan since Pa died and for once I agree with her. He starts his new job on Monday, with a firm of tea merchants in Mincing Lane in London. He's going to live at Aunt Dolly's in Earls Court, the lucky thing, but come home on Saturdays. I shall miss him, although he makes such a noise and is always playing silly practical jokes. Suki is captain of the second eleven at hockey (she would be), she'll end up captain of games for certain. Games and dogs is all Suki thinks about nowadays. I heard Mother say to Mrs Peters at tea the other day: 'I sometimes wish my little Suki wasn't quite such a hearty – she's such a dear child.'

'Be thankful, Elvira,' says Mrs P., 'she's not another Lally. You'll have trouble with that one or my name is not Amelia Peters.' Mrs Peters is rather common, but quite nice really. Anyway, I like to think I might be trouble one day; it's so dull to be good. (I promised myself this diary is going to be absolutely, entirely honest – like Pepys, only not in code – that is why I wrote the last bit.)

And me? Poor little me? So bored and flat. There must be

something more to being grown up than this – but what? I went to see dear Polly just before Christmas. Polly came with us from No 4 (Milne and the others had to leave, Mother couldn't afford them, and darling Nanny went to live with her widowed sister in Chippenham and died of pneumonia a year after Pa), and now she, Polly, is married to a postman called Ted and lives in a funny little house behind the station. She has two babies, Tom and Bella and a dear little dog called Ruff. I go and see her quite often. Mother says I shouldn't be so friendly with a servant, even if she is Polly, but I don't see why not. Anyway, Pol says it won't be long before I bump into Mr Right.

'You're something special, Miss Lally, always have been.' (Pol's the only one who thinks this, but never mind.) 'What you need is an experience – be swept off your feet, like – no time to argue.'

'Have you ever been swept off your feet, Pol?' I asked. We were peeling potatoes for Ted's midday dinner, he has a big one after his round. 'I was by Arn,' she said, 'and once is enough.' (Arn was killed in the Transvaal soon after we moved.) 'But then I'm not like you, Miss Lally.'

Oh how I should *adore* to be swept off my feet by a man! But the boys I meet aren't *men*. They are just grown up babies, who are only interested in how Surrey is doing at cricket, or ragging, or how the new people up at The Rise made their money, or . . . Oh, I don't know, they're so stupid I can't even think, what they are interested in.

And the girls at Mrs Lambert's are no better. Mrs Lambert runs what she calls a 'Secretarial College for Young Ladies'. There are only six of us, so it's not really a college. We learn typewriting and Pitmans shorthand, and how to help fat old men in stuffy old offices, and how to 'keep our distance'. 'You may have to earn a living, my dears, in the great world outside, but always remember – you are still ladies.' Pooh! Anyway, I suppose being at old Mother Lambert's is better than being boxed up with my moaning mother all day, and I quite like typewriting. I'm ever so fast at shorthand, much faster than the others, somehow I can never read mine back so it's not much good. We learn French, too, and book-keeping. A man teaches us French, a Mr Lark. Quite a sensible one as men go. He has lovely soft, wavy hair and a gold moustache and ever such sad blue eyes. The others say he's a sissy, and fancy wearing a celluloid collar, but I think he's nice. He has a secret smile sometimes, and I'm sure he laughs at Mrs Lambert. One day last term he left his notes behind on a chair, and he'd drawn ever such strange little pictures on the back of his sheet of irregular verbs. They made me feel quite funny.

There's a party tomorrow night at Mrs Peters'. 'Just a hop, my dears, nothing out of the way, but Bunny wants to try out his new gramophone' – Bunny is her spotty son – 'so come prepared!' For what, I wonder. But even a party given by Mrs P. and spotty Bunny is better than nothing. Back to college next week. Oh darling Pa, shall I go on missing you always? *3rd January* Poor Mrs Wolf is dead. Mother had a letter from Granny Morgan this morning; it was in *The Times*, she says, last week. 'A merciful release,' writes Granny, 'the poor soul never recovered her sanity and died in the asylum they moved her to after Broadmoor.' Mother gave me the letter to read.

'You are a grown-up now, Alice, you had better see this.' Then she went upstairs and shut herself in her bedroom until tea. Granny Morgan goes on to say, 'No doubt that frightful man will marry again, now he is free at last to do so. Lady Stedman – she chairs our Hospital Committee, charming woman – says her husband sees Wolf from time to time at his club – how he managed to become a member no one seems to know – and the buzz is that he has made another fortune, this time out of the South African War. God certainly moves in a mysterious way. One can only hope, dear, the man will one day be punished for his wickedness, if not in this world, at least in the hereafter . . .'

I know it's wrong, but sometimes I wonder if there truly is a God. Poor Pa and Mrs Wolf, both so good and kind, yet it's horrible, vile Mr Wolf who flourishes like the green bay tree.

This afternoon I went down to the beach. The sky was wild and ragged and the wind bitter cold. I took off my hat so my hair blew about in the wind, and picked up my skirts and just ran and ran as fast as I could along the shore. There was no one about, the only sounds were the wind, the crunch of the waves breaking on the shingle and the cry of seagulls sitting on the sea wall. I felt better after that, although my face stung with cold and my ears and fingers were numb.

On my way home, who should I bump into but Mr Lark! 'Good afternoon, Miss Morgan. Braving the elements, I see.' He was certainly looking at me hard enough, and it wasn't just at my hair sticking out any old how from under my hat, and my wet boots. 'I love the sea like this,' I shouted above the crash of the waves, 'it's so exciting.'

'You like excitement, then,' he said, holding on to his hat. 'I thought perhaps you might.' And then we just stood there staring at each other for simply ages. I've never been looked at like that by a man before and don't yet know whether I like it.

'Are you interested in art, Miss Morgan? Just a thought. There's a small exhibition of work by an up-and-coming man, to be held in the Pavilion next week. I've two tickets for the private view – wonder if you'd care to come? Seven-thirty for eight, dress informal, only a small affair but could be quite amusing.' Well, of course I said yes, but shall I tell Mother? Better not; she'd think Mr Lark common, (he is, I suppose, a bit.) But supposing I meet someone I know? I have it, I'll tell Mother Mr Lark is the brother of one of the girls at college and we're going back to his parents' home afterwards. Has Mr Lark parents? It's hard to imagine them if he has.

Time to change for Mrs P. and Bunny. I think this afternoon has done me good; I don't feel so angry about Mr Wolf now . . . Poor Mrs Wolf – somehow I cannot seem to hate her.

8th January   Mother and I not speaking. Ever since Granny Morgan's letter Mother's been in a mood. What am I supposed to do? I miss Pa more than she does. I sometimes don't think she misses him at all, it's just the scandal she hates.

The party at Mrs P.'s was quite enjoyable. Some ripping music too. How I love ragtime, it makes me feel so alive.

We saw Bob on to the 5.15 train to town. He looked ever so smart in his new suit and bowler hat. Oh, how I *wish* and *wish* I were a man and could go to town and make my fortune. Mother cried as the train moved out. 'Who will be my prop

80

and stay,' she moaned, 'now darling Bob has gone?' I knew she wanted me to say I would, but somehow I couldn't. I don't want to be anyone's prop and stay, ever. 'Please don't cry, Mother,' says Suki, and cuddles up, 'you still have Lally and me.'

Tomorrow I meet Mr Lark. Wot Larks!

10th January   Well, I don't know. Quite odd, really, the whole evening, and I'm to meet Mr Lark (I must remember to call him Walter) again this very afternoon at Welland's Rock! My goodness gracious me, Miss Lally Morgan, whatever are you a'doing of?

I have never been to a private view before – not even to a picture exhibition for that matter. Some damned funny folk were congregated there, I must say. Sad ladies in purple with interestin' faces and dowdy hats, a sprinkling of foreign-looking men, Mr Jones who runs the pier and looked bored to death, and some rather ragged young men who looked as if they were sheltering from the rain. The artist himself, a pale, nervous person in a threadbare suit, sat alone in a corner and never spoke.

I met Mr Lark at the door. He winked at me, which I didn't much like, but as Pol says, a girl can't 'ave it all ways. 'Isn't this topping, Miss Morgan!' he says, taking my arm and squeezing it tight. 'Let's go where the fizz is.'

'I thought we had come to see the pictures,' I say – he was getting above himself and needed deflating, 'is Mr Boothroyd well known?'

'People have been known to cough up a pony or two for one of his works,' says Mr Lark, leading me rapidly through the throng to where a splendid lady in black and feathers was dispensing champagne and little sponge cakes with cherries on the top. 'Do you like bubbly?'

'I haven't had it very often,' I say (only once, actually, and it made me sneeze.) But after two glasses of the stuff it didn't make me sneeze any more and I felt absolutely ripping; the cakes were good too. I noticed Mr Lark ate several, as though he hadn't eaten for some time.

And the pictures? Rather 'greenery-yallery'; funny, elongated ladies leading tiny prancing dogs, or sitting about under striped umbrellas. But, as I heard one of Mr Lark's shabby friends say, they had a certain power. By the time I'd finished my third glass of bubbly, however, I had forgotten the pictures, but felt ever so jolly and laughed like anything at whatever Mr Lark and his friends said.

Then suddenly it was over and we were outside in the rain, with Mr Lark sheltering under my umbrella. 'It's been grand, Miss Morgan,' he said. 'May I call you Lally?'

'Perhaps,' I said, 'if you behave yourself.' Mr Lark looked sad. 'What else can I do?' he said. 'It's damnable, but I'm cleaned out of the ready. May I see you to your omnibus?' This was a let-down; I had hoped he would be taking me on to supper, perhaps even drink champagne out of my shoe. 'If you must,' I said, crosslike, 'but the stop is only round the corner.'

'Please, please don't be angry,' he said, 'you see, your esteemed preceptress' (he meant Mrs Lambert) 'does not pay me until next week, and all I have has gone to my widowed mother in Paris.' So then, of course, I felt ashamed, and squeezed his hand. 'Meet me tomorrow at Welland's Rock,' he whispered urgently (the rain was dripping down from the rim of his bowler on to his beautiful moustache; every now and again he licked it off).

'If I can,' I shouted as the bus came round the corner, 'but I'll not promise.'

'Three o'clock!' he shouted back, waving his sodden hat in the air. So there we are.

'Did you have a good evening, Alice?' asks Mother. 'Perhaps your friend would like to come to tea?'

11th January Oh goodness me. I think (indeed, I am certain) disaster has been and gone and struck, and I await the end with what courage I can muster. Mr L. and I have been found out! Mrs Lowndes-Digby and her botany group witnessed us cavorting together on the beach this afternoon. Alas, it seems I am undone!

I met the man at 3 o'clock, as arranged (I wore my fur hat and a long, green scarf that simply *floated* round me in the wind). Mr L. said I was his Ondine, and did I have a merman to go back to in my home under the sea? *Très romantique!* Then somehow, I don't quite know how, I had kicked off my shoes, thrown my hat upon the ground, twined my long scarf round Mr L.'s neck, and we were dancing together, barefoot, on the wet sand. It was then, appearing unexpectedly from behind Welland's Rock, that Mrs Lowndes-Digby saw us. *And* she said nothing, just looked – it was really rather frightful. Then she shouted to the botany group trailing behind her: 'Nothing here of interest, ladies, let us go back', and disappeared from view.

Mr Lark is certainly no 'gentil parfit knight'. He had put on his boots and jammed his hat back on his head in a trice, and all he could say was: 'Oh my God, I hope the old dragon don't tell Mrs Lambert!' Of course she will, and Mother too. What will happen; shall I be sent away? But where to? It's certain poor Mr Lark will get the sack from old Ma Lambert's. Oh horrors, it's all my fault. Not quite all, but a big bit of it.

It was fun, though, while it lasted. I know Mr L. is silly and a bit of a bounder, but all the same . . .

12th January   The worst has happened and I'm in terrible disgrace. This morning, on my way home from the library, I saw Mrs Lowndes-Digby come out of our house. I quickly hid behind a lamp-post and watched her stride up the street, then let myself in as quiet as a mouse. I was just tiptoeing up the stairs when: 'Alice, come into the morning room at once, I wish to speak to you.' (Actually it's just a parlour, but Mother likes to call it the morning room.) 'Is this true? I simply cannot believe it, even of you. Tell me that what Mrs Lowndes-Digby says is wrong. It's not true that she saw you dancing barefoot on the beach yesterday afternoon with the French master from your college?' It's funny, but for a moment Mother looked as Mrs Wolf had done all those years ago; the same terror in her eyes, as though the whole world was against her and she was powerless to defend herself. Suddenly I felt sorry; not at what I had done, why should I? – Mr Lark and I had meant no harm; just sorry that poor old Mother should suffer so. I felt angry too, that stupid, pointless convention could cause so much pain. I think in that moment I grew up.

'I'm sorry, Mother,' I said, 'I'm afraid it is true. Mr Lark and I went for a walk on the beach, that's all – '

'All! But you were seen dancing barefoot with your arms round each other! Mrs Lowndes-Digby said . . .' And so on and so on. Apparently we'd been seen at the Pavilion too, 'drinking alcohol with louts from the town'. Mrs L-D. it seems, has her spies everywhere. I stood there and let the storm break over me, but I determined there and then that I would never, never, never be bound by convention in the way Mother and Mrs L-D, are.

At last Mother seemed to be running out of steam. 'Go to your room, Alice, and stay there until I have decided what is to be done. You will not, of course, return to the college on Monday; under the circumstances, that would be quite out of the question – despite the fact that Lark has already left Bigbury. A note sent round to his lodgings this morning by Mrs Lambert was returned unopened. It seems the man left for town by the early train, taking his luggage with him. If you are entertaining thoughts of eternal love, therefore, you had better forget them. He only wanted one thing.'

'Do you think I didn't know that?' I shouted, really angry now. 'And it wasn't my money either. I'm not a fool, Mother, whatever you may like to think. I merely wanted some fun, and so did poor Mr Lark. The Lord knows there's not much to be had in this place, so we took it in the only way we could.' It was then that Mother slapped my face. It really hurt and made my eyes water for a moment. 'You wanton, wicked little bitch, you didn't. . . ?'

'No, I didn't. I'm sorry to disappoint you and Mrs Lowndes-Digby, but he never even kissed me.'

'Get out!' she screamed. 'Get out. I never want to set eyes on you again!'

So here I am awaiting my fate in my cold little dimity bedroom, with the picture of 'Bubbles' on the wall, and the white lace crinoline-lady pincushion that Suki gave me for Christmas on the dressing table.

Mrs Peter's been summoned, and sundry telegrams sent. Am I to go to prison, I wonder, or be whipped, naked, down the High Street, clinging to Mrs L-D.'s chariot wheels? So Walter Lark has upped and gone; I'm sure I don't blame him. He seemed an odd sort of person to find in Bigbury-on-Sea in the first place; the 'Great Wen' is surely more his cup of tea. Or Paris, I suppose. I wonder if he really has a widowed mother living there. He might have, he certainly spoke French like a native; he certainly had a beautiful moustache, too, for that matter.

Quick! Someone is unlocking my bedroom door. Is't to bring me bread and water?

Friday, 18th January   The Rectory, Little Westhrop
Misery, oh misery, I've been banished to Granny Lloyd's. I arrived three days ago and haven't thawed out since. Among the million things Grandfather Lloyd disapproves of is ladies sitting too near the fire. Backbone is all, he says, warming his bottom before the roaring blaze in his study. Granny L. is simply covered in chilblains and so are all the servants.

This morning, however, wandering about outside in the frost (I don't think anyone knows quite what to do with me), I found a haven – a tiny ray of light, as t'were, in all this sodden wilderness. In short, I found the harness room and in the middle of it a roaring, red hot stove (does Grandfather L. know about this?) with Ball the coachman sitting beside it, smoking his pipe and reading the *Sporting Times*.

'Please don't get up, Mr Ball,' I shout (he's very deaf). 'I only want to warm my hands.' At that he winks – odd how many men do this – and tells me to sit down now, and would I like a mug of coffee? And oh, how good it was! We don't talk much, Ball and me, just smile at one another now and again, but it was the nicest time I've spent since Mrs L-D. jumped out from behind that rock.

What is to become of me? Shall I run away to London and become a lady milliner? Is my typewriting good enough for me to become a lady typewriter in an office? I have my doubts on that score, but I suppose if I smile enough I might get me a position. Meanwhile, prayers morning, noon and night, half-cooked meat with gristle in it for dinner, and this afternoon I serve on the white elephant stall at a bazaar in aid of missionaries in China. I would have thought there were more worthy causes nearer home than converting the heathen Chinee, who probably doesn't want to be converted anyway – but I keep them sentiments to myself.

23rd January   The unbelievable has happened! The most spiffing, ripping, fizzing thing I ever could have imagined. I am to go to finishing school in Paris!! How can this be? I hear you cry. Surely such splendiferous things are not for the likes of her – one who cavorts lasciviously upon the sands with lewd, seductive French masters? But they are, my friends, THEY ARE!

Dear Granny Morgan it is who has worked the miracle. I do not know the details, what I do know has filtered down to me through Granny Lloyd. 'My dear,' she says after breakfast this morning, 'a word in my room, if you please.' Palpitating, I follow her, wondering what on earth it is I've been and gone and done now.

'A letter came this morning from your mother,' she says, not looking at me. 'It seems your Grandmother Morgan has very kindly offered to send you to school in Paris for six months. You are a very lucky young woman indeed, and must write and thank Mrs Morgan immediately. No, don't interrupt, dear, until I have finished. The school, I understand, is run by an old friend of your grandmother. The discipline is strict' (she gives me a look) 'but the education is wide and you will, of course, be able to perfect your French. You are to leave on the boat train from Victoria on Monday morning, accompanied by one of the instructresses from the school, who has been in London for the last few days. What luggage you need from home will be sent on. Now cut along, dear – it is your day, is it not, for doing the flowers in church?'

And that was that, but oh, isn't it enough!

1st February   Pension Lancaster, rue d'Abelard, Paris
Well, here I am at last. But oh, it's so cold and *caging*! This house was once a convent, and hasn't changed much either. Hard, narrow, lumpy beds in cubicles (bars on the windows), a carpet in the parlour where Madame sits but nowhere else, and great big echoing rooms and drafty corridors.

Miss Sutcliffe accompanied me from London, a stiff old stick in black bombazine. Poor dear, she was ever so sick on the Channel crossing and seemed quite grateful when I offered her a peppermint and my travelling rug. She looked as though she wasn't used to people offering her anything, except perhaps a rap over the knuckles. I didn't feel sick at all, and met two such amusing men, one tall and thin, the other short and fat, and both of them wrapped up to the eyes in ulsters and scarves. The tall one's hair was dyed, I'm sure; it was certainly a very odd colour. They insisted upon calling me 'girlie' and are on the music halls.

'Come and have a b and s in the saloon,' the fat one said, 'it's brass monkey weather out there.' So I said thank you very much, and it warmed me up (the b and s) no end. They told me they were on their way to a four-week engagement at a café in Paris – 'Money's none too clever, but what about those Frog Mamselles!' – and gave me their card: The Banjo Brothers Comedy Duo. 'Of course we ain't really brothers,' says the thin one. 'My name's Reg Potter and this 'ere's Bert Starling.' I told them about me going to finishing school and they winked at each other and said they'd have a job to keep that little bird in her cage.

Anyway, in their company the journey flew by; we were so merry that I nearly forgot all about poor Miss Sutcliffe wilting away in the ladies' lounge. Bert and Reg gave me a sample of their 'turn' (out of the wind, behind the lifeboats). Actually, I thought they were much funnier as themselves, but never mind that.

'Tell your friends about us,' they shouted as we waved goodbye, 'and mind how you go.'

Then there were porters in blue overalls all shouting at once (in French too!) and then we were hissing and puffing through the dark on our way to Paris.

We took a flacre at the Gare du Nord and oh, the bliss of everything! The lights, the boulevards, the crowded pavements. How I longed to jump out of the cab and sit outside one of the cafés and just watch and watch and watch the people going by. Much too soon we're over the Seine; as we crossed a bridge I craned out of the window to look at the towers of Notre Dame. 'Don't do that, dear,' says Miss Sutcliffe, 'it is unladylike', and puts a paw on my arm. I sit back and close my eyes, and soon, too soon, we are in quiet, boring streets between tall, gaunt houses, all with heavy shutters on the windows, and then suddenly up looms the Pension Lancaster and we're there.

'So like your dear father,' says Madame Lancaster, kissing me on the cheek while Miss Sutcliffe twitters away in the background; 'blood will out, I suppose.' Madame Lancaster is very fat, and still dresses in the style of the Second Empire. I think she wears a wig. But she must have been beautiful once, and she does have naughty eyes.

'Supper and bed for you, my dear, you will be exhausted by your journey. Wait until morning to meet your fellow pupils.'

Supper was sparse but very good, and I was allowed a glass of wine with it.

I can't write any more, I'm too sleepy . . .

7th February   Pension Lancaster
So busy – no time to write my diary.

I've made a friend, Mary Wentworth. Mary has the cubicle next to mine; she's clever and funny and rather plain, but ever so stylish. She says we are two of a kind – no one knows what to do with us! The other girls are frightful snobs, and spend their time talking about 'Home', and being presented, and what Mama said to the Duke of Athol out hunting, and how Papa shoots with the King.

The first morning, one Bunty Moncrief looks me up and down and asks: 'And where's *your* family place, Alice?'

'Bigbury-on-Sea,' I reply, watching her face, like. 'No 19 Ladysmith Road, to be exact.'

'Really,' she says, 'how frightfully odd.'

'I don't see why,' I say. 'Where's yours?'

'Fleet, of course,' she says, opening her eyes very wide, 'we've lived there since the Conqueror.'

'Poor you,' I say, 'how very uncomfortable', and she jounces away in a huff.

'Dr Livingstone, I presume,' says Mary, coming up – she'd been listening, and that was how we met.

Am I just a tiny bit disappointed in the place? I mustn't be, I know it's wrong; I'm ever so lucky to be here. But we never meet anyone outside the school, it's all lessons, deportment, and visiting museums (we walk in a crocodile with a mistress at either end). We do have dancing in the evenings, but we only dance with one another. It's ever such an old-fashioned school, even St Ethelberger's at Bigbury was more up-to-date; no wonder Madame's clothes are Second Empire – the whole place is; I'm surprised we aren't all rigged out in crinolines. Mary Wentworth and I did manage to escape from the Louvre on Thursday afternoon to sit in the Tuileries, but we were caught in no time and given ever such a ticking-off.

Can I endure it for six whole months? Of course you can, Miss Lally, you ungrateful child. Brrh, but it's cold. Perhaps when spring comes it will be better. Spring in Paris . . .

Saturday, 23rd March   And it is! Better in spring, I mean.

So's my French (it d—d well ought to be, I hear Pa say).

We went to Fontainbleau today and oh, it was beautiful. I wanted to dance barefoot in the woods amongst the flowers, but thought better of it; look what happened last time.

Not much news from Bigbury. Things jog along as usual. Mother writes that Suki has taken up badminton and Miss Carter says she has the makings of a champion (!) Bob writes that he's met a 'ripping girl called Topsy' and is madly in love, but not to tell Mother, she might not approve. Ho hum . . . Granny Morgan writes Would I like to stay with her in town for a month in the summer and help sort out her papers? Now Grandpa Morgan is dead, Granny has taken a house in Bayswater and there is 'so much to do'. *Would* I!!

Mary and I have decided that if all else fails we will take a little flat in Chelsea and do our own cooking and have Bohemian parties and join the Women's Suffrage Movement and . . . and . . .

18th April   Something extraordinary has happened. I feel so dithering and strange. Oh, that Pa were here to advise.

Since I last wrote, Mary and I have worked out a way of escaping for half an hour or so in the afternoons (it was a case of find a plan or die of boredom, actually). It's really rather clever. What we do is this: when the crocodile splits in two, as it usually does at some point in the afternoon, with a single mistress in charge of each group, Mary and I pretend to split with it, but in fact one of us escapes, leaving the other as an alibi. For example, if it's my turn to go, when asked where I am by Miss Sutcliffe or whoever else is on duty, Mary simply says that I have decided to go with the other group – and vice versa. It works, too.

Today it was my turn. Group A were visiting Notre Dame (for the umpteenth time) and Group B the Conciergerie; they were to meet afterwards in the square outside Notre Dame in one hour's time. Standing discreetly behind a large lady in an ostrich feather hat who was feeding the pigeons, I watched my fellow prisoners file reluctantly into the church. The last one in, and I was away over the Petit Pont and running along the left bank. Then, turning left at the next bridge, I joined the crowds milling up and down the boulevard St Michel.

The sun was shining, I was wearing my new spring coat and

skirt (paid for by dear Granny M.), and I felt quite a few men's eyes on me as I strolled along (a not unpleasant feeling, in moderation). It was when I decided to stop at a café that the thing happened. Mary and I don't usually do this, it's too risky, but today I felt reckless; besides, I was thirsty. I sat down at a table sheltered by a bay tree in a red tub, not too near the edge of the pavement, and clicked my fingers at a passing waiter. The waiter came towards me, smiling; then – and I can still hardly believe this – turned into Julian Wolf!

He recognised me at once, too, although it is six years since we last met. But as soon as he did, his face closed up and he turned away, pretending he hadn't. The idiot, it isn't him I hate, it's his father. Anyway, I had to discover what he was doing working as a waiter in Paris when horrible Mr Wolf is so rich; so, not caring about anything, I jumped up from the table and ran after him. 'Julian, Julian Wolf, come back! It's me, Lally Morgan.' Of course, he had to turn round then, all the people in the café were looking at us.

'Hullo,' he said, 'you haven't changed much. I've still got that cricket bat, by the way.' He was trying to sound cool and calm, but I could see he wasn't really. He was blushing like anything, and his eyes had that hunted look Mrs Wolf's used to have. 'You haven't changed much either,' I said, 'except you're taller . . .' Then suddenly I couldn't think of anything else to say, and there we stood, just looking at one another like a pair of idiots.

'What . . ?' 'Are you . . ?' We both spoke at once, and that made us laugh. 'I'm at finishing school,' I said. 'I've escaped for an hour, the others are looking at Notre Dame; I have to be back there by a quarter to four.'

'You wicked thing,' he said, 'but you always were a graceless brat.'

'I wasn't,' I said, 'but you were. I remember . . .' Then we both remembered, and both blushed. 'Look here,' he said, 'sit down for a minute and have some coffee. I think I can swing it with the *patron* and get a few minutes off; we're not busy and he owes me some favours. Then I can walk you back – that is, if you'd like me to.' Of course, I said yes. I couldn't be angry; somehow Julian never seemed quite to belong to Mr and Mrs Wolf anyway; you couldn't blame him for what happened to Pa.

'Very well,' I said, 'I'll have an absinthe while I wait.'

'How very daring,' he said. 'I'll send Alphonese.'

I didn't like the absinthe much, it tasted like Nanny's cough mixture, but I felt I needed something to calm my nerves and it did do that. Then there was Julian again; quite smart, with a boater on the back of his head and a flower in his buttonhole. 'Pinched it from a table,' he whispered, 'we'd better hurry.' I looked at my watch. 'I only have half an hour left,' I said.

So we went to the Luxembourg Gardens as they were only just round the corner. When we got there we sat down side by side on a seat, as stiff and silent as a pair of tailor's dummies, while two noisy French boys bowled their hoops up and down the gravel path in front of us.

'Pardon, monsieur.' One of the hoops, out of control, bumped into Julian's legs. In fast, idiomatic French he ordered the boys to bowl their hoops somewhere else. What he actually said was, I think, rather rude, but unfortunately I only understood about one word in ten. Whatever he said, however, worked. The boy put his fingers in his ears and stuck out his tongue at us, but he picked up the hoop and ran away, followed by his friend. At least all this helped to break the ice between us; it made me giggle. 'Why are you working as a waiter, Julian?' I asked. 'I need the money,' he said, throwing a pebble at a passing pigeon. 'I'm trying to make my name on the stage in cabaret, you see, as that's all I seem to be good at. At the moment, however, the great Parisian public aren't exactly flocking.'

'But your father . . . ?' Both of us blushed again and I felt awful. 'I haven't seen my father since I was fourteen years old,' he said stiffly, as though I were a complete stranger, 'not since I heard what happened to . . . to . . . He said it was a dreadful accident, but I knew it was his doing. He came out to my uncle's in Hamburg to tell me, and I went for him with a knife. It was all hushed up, of course – you know Father. They said . . . they said I was like Mother. Then I ran away and joined a circus, and I've been on my own ever since.'

I wanted to cry out, to put my arms round him, love him – anything but just sit there feeling his pain, knowing how much luckier I was, even though I'd lost my Pa. But I didn't dare even put my hand on his arm; he was like a young, unbroken colt, shivering with life, wanting reassurance but terrified even of being touched.

There was another long silence while we watched a cross-looking over-dressed lady pass by, pushing an equally cross-looking over-dressed baby in a perambulator. Then I could stand it no longer and said the first thing that came into my head. 'It's nice to meet another person with red hair' (Julian's hair is even more ginger than mine is) 'all the girls at the Pension Lancaster are either statuesque blondes or petite brunettes; ginger hair and freckles are definitely out this season. Shall I buy us a toffee apple?'

'You *are* a graceless brat,' Julian said, 'you haven't changed a bit. Toffee apples, my eye!' (And he sounded so like Nanny, I started giggling and couldn't stop.) 'Whatever can you be thinking of, Miss Lally, and you in your Sunday best.' Then we were both laughing and everything was all right.

After that I told him about Bigbury-on-Sea and St Ethelberger's and Bob, even about Walter Lark. And he told me about the circus; how at first he had just looked after the animals, but later trained as a clown. And how one night last year, when the circus was in Lille – it travelled all over Europe – a man called Monsieur Duraton, some sort of theatrical impresario who books acts for the Paris music halls, came round after the performance. He said Julian had talent and should work on his own, and if he came to Paris he would get him a job. So after that he left the circus and came to Paris to find Monsieur Duraton, who turned up trumps and gave him a booking at a music hall in Montmartre for six months. Then M. Duraton lost all his money in some business venture, and Julian was out of a job and had to work as a waiter to keep body and soul together. But now, at last, he had got himself a booking; his own ten-minute spot in a cabaret on the boulevard de Clichy – 'some impressions, monologues, a bit of mime, and a few enlightened gentry seem to like my stuff' – but the money, even with tips and a meal, was not enough to pay for his lodging, so he had kept on his job as a waiter during the day.

I longed to hear more about his life, but much too soon it was time for us to go. 'I'll walk you to the bridge,' he said, 'and by the way – and we won't mention it again if you don't mind – I know my mother is dead. My Aunt Chrissy writes from time to time with news from home.' I could think of nothing to say to that, so squeezed his hand instead. He smiled, and put his arm round my waist. 'Everyone else is doing it,' he said, 'so why not us?' And he was right, I had not noticed before, but everywhere amongst the jostling boulevard crowds there seemed to be lovers.

I think I half fell in love with him then.

But how absurd! Julian is almost ugly. When I try to think of his face, I can't see it properly. I can see his curly red hair, though, and how tall and thin he is, and somehow I can feel him . . .

Now, where was I? Do not ramble on so, Miss Lally. Well, we said goodbye at the Pont St Michel, by the flower-sellers. I gave him my address. 'I'll come and call on Sunday,' he said. 'But you can't,' I had to shout above the noise of the traffic, 'they would never allow a gentleman caller.'

'I'm not a gentleman,' he said, 'so we'll see.' Then he had gone, and by running all the way back to the Conciergerie, I got there with just half a minute to spare.

'Are you all right, dear?' asks Miss Sutcliffe, when we joined up with the group from Notre Dame. 'You look a little flushed.'

'The heat, Miss Sutcliffe, and I found the prison – Queen Marie-Antoinette and all those poor aristocrats – just a little upsetting.'

'Dear child,' says Miss Sutcliffe. 'Come on, girls, let us for once be a little naughty and treat ourselves to a glass of iced lemonade.'

1st April – late   He came! And I'm still laughing. He stayed for ages, too, and my stock has gone up no end. Well . . .

Yesterday morning Madame called me into the parlour. 'Alice, my child, I have received a letter from a young man begging permission to call on you. You did not tell me you had friends in Paris?' I made a sort of noise in my throat and smiled sweetly, hoping she wouldn't expect an answer. She didn't (lucky for me, as I had nothing whatsoever to say). I knew the letter must be from Julian, but how. . . ? A music hall artist working as a waiter? Old Ma Lancaster was holding the letter up to the light; the paper certainly looked thick and expensive.

'Such a charming note. Mr Wineberger is staying at the Meurice – so comfortable, he says, of course they know his ways. "Miss Alice Morgan will remember me well," he writes, "my dear father and hers were such very great friends when we lived in London. My stay in Paris is but a short one, but when I left our home on Long Island my parents expressly bade me pay my respects to Miss Morgan. Her Mama had written to mine – they are such close correspondents – that Miss Morgan was lucky enough to be a pupil at your establishment".'

Wasn't he overdoing it a bit? How I longed to giggle, I felt quite *ill*. But no, Madame never blinked an eyelid.

'The upshot of all this, dear, is that I have despatched a note asking the young man to take tea with us tomorrow afternoon. Marcel will prepare the little salon, then perhaps a stroll in the garden . . . The Winebergers of Long Island – one of the old New York families, of course, and enormously rich. Oscar Wineberger was a beau of mine many years ago before I married – this young man's uncle, perhaps.' And so on in the same vein, with me sitting there nodding and smiling like a demented mandarin.

Of course, I was on pins all that evening, and all through church and *dejeuner* the next day. The girls were ragging me like anything and dying with curiosity about what 'Lally's millionaire' would turn out to be like. Mary too; I haven't told her yet about my meeting with J. Silly, really, but somehow I couldn't.

Comes three o'clock and there we all are, squinting out of the only window that looks on to the street – me feeling an absolute ass, all dressed up in my Sunday best – when this magnificent motor pulls up outside the front door and out of it jumps the most exquisitely dressed young man you could imagine. Waving nonchalantly at the liveried chauffeur to wait, he treads across the flagway – his hat tipped ever so slightly over his nose, a perfect red rose in his buttonhole – and bangs on the knocker, and we all tumble back into the room squawking and giggling like a parcel of idiots. I notice Bunty M. gives me a pretty sharp glance. 'Oh Lally, he's beautiful,' lisps Maudy Winston '*and* so rich. I thought he would be hideous and covered in pimples.'

'Personally, I've always loathed men with red hair,' says Bunty, and picking up a book, slams out of the room.

'Madmoiselle Alice, please to come down.' I feel sick with fright as I follow Marcel downstairs. In the parlour Madame is purring away like an overfed cat – what on earth has the wicked boy said to her?

'Miss Lally, but you're so grown up and – dare I say it? – so beautiful.' Julian, a vision in grey, transformed into a character from one of Mr Henry James' novels, steps gracefully forward with his hands outstretched and grasps my two limp ones. 'I'm sure chère Madame Lancaster will forgive me for talking so free, she knows us simple colonials like to speak out what is in our hearts. She knows, too, my Great-Uncle Oscar!' At this he and Ma Lancaster both laugh heartily, and I stand there holding Julian's hands, feeling more ridiculous than I've ever done in my life.

'But Mr Wineberger', I manage to produce at last, all wide-eyed and gushing (if he can play at that game so can I), 'how you have grown too, and how pleased my Mama will be to hear that you have called', etc etc. And we all go on like that for at least ten minutes, until the pain of not laughing is so bad I could gladly die. Even J. twitched a bit (not much, he really is the most marvellous actor). Anyway, when I'm sure I can stand it no longer, Marcel appears on cue to say that tea is served in the *petit salon pour madmoiselle and monsieur*. Ma Lancaster, laughing roguishly (is this the effect J. has on women?) begs us to behave ourselves like good children and she will join us shortly for a stroll in the garden.

The little salon smells of damp, with a whiff of drains and garlic; it's obvious no one has sat in there for years. The door closes behind Marcel; I arrange myself fashionably on the little Louis Quinze sofa, the tea tray on a table in front of me, one hand delicately poised over the silver teapot. Julian lounges elegantly by the window seat, one hand twirling his gold watch-chain; a ray of sun glinting through the bars catches the lights in his red hair; there's a look of simple, boyish admiration on his face. Then, as Marcel's footsteps die away down the stone passage, suddenly he is Julian again; wicked, gamin – triumphant. 'I *told* you I could do it, Lally Morgan, I told you. What have you to say now?' Then another lightning change and he is old Ma Lancaster, winking naughtily, one hand gently caressing an over-stuffed bosom. 'Oh Mr Wineberger, dare I say it, but your dear Great-Uncle Oscar was just the teeniest bit of a rake – '

'Julian, Julian Wolf,' I screech, 'stop it at once. I can't, I simply can't bear any more.' And I hurl the contents of the sugar basin at his head. Then he's down beside me on the sofa and we're laughing, laughing until the tears pour down our faces, and I'm picking the sugar lumps out of his hair.

'Come and see my act, Lally,' he says at last, 'it'ud be such a lark.'

'It would too, and I should be expelled and sent home in disgrace.' But of course I was tempted, who wouldn't be? After that he told me how he'd borrowed the car and clothes from a rich American he'd met at Le Chat Souriant (that is the name of the café in the boulevard de Clichy where he does his act), a Mr Johnson P. Wyatt, commonly known as 'Pills' Wyatt (because his father invented Wyatt's Liver Pills) who liked his performance and comes to the café to see him nearly every night.

'He's a damned sound chap, is old Pills. That's who I lifted the accent from, by the way, and it was he who thought of young Wineberger. He lets me have a bath from time to time in his suite at the Ritz. They only run to a cold tap in the courtyard in the superior slum I temporarily reside in, and a good wash does much to help the inner man, I always say.'

But there was so much to say, and so little time to say it; I can't remember any more. We'd barely tidied ourselves, and J. eaten the last of the little cakes (I couldn't eat a thing), before Ma Lancaster, sprightlier than ever and a little flushed (the buzz is, she drinks) was back, ready and panting for our stroll in the garden.

Of course, after that we could only talk rot. Except that J. did manage to get me behind the mulberry tree for a second while Ma Lancaster teetered about round the lily pond making cooing noises at the goldfish. 'Well, are you coming to see my act if I can arrange it?' he hissed in my ear. 'I'm not on until past eleven; I could easily get old Pills to fetch you, he's always game for a lark. Everyone here would be in bed by then, surely? They would never know you'd slipped out.'

Like an idiot, I said yes. 'Good girl, I'll write instructions', he whispered as we joined Ma Lancaster. 'One evening next week.' And so I am committed.

After that, it was all goodbyes and tra la la. 'Such a delightful afternoon, Madame, I cannot recall when I have enjoyed myself more, and I will write this very evening to Mother. Miss Lally' (he squeezes my hand) 'Mother will be so pleased to hear I have seen you.' Then he's drooping over Madame's tiny paw and giving me a quick pinch on my behind (how *dare* he) and then he's gone – up the street in a cloud of exhaust in Pills Wyatt's silver Rolls Royce. And suddenly everything is quiet again.

'Papa has *two* Rolls Royces,' says Bunty M., giving me one of her fishy stares. 'He can't manage with one.'

Oh lor, what have I let myself in for? But it's fun, all the same, it *is* fun . . .

24th April Everything is arranged for tomorrow night! The garden boy gave me a note this afternoon. How quite ridiculously romantic – except that Julian isn't romantic, is he – how can someone who makes you laugh be romantic?

The note says I must be at the gate in the garden wall – the one that opens on to the back alley – at a quarter to eleven, and Pills will be there in person to collect me. 'Pills and I,' J. writes, 'formed a reconnaissance party yesterday afternoon – Pills happens to be an old army man – and we're of the opinion that an agile brat of the likes of you – of course old Pills doesn't know you're the latter, but I do; I well remember you shinning up that monkey puzzle tree in the Frenches' garden at No 10 with poor old Bernard's cap – could make it over the wall without the smallest difficulty. And Pills, stout fellow that he is, has agreed to be on the other side to catch you, so there's not the slightest need for worry on your part. There won't be anyone about at that hour, by the way. While snooping, we had a chat with the porter (a little money changed hands) and he says he locks the gate at ten o'clock, after which he strolls along to his favourite café round the corner for an hour or two before turning in. *C'est ça, mon enfant – tu comprends*?'

Julian Wolf is a devil, truly he is. The whole idea is quite preposterous, and yet I can't resist it – as I am sure he knows.

And I have to admit the wall in that particular place is not too high, and there is a sort of bin I can clamber on . . .

25th April I have told Mary – I had to; she must cover for me if anything should go wrong. She's wild, of course, that I haven't told her before. 'Oh Lally, couldn't I come too? Le Chat Souriant – Montmartre – jumping over walls into the arms of American millionaires – I shall go insane with jealousy!' But she promised to help all she can. What a brick she is.

And now we wait. How lucky my cubicle is at the end of the dormitory by the door. Easier to slip out . . .

27th April I couldn't write yesterday; too tired. Besides . . . Oh, I don't know . . . Suddenly things aren't funny any more. Have I fallen in love with Julian Wolf, or do I hate him? I have certainly been a fool, that at least I know. And yet, and yet, every time I close my eyes I see his naked body, white in the candlelight, his face close to mine, brown eyes pleading. 'Love me, Lally, please, please . . .'

Come on, Lally Morgan, don't wax poetic, it don't suit you; just state the facts. And I wasn't caught, that's something. But I do wish (do I really?) that I had never gone.

It was all so easy.

Everyone in the house was asleep by ten o'clock; not a creak nor a rustle as I tiptoes downstairs and out through the garden door. The night was dry and cold, with a full moon. Hitching up my skirt, I was up on the wall in a trice and looking down on the alley. 'Good evening, Miss Morgan,' hisses a large figure in a Homburg hat, standing under the gas lamp. 'May I say at once what a plucky young lady I think you are. I – '

'Never mind all that,' I hiss back from the top of the wall, 'get me down before anyone walks past.' So the figure galvanizes itself into action and gentle as anything, lifts me down. Pills Wyatt is large and slow, but his heart's in the right place, as Pa would say. 'I've left the motor round the corner,' he says when I'm safely down, 'I thought it might attract attention.'

And what a lovely ride it was, right across Paris, almost to Montmartre. We have never visited Montmartre, 'too many undesirables,' sniffs Miss Sutcliffe, 'besides, the church is not yet finished and of no great architectural merit.' I've never seen Paris by night, not properly, and oh, but it's splendid. So alive and, truth to tell, just a little frightening. All very fine to be seated in a Rolls Royce high above the commonality, a millionaire at one's side, but alone. . . ?

The boulevard de Clichy is a noisy place, and wicked too, if the look of it is anything to go by. So much traffic, so many people; rich-looking men (young and old, some *very* old) in silk hats and opera cloaks, ladies wearing very little (aren't they cold?), negroes, ordinary-looking men in butterfly collars and bowler hats, brigands, beggars, drunken old women, ragged children, cats and dogs and birds in cages; rubbish in the gutters, flashing lights, and music, music, pouring out of everywhere.

Le Chat Souriant is right in the middle of all this. And in case you might mistake it, over the entrance sits an enormous black cat, with green electric lights popping on and off behind his eyes, and his mouth slit into a huge red grin.

Pills' chauffeur was waiting outside for us. He touched his cap most respectful-like at me. 'Good evening, miss . . .'

'Mission completed so far, Granger,' Pills winks at him. 'You had better be here by two; go get a bite to eat.'

'Very good, sir,' says Granger, jumping into the driver's seat, while Pills and I push our way up the steps into the café.

Inside, it's one enormous, smokey, stifling room, the tables packed so tight that people are nearly sitting on top of each other. At the end is a small stage with a space at the side for a three-piece band and the fat lady with golden hair and a red silk blouse who plays the piano. The music is so loud you can't speak, but it makes you want to dance. I follow Pills to a table near the stage, and a sweating waiter eels his way through the crowd. 'The usual, monsieur?' The waiter has to shout above the din. Pills nods, and in a trice the waiter is back with two large glasses of brandy and a dirty saucer with little lumps of cheese and a few gherkins on it.

'Is this for the Laughing Cat?' I shout, pointing to the cheese, trying to make a joke of it, for actually I am beginning to feel a little nervous. 'Hush, my dear,' says Pills, grave as a bishop, you'd think Our Lord himself was about to appear, 'it's time for the show to begin.'

With a roll on the drums, the music stops; people are stamping their feet and banging on the tables; others rush in from the street outside, and everyone is telling everyone else to be quiet. Then the lights dim, and all at once there's Julian standing alone in the centre of the little stage, wearing just an ordinary, everyday suit, looking like Julian. And suddenly I see again the frosty trees in Kensington Gardens, the violets in Mrs Wolf's fur hat: 'Oh dearest boy, please stop, whatever would your father say. . . ? And the performance has begun.

And what was it like, the performance? Well, as Julian described it, I suppose: a few impressions, a monologue, a bit of mime. But there's one thing more; it was sublime. For in those brief ten minutes, Julian Wolf became a wizard, a warlock, a magic man. He seemed to have the power to turn himself into anything he chose before your very eyes – man, woman, child, even a flower or a piece of machinery. One moment so funny your sides ached with laughing, the next so sad you could not bear to see or hear any more. And I truly believe that if at the end of his act he has asked the audience to stand on their heads, they would have done it.

But suddenly, too soon, it's over. The lights come on, the lady in the red blouse flexes her fingers in preparation for another assault on the piano, and everyone is clapping and cheering. Pills is shouting, 'Bravo, old lad, bravo', at the top of his voice, and Julian is standing beside us, blinking, his hair on end, sweat pouring down his face. And me? I'm blubbing like a school kid. Luckily the others didn't notice, what an ass they would think me if they had.

'So you came, then.' Julian slumps down in a chair as though the life had been drained out of him. 'Word of a Morgan,' I answer back, suddenly feeling cross and rather shy. 'When we say we will do something, we do it.'

'She's a real plucky kid, Ju.' Pills signals to the waiter for more drinks. 'She was up and over that darned wall as quick as a jack rabbit.'

'I'd liken Lally Morgan to a number of things,' Julian says, showing signs of life, 'but a jack rabbit ain't one of 'em.' I stick my tongue out at him and we all laugh and I feel better.

'Anyway, here's to her,' J. shouts, suddenly leaping to his feet and waving his arms about, 'and if the inebriated old party what runs that school of hers pushes her out for this night's work, she can come and join the circus.' Then he drinks down two glasses of absinthe, one after the other, just like that, and I jump on my chair and strike a pose. 'I'll come and join the circus – who cares a fig for the stupid old Pension Lancaster, anyway.' People round us start to clap and someone shouts 'Bravo!' but Pills looks grave again (J. is drinking another absinthe). 'Please sit down, Miss Morgan – Lally,' he begs, gently pulling at the tail of my jacket, 'this is a rough place, they're not used to young ladies.' He turns to J. 'Give the drink a rest, old man, won't you. Remember you're on again at two.' And J. shakes himself like a dog coming out of the sea and puts his empty glass down on the table, and I climb down from my chair feeling rather foolish.

'Let Lally come and watch me have supper, Pills. Word of a gentleman, I'll behave. I can't eat in this infernal din.'

'If she wishes,' says Pills, 'it's for Lally to decide.' Do I wish? I don't know, but all the same I nod. 'I'll come and watch you eat, Julian, I might even have some food myself.' So we all get to our feet. 'Look after her, old man,' Pills says. 'Your word . . .'

'Word of a Wolf.' And for one terrible moment Julian looks like his father (but I imagined that, I must have). 'I'll be with my friends in the corner, then,' Pills says, 'Granger will be back with the car just before two.'

Then I'm following Julian through the door at the back of the stage and along a dark passage that smells of cats and drains. We stop outside a noisome kitchen and J. collects a tray of food from a cross-looking woman you can only just see through the clouds of steam. The woman wears a grimy apron and has silver rings in her ears. She shrieks something I don't understand, in a voice like a parakeet.

Then on, up a long, steep staircase, Julian in front, one hand on his hip, the other balancing the tray on one finger above his head like a waiter, with me shouting after him, 'Be careful you ass, you'll drop it!' He doesn't of course; after all, he was trained in a circus. And then at last we're in a lovely little attic room at the top of the house, with a view right over Paris. There is only a rough table, a couple of chairs, and a battered old couch in the corner, but all the same it's lovely, and suddenly so quiet too.

'I feel like Trilby,' I say (I really did).

'Well, I'm no Svengali, m'dear, nor Little Billee neither,' J. says, taking the cover off his food and settling down to eat. 'I do agree however, that the place smacks a little of La Vie de Bohème. I discovered it after I'd been working here a couple of weeks; no one else uses it. The harridan in the kitchen downstairs don't approve, that's why she was shouting. Have some wine?'

And it was so peaceful sitting there, the two of us side by side at the little table, the solitary candle making shadows on the wall behind us; the blaring café down below was another world. We talked and talked, while J. ate and I sipped my wine. When at last he had finished, he said: 'Your Pa was a wonderful man, Lally. Not just . . . not just because he tried to save my mother. I remember how I wished he could have been my Pa. I used to watch him come out of your house in the morning to go to the office, his hat on the back of his head, brolly over his shoulder; down the steps two at a time, always in a rush, always so happy . . . and then I would think of mine – '

'Don't, Ju' (I'd never called him that before, why now?) 'It does no good; it's over, truly it is – '

'But it's not over, is it?' he says, refilling his glass and drinking the wine in one gulp. 'The bastard's still alive.' I put my hand on his arm; he's trembling like a terrified child. 'Ju, you must forget – you *must*.' And suddenly somehow we're in each other's arms and he's half carrying, half dragging me over to the couch, my skirt wet with spilt wine, my hair down on my shoulders. 'Love me, Lally, please, ah, please. You're so strong, so full of life; spare some for me . . .'

Then? Well, I suppose we committed the unforgivable, the thing everyone thinks about but no one dares to name, and as a result I'm sore and aching and wishing I hadn't. But that's now; then it was different. Then I wanted to give and give and give again, and so did Julian, I know he did.

All right then, Miss Lally, what was it like, this all-important, nameless thing.

So difficult to explain. But it was as though Julian and I were climbing together up a tremendously steep, tremendously dangerous mountain; holding on to each other, strug-

102

gling, slipping now and again, crying out in pain, falling back, but always climbing, always together, helping each other on. Then, when at last we reached the top of the mountain, the view was so marvellous, so breathtaking, we could only bear to look for a second and then we were falling, falling, falling into space and there were no longer two of us but only one. Then suddenly I'm me again, just ordinary Lally Morgan, and my thighs are wet, and there are drops of blood (mine?) on the flowered cretonne cover of the couch. And Julian is sitting up, running his fingers through his hair and looking sheepish. 'I told you I wasn't a gentleman, Lally, but on my honour I didn't mean this to happen.'

And this makes me angry, so angry that for a moment I want to kill him. 'It happened, Julian Wolf, because I let it happen.' I'm standing, now, on the bare boards, my petticoats round my knees, my top half wholly exposed to the cold night air. 'Just because you can make a few people laugh now and again doesn't make you God Almighty, you know – and it wasn't pity either.' That makes *him* angry, and I'm glad. He leaps off the couch and puts his hands round my throat so tight I'm choking. 'Don't you ever pity me, do you hear, or I won't answer for the consequences.' 'Don't be so damned melodramatic, Wolf, we're not on the stage at the Lyceum' – suddenly I hear Pa's voice quite clearly inside my head, and somehow it makes me giggle. For a moment J. looks shocked, then he's giggling too.

'Oh, Lally, Lally, Lally, you're so . . . splendid. Much better than a dozen absinthes – better than anything.' And then suddenly we remember the time, and it's all rush and go and trying to tidy ourselves up. 'You're as plump as a partridge,' says J., trying to tie my stays by the light of the candle.

Downstairs in the café, the music is louder than ever and Pills is drumming his fingers on the table, looking anxious. 'Julian, they're calling for you, we were about to send out a search party.'

'I'll write, Lally.' Julian squeezes my hand, but his eyes are far away. 'Thank you for . . . thank you for coming to see my act.' Then he's gone, swept into a crowd of admirers, and I am being firmly propelled towards the door and the waiting motor.

This time Granger drives, Pills and me sitting together in the back. So much has happened that I don't understand, I feel numb; all I long for is bed and my little cubicle and to be alone. Pills seems to understand; he only speaks once and that is to say that Julian has the making of a great artist in him and is wasted where he is. 'I'm in touch with agents back home, there's a great future ahead of the boy if he wants it.' It was Granger who gave me a respectful leg-up on to the wall. 'Just put your foot on my hand, miss, and we'll have you up and over in a jiffy.'

The old house was still sleeping when I let myself in through the garden door. Nothing at all had changed; Miss Sutcliffe still snored gently in her little room at the end of the passage, my bed was just the same as when I had left it, with the bolster struck down under the covers; the moon had moved across the sky a bit, that's all. But I had changed; oh, I had changed.

Please, please, please, Julian, write. Tell me you don't think me cheap. I felt so bold and strong when I was with you in that little room – but now??

Sunday, 28th April   A blank day. But what did I expect? I have told Mary everything. She wasn't shocked in the least. 'My dear, how very grand and brave you are.' Of course, her people are awfully advanced; her mother is in the Women's Suffrage Movement. 'Might I have a baby, Mary? Does one alway after. . . ?'

'Of course not, you goose. We must just wait and see if your monthly comes.'

'And if it doesn't?'

'Just wait and see.'

But it's all waiting, and I find it hard to bear. Surely he could have written by now.

Thursday, 2nd May   He has! Only a short note. Can I meet him at La Bonne Femme (the café where he works as a waiter) tomorrow afternoon? I suppose I can, but where, oh where is it all going to end?

3rd May – very late   Julian is going away! A German impresario has seen his act and has offered him a job in Berlin. 'Lots and lots of money – enough to buy a motor – even to eat!' I'm pleased for him, truly I am. Why then do I keep crying?

104

I was forced to catch a bus up the boulevard St Michel, there was so little time. We visited the Louvre again today and I thought I should never get away. They were awfully busy at La Bonne Femme, and I sat and waited for ten minutes before Julian came. When he did, he looked so happy and excited I couldn't be angry.

'I've cracked it, Lally, can you believe? No more penny-pinching, no more scavenging. I'll buy me a Mercedes and a fur coat and smoke cigars – '

'Let's go to the Luxembourg Gardens,' I said, 'I haven't much time.' We walked up the boulevard, not talking; every now and then J. would look at me out of the corner of his eye, like a child who has been naughty and is unsure of his welcome. It was raining, which didn't help, and neither of us had an umbrella.

We found a seat under some trees, but my boots were wet and rain dripped down my neck from the brim of my hat. The seat was wet too, and the silence between us seemed to stretch into hours. At long last J. spoke (not looking at me, but holding my hand). 'Lally, don't be angry about the other night. It was wrong of me, I know that. Ever since, I've been kicking myself for being such a cad – taking advantage of you. It's just . . . after a performance something happens to me – I can't explain it – '

'I'm not angry!' I was shouting again; why does J. make me shout? 'I'm proud. We . . . we did what we did together, the both of us – can't you see? Don't spoil it.' Then suddenly we're kissing, and my hat falls off and my blouse comes undone, and I'm all wet and oh, I could have *died*. Just as suddenly it was all over, both of us trembling and talking at once.

'I must go to Berlin, Lally, I must. It's such a ripping chance. You're the finest, most beautiful girl I've ever known, but it wouldn't do – you and I – we both know it.' I knew he was right, of course, but somehow, for just a moment, I couldn't bear it.

'When do you go?' J. squints and looks across the sodden grass towards the Palais. 'Tomorrow, as a matter of fact, on the night train – first-class like a real toff.' I'm shivering a bit now, while I try to fasten the damp buttons on my blouse.

'Safe journey.' There doesn't seem much else to say. He squeezes my hand. 'And you? What will you do?'

'I'm going to be companion secretary to my Grandmother Morgan' (I am, she wrote and asked me to). 'She has a house in town now, north of the park.'

'But that's splendid! You'll like that' (jolly, over-eager) 'parties and dances and all that rot. Lots of young men to play with.'

'Yes,' I say, 'I shall like it most awfully.' J. takes off his hat and shakes the water out of it; his damp hair has gone into little curls; he bangs the hat back on his head. There is another long silence. Two tramps walk past, hunched against the rain; one of them has an old newspaper draped over his head.

'I know it's something that chaps don't talk about to girls – girls of your sort.' J. is blushing and looking at his knees. 'But I don't think you need worry about, well, about – '

'Having a baby?' And I'm blushing too. 'I'm no end glad to hear that.' (The voice – sarcastic, jeering, bitter – surely isn't mine?)

'Oh God, Lally, *please*. Please don't take it hard. If anything happens I'll send you money, I swear I will. I don't know what came over me the other night, truly I don't. I suppose it was so ripping meeting someone from home; someone who had known Mother – I never knew I missed it all so much until you came running after me that afternoon in the café. And you're so pretty and now – oh, I don't know – it all came together. And do you know, the night you came to see my act, the night we . . . well, I gave the best performance of my life. I knew it at the time – God damn it, I could *feel* it! – and Herr Richter was there and came round afterwards. So you brought me luck, Lally, doesn't that count for anything?' I think I knew I loved him then – will I always? I hope not, I don't think he brings *me* luck.

'I must go,' I said, getting up off the seat. 'Will you write – c/o Mrs Stanley Morgan, 58 Ilchester Crescent, Bayswater?'

'Of course,' he says. 'Look, the rain's stopped.' And so it had, the sky above the gently waving trees was as blue as blue could be.

We kissed goodbye at the park gates. At the last moment J.

pulled something out of his pocket and dropped it into my hand. I opened my fingers, and a tiny replica of the grinning cat outside the café, Le Chat Souriant, grinned up at me. 'It's not much, not even real silver, just a souvenir for tourists, but it's something to remember me by, and it might bring you luck.'

'It might,' I say, putting the ugly thing in my pocket and trying not to cry. Then I turned and left him standing there by the shouting newspaper-sellers, looking down at the wet pavement, his hands in his pockets, his hat on the back of his head, jostled by the busy afternoon crowds . . .

'Morgan, my child, how on earth did you manage to get so wet?'

'I slipped in a puddle, Miss Grobie' (Miss S.'s number two). 'I'm ever so sorry.'

'No need too apologise, Morgan, you're the one to suffer! Now then, girls, full speed ahead to the omnibus stop before the next shower.'

5th May I feel so very low. There's nothing whatever to write and nothing whatever to say, but how I long to leave this horrid place.

Yesterday, Mary showed me a copy of a newspaper she had found on the table in Marcel's pantry. 'He is rather adorable, but wicked too,' she said, thrusting the thing under my nose and pointing to a photograph on the front page. And there is Julian waving his boater out of a train window and pulling a silly face. Underneath: 'The sensation of Le Chat Souriant waves goodbye to admirers. Young comedian, M. Julian Wolf, snapped up by the well known German theatrical impresario, Herr Max Richter, leaves for Berlin on the night express.' In smaller print: 'Many pretty girls wept openly as the Berlin express pulled out of the Gare du Nord last evening, carrying with it the new young sensation of the Paris music halls, M. Julian Wolf. But do not despair, young ladies, for he will be back before too long. He told your reporter, "Paris is my home – it is in Paris after all, that fortune found me".' etc etc. Such rubbish.

'He looks a dear,' said Mary, reading over my shoulder, 'but what about Les Girls?'

'He isn't a dear,' I said crossly, 'and how should I know about Les Girls?'

11th May   Letters from Mother and Granny Morgan. I am to travel to London on 1st June – Mary too. Then to Bigbury for a week, 'for Mrs Gamble to run up a few frocks', then on to Granny's on the 8th.

'You must work your passage, dear,' writes the latter, 'no slacking! There's oodles to be done and your typewriting will be such a boon with all the comittee work I have to get through. I had a young man, one C. Perkins, who came in three mornings a week to help, but he was not a success. He spent his time perusing the butler's sporting newspaper, and when not engaged in that, squeezing the new housemaid in all the most uncomfortable places. Now one hears with some relief he has upped and gone to Africa.

'Dear child, it will be such splendid fun to have you with me. We have all been so busy fitting out a smart little office for you, complete with brand new, spanking typewriting machine and lots and lots of paper. And Dunnings have papered your bedroom in blue and white, and I have bought from Heals (I couldn't resist it) the prettiest bed you ever did see to go with it. Oh, and I nearly forgot, there just might be time for a dance or two and a few young men to tea, and there's always my Thursday Afternoons . . .'

How lucky, how unbelievably lucky I am to have such a wonderful grandmother. And all I can do is drag about and weep and oh how my tummy hurts. Mary says it's only to be expected – how can *she* know?

Wednesday, 15th May   A stain of blood on the sheet this morning. Halfway through French history, such a flow that I could stand it no longer and asked to be excused. Now I lie on my bed with a cold compress on my forehead while the life flows out of me. Am I glad or sorry? I don't believe I know . . . but wait, of course I'm glad. It's just – oh, there's nothing left now, is there, of that wonderful, frightening journey we made, Julian and I, nothing at all, nothing but that silly, grinning, ugly little cat.

31st May   Goodbye, old Pension Lancaster! I am just a little sorry to leave you, but not much. I've made one real friend (Mary), my French is *much* improved, I know the most enormous amount about Italian Primitives, Sèvres porcelain and the last days of Queen Marie-Antoinette. I can climb in

108

and out of a landau without tripping over the hem of my skirt, and . . . well, that's all really. Except, of course, that other thing, the important thing, the secret thing. If I marry one day, will my husband know what I've done without me telling him? If he does, what will he say? Pooh! I don't care. If he loves me enough . . .

Nearly all the others are to be presented this season. Not Mary, her people don't approve; and not me. I'm to my typewriter. I think I shall become an authoress, or join the Women's Suffrage Movement, or both. But every night, in my narrow, lumpy bed, half waking, half sleeping, I dream of Julian Wolf see again his pale skin in the light of the candle, his tumbled hair damp with sweat; rub my cheek against the soft, golden down on his chest, kiss his poor haunted eyes and laugh at his funny smile. Shall I tell Polly about him when I get home? I think I shall, she's the one who'd understand.

Monday, 10th June 58 Ilchester Crescent, Bayswater, London

London, dear old London, what fun you are! Smoky and dirty and smelly and noisy and so much to be done, but still I love you. And Granny and my 'office' and my brand new, spanking typewriter and . . . oh, everything.

'You look a little seedy, dear,' says Granny with one of her looks, 'you have not fallen in love again? Emily Lancaster assured me – '

'Of course not,' I shout, pink in the face, 'you cannot surely imagine, Granny, I ever was in love with poor old Walter Lark?'

'Well, dear, your mother did hint – '

'No doubt she did,' I say, subsiding a bit, 'but you know Mother.'

'Your mother has had a lot to bear, dear – always remember that,' says Granny. 'And we shall see.' I wish people of Granny's generation were not always so enigmatic. I suppose it's because of their straight-laced upbringing – never under any circumstances say what you think. How glad I am I live now and not then.

I'm writing this in bed. Louise, Granny's French maid, has just brushed my hair, and I feel ever so comfortable and sleepy. I do believe, too, that quite a bit of today I did not think of Julian. We progress! I have hidden the little cat in my treasure box, it would not do for Granny to find him.

Tomorrow we go shopping; 'as a dressmaker, dear, Mrs Gamble is no doubt good enough for Bigbury-on-Sea, but for town . . . Your dear grandpapa, you know, left me most comfortably off, and without The Poplars to keep up . . .'

1st July Mercy me – a postcard from Julian! Two fat German frauleins on a tandem bicycle. Chivers brought it into the morning room all by itself on a silver salver. 'For you, miss, it arrived by the late post.'

'Thank you, Chivers,' I manage, but knew I was blushing like anything, and my hands shook. Granny, however, chose to say nothing, merely picked up her lorgnette and went on with *The Times*.

And the postcard? So absurd (and in French). 'Good luck, my little cabbage, in everything you do. Berlin is too hot for a fur coat, but I have bought a motor. We open Monday next, so pray for me, will you – J.' And underneath, a tiny black cat with 'Mee Aowww!' coming out of his mouth. That's all. Afterwards I walked alone in the park with my hands behind my back, pondering . . .

2nd July 'You have a friend in Germany, dear? Such an interesting country, I always think, and of course there's the music . . .'

'The b . . . brother of a girl at the Pension Lancaster, he's, er, studying German before going into the Foreign Office.' Granny smiles sweetly and goes on buttering her toast. 'So useful to have several languages at one's fingertips . . .'

12th July So busy – the days rush by. And so many people! And although I says it myself, I have got the office in apple pie order. What a mess it was in, too. IOUs in the Whitechapel Mothers file, and a lady's(?) stocking in the Better Drains for Wandsworth Elementary Schools file. That Mr C. Perkins must have been a One! I even found a tear-blotched love letter in the cashbook. 'Dere Cris I luv you so everso plees cum tonite ile be wating at the corner. Yr luving Maudy.' How very sad, how very, very sad.

I have met two (tolerably attentive) young men (suitable to play with, says Granny, but no more). One took me to Hurlingham – it rained – and the other skating – he fell over while executing a particularly dashing twirl and broke a tooth. I met a real live poet yesterday at Granny's Thursday. He said over a cucumber sandwich and a cup of Granny's best Ceylon tea that he considered me to be the epitome of the New Woman and I frightened him to death – the rude thing.

Tomorrow the Talbots' dance (my first proper one). Mother writes that she hopes I appreciate all that is being done for me. I do, oh but I do.

14th July Now, there's a thing! I've met Rupert Eagon again at the Talbots' dance.

Up the stairs at Talbot House we go, Granny and me, awfully grand-like – white gloves, flowers in the hair, sparklers in the ears and all that. At the top (I'm panting a bit and Granny's wheezing): 'Mrs Stanley Morgan and Miss Alice Morgan', and there's Lady T. painted like a Red Indian, encased in mauve satin and diamonds; Sir John, baggy eyes and wicked, winks at me and squeezes my hand most awfully tight.

'Ned Morgan's girl, eh? Capital, capital. You're a beauty, m'dear, but you know that, I expect. You must come down to Bathgates – play a spot of lawn tennis – you like lawn tennis?' Then on through the archway, and up charges Bob out of the crush (he'd dined earlier with friends), dragging a tall young man behind him. 'Here they are, Rupe, old man. Here's my little sister, back from the fleshpots of Paris.' And there is Rupert Eagon, bowing over Granny's hand. 'So you've brought her back to us, Mrs Morgan, how very good of you.'

And goodness me, but he looked lovely! The handsomest man I ever did see. Six feet tall, flower in his buttonhole, hair a sort of browny-gold, eyes as blue as you could wish, and mouth – well, perhaps just a little bit too full for my liking, but pretty good all the same, and the jaw underneath quite perfect, with the dearest little dimple in his chin (I'd forgotten the dimple). All in all, enough to turn a girl's legs to water, even a world-weary one such as I.

'Hullo Rupert,' I says as bold as brass, 'was it you who sent me that Valentine?'

'Who else?' says he, reaching for my dance programme. 'May I fill this in? I'd like to be first in the race, if I may.'

'Don't rush the child,' says Granny, 'there are other young men here tonight, you know, Mr Eagon.'

111

'That, Mrs Morgan, is what I am afeared of – '

'I think it's silly having programmes for dances, anyway' (and I have to admit my heart is beating like a drum) 'I think girls should be able to ask men to dance, not all this stuffy formality.'

'You do, do you, Miss Lally Morgan? Well, I could take you somewhere where there's none of this stuffy formality, if you'd care to come. D'you like ragtime?'

'Does she!' Old Bob's grinning like a Cheshire cat. 'You should see her do the bunny-hug.'

'Be quiet, children, and behave yourselves, and don't mention ragtime to me,' says Granny. 'If the lower orders care to cavort like natives in the jungle, that is their affair, but try to remember that you, at least, are ladies and gentlemen.' Then we're all laughing, and people are coming up and talking, and then Rupert and I are waltzing, just as we did at Mrs Wolf's party, only better, and it is, er, really rather splendid.

'I was fearfully cut up to hear about your father,' said Rupert at supper. ''M'govenor told me; said it was a dreadful business and Mr Morgan behaved like the gallant gentleman he was. They say that frightful rotter, Wolf, has married again and – '

'I'd rather not talk about it, if you don't mind.' But I was pleased he mentioned it, all the same.

It was daylight when we drove home. And afterwards I stood at my bedroom window listening to the birds in the park and smelling the scents of London early on a summer's morning. Below, in the empty, clean-swept street, a battered old handcart trundled by, loaded with broken-down sticks of furniture. On top of this crouched an old woman with a sack over her shoulders and a man's cap on her head. The cart was pushed by a pale, tattered young man followed by a gaggle of ragged children. What were they doing? Where were they going and what had happened to them? Why, oh why, is life so unfair and cruel? I turned back into my blue and white bedroom with its dainty Heals bed and muslin hangings, and slowly, one garmant at a time, stripped off my clothes until at last I stood quite naked in front of the long mirror. Then I climbed into bed, and although I felt so wide awake and thought that sleep would never come, I fell asleep at once and dreamed of. . . ? Nothing.

17th July Rupert Eagon has called twice and we have visited his people in Onslow Square. Mr Eagon is a dry old stick who doesn't say much, just looks, and every now and then releases a short bark of laughter like a fox. Mrs E. is still rather beautiful in a ravaged sort of way. She's ever so deaf (you have to shout really loud, as she won't use a trumpet), but despite that she talks a great deal, and you can see she simply dotes on Rupert. Rupert's brother, James, is in the Indian Army out in Calcutta, but I was shown a photo of him, very stiff and starched in full regimentals. Then there are the sisters, Rosa and Con, who are quite *wild* (especially Con) but such fun. They have six dogs between them! 'And how they hate old London,' Rosa said, 'they long to be back at Bengers' (the Eagons' place in the country). 'D'you play tennis, Lally? Con and I are most frightfully keen, there's a chance I may play for the county next year.'

'Vicarage tennis is more my line, and I'm not much of a hand at that. But I love dogs.'

'I say, you are a scream,' says Con, 'Rupe told us you were.' Am I a scream? I don't know. But I rather like the Eagons, at least they're not stuffy.

Yesterday, I met the two girls in the park. Their rough-haired terrier, Mr Moke, had just jumped into the Serpentine in pursuit of one of the ducks. Con was standing on a seat, waving her hat and shrieking, while Rosa besought a pink-faced young man in a celluloid collar and bowler hat to jump in after him and 'save the day'.

'Jump in yourself,' he said rudely. 'If you can't keep the creature under control, you shouldn't have brought him here.' Then he removes his hat, takes out a packet of sand-wiches from inside it, puts the hat back on his head, and commences to eat his lunch! Of course this made us giggle, and then somehow we couldn't stop; we just went on and on, and forgot all about Mr Moke, until he suddenly emerged panting from the water and shook himself over the lot of us, including the rude young man. Apologies seemed inappro-priate, we were laughing too much anyway, so Rosa quickly fastened the brute's lead and we ran as fast as we could for the park gates, where we collapsed in a breathless heap on one of the seats. And suddenly it was so ripping to be laughing and playing in the park again after all those years, and somehow the shadow that has been with me ever since Pa died, lightened a little, and I felt he was somewhere about quite near.

'Young Eagon is very attentive,' says Granny. And so he is . . . and so he is.

26th July Rupert and I danced together last night at the Springfields' and I am almost sure I fell in love.

'Explain,' said Mary when I told her (I see Mary almost every day, the Wentworths' flat is just round the corner). I tried to, but it wasn't easy. 'Oh, I don't know: something just happened, that's all; someone pressed a switch, pulled a lever, a penny dropped. Perhaps it's the way Rupert's hair curls round his ears, or the way he laughs, almost a chuckle, really, but it makes you want to laugh too, even if what he says isn't very funny. Or perhaps it's his drawly voice, or his bright blue eyes, or even the dimple on his chin.'

'I see him,' said Mary, making circles in the air with her pen, 'as a beautiful young sun-god, whom all the other gods indulge because he is so beautiful. Have you ever wondered what would happen if he were crossed?'

'But he's awfully good-natured,' I chip in quickly, 'his sisters rag him like anything and he doesn't mind a bit.'

'Humph,' says Mary, and turns back to the tract she's copying for her mother.

Rupert has invited me down to Bengers in August. 'I promise you won't have to play tennis unless you want to, and it would be so ripping to have you there.'

'I don't know if Granny can spare me,' I say, hedging a bit, 'and Mother wants me for a week . . .' But of course I know I shall go, and so does he.

29th July 'How quite extraordinary,' says Granny at breakfast this morning, 'there's a piece in *The Times* about a young English comic artist by the name of Julian Wolf. It says he has become quite the rage of Berlin. "His talent" (she reads) "is prodigious, although strictly not for the prudish. Tickets for his performances are as gold dust, and the young man has been taken up by such luminaries of the avant-garde as Madame Isadora Duncan and Mr Gordon Craig".'

Frozen, I stare down at my plate. Granny goes on: 'Could this possibly be the Wolf boy? I do remember him as such a talented child, he used to have us all in fits. People said after Ned's death that the boy had run away from his people, and who can blame him?' Then she looked up suddenly from the newspaper and caught me unawares. 'Do you know anything of this, Lally?'

'I think it probably is Julian,' I mumble, 'he was in Paris when I was there, actually, working as a waiter, but on the stage as well. A German impresario heard him performing at a . . . a café and – '

'How do you know this? The truth now, dear; it's always best.'

The truth!

'I happened to bump into him, Granny, by chance of course, it was really quite extraordinary, and . . . and we went for a walk in the Luxembourg Gardens' (this at least was true).

'It was Julian who sent you that postcard from Berlin?' I nod, feeling like a naughty child found out. Then suddenly I'm angry, angry for being such a coward, for lying. 'And I'm glad Julian is such a success, he deserves every bit. He's worked so hard, without any help – he trained as a clown in a circus and . . . and he's had such a rotten time, and it must be awful having a father like Mr Wolf.'

Granny was silent for a long time. I looked down at my plate, but could still feel her eyes on me. 'To have Wolf senior as a father is certainly a fate one would not wish on one's worst enemy,' she said at last. 'And Lally, never be ashamed to stand up for those you . . . admire. I am, however, a little surprised that you have not mentioned the young man before. So interesting and so brave, and now it seems so talented.'

'I thought it might upset you,' I mumble, 'remind you of Pa and . . . and I never thought he would become famous so soon. He is marvellous, of course, but – '

'You have seen his performance?' Oh fool that I am! 'No, no of course not, but he has a friend, an American called Pills Wyatt' – Granny's eyebrows go up ever so slightly – 'Johnson P. Wyatt, actually, his father makes those liver pills.' 'Ah,' Granny nods politely. 'Well,' I continue, 'I met Pills too, you see, and he told me how . . . how really good Julian is.'

Then, surprisingly, Granny smiles. 'Ned always said the boy would go a long way, and so it appears he has. One only hopes Wolf senior will not see this and try to get in touch with the boy.'

'Oh no!'

'Quite so,' says Granny, in a voice as dry as dust, 'quite so', and with that she rings for Chivers to clear, picks up her newspapers and departs for the morning room.

But, but, but I have sworn I will *not* concern myself with Julian and his horrid father. Pa did, and look what happened to him. I am simply glad of J.'s success, that's all. I cannot even write my congratulations; he did not choose to give me his address.

Tomorrow I dine at Onslow Square with the Eagons *en famille*, then to the Savoy Theatre to see *The Yeoman of the Guard*. 'The only time the governor perks up a bit,' says Rupert, 'is when he hears one of those damned rumti-tum tunes. This is the old man's birthday treat, we do it every year. Mama don't hear much of the music, but that don't worry her; she likes the clothes and the glitter.'

28th July I am definitely to stay with the Eagons at Bengers – two weeks from the 9th August. Granny is spending a month with friends at Leamington Spa, and the house is to be shut up. I do believe I love Rupert more every day. What about marriage, then, Miss Lally? Oh, I don't know . . . I don't *know*.

7th August Everything is packed. The servants will go on holiday too, once they have covered everything in dustsheets. Chivers is to visit his widowed sister, who keeps a boarding house in Margate. 'Will you enjoy it?' I ask. Chivers says nothing for a moment, he seems to be thinking, then: 'I hope to find the ozone beneficial, miss.'

'But what about your sister, does she – ?'

'There goes the front door bell, Miss,' he says, looking relieved, 'perhaps you would be good enough to excuse me?'

8th August I have written to Julian; only a short note, care of the theatre in Berlin. Just to thank him for the card and say Congratulations. It won't matter in the slightest if he never gets it.

15th August   Bengers Court, Mosbury, Devonshire
How very nice and pretty the country is! I never was in it
properly before. Such trees and grass and cows and mossy
banks, and not an iron railing nor a park bench in sight! Too
much killing, though, and the Board School children none too
healthy.

Bengers is a funny house – a Bigbury-on-Sea villa multi-
plied ten times over. There's a 'gazebo' at one end, with a
flagpole stuck on top like a sandcastle, a grass tennis court, a
croquet lawn, a fruit cage, commodious stables and harness
room and a special room where Rosa and Con feed their dogs;
then indoors there's a study for Mr E., a boudoir for Mrs E., a
billiard room for the men, a 'play' room for the children (us),
and heaps of other rooms all stuffed with furniture that's
mostly covered, in dog's hairs. Soft beds, potted palms, tiger
skins, photographs, and big, dark pictures of the Nelson-
dying-at-Trafalgar and Wellington-at-Waterloo variety.
What else? Lots and lots of too-rich food which no one eats,
and prayers every morning which no one attends (except for
Mrs E. and yours truly). And do I find it all the tiniest bit
suffocating? Well, perhaps. But there's always heavenly
Rupe – laughing at me, beating me at croquet, chasing me
through the orchard, teaching me the jungle-bunny hop,
pushing notes under my bedroom door at six o'clock in the
morning: 'Get up, lazy bones, it's time to pick us some
mushrooms for breakfast . . .'

There's to be a cricket match in the village on Saturday,
Rupe to captain our side (of course) and a dance in the
evening at the local Big House. There are tennis parties and
garden parties and pretty-maids-all-in-a-row parties; Mr E.
nods, Mrs E. beams and calls me a d---d good-looking gel
(Mrs E. used to hunt 'at home' in Ballybunnion).

And yet . . . and yet. It seems there is some devil in me I
didn't know of until now. A devil who every so often creeps
up and rattles the windows of my soul; clawing with its skinny
hand, thrusting its dark and slimy shape between me and the
bright, opulent world outside; whispering treacherously in
my ear that the real world is not like this, the real world is
cruel and terrible and infinitely callous.

Tea yesterday on the lawn: honey sandwiches and damp seed cake. I happens to pass a remark about the village children. I'd seen a little girl crying, barefoot in the rain outside the Post Office; she'd a big bruise on her cheek and looked half-starved. 'One of the brats from Back Lane, I expect,' says Rosa. 'Back Lane's an absolute disgrace. The men are all shirkers, and spend their days drinking or hitting their wives, and their nights poaching, and the houses are little more than hovels. Honestly, Lally, if you could see the place.'

'Who's the landlord?' I asks, innocent-like, biting into my macaroon. 'I mean, shouldn't something be done?' Rosa opens her eyes wide. 'The Rigbys, of course, they own the village. But I hardly think that old Sir George . . . You can't expect his agent to waste time on people like that – people who won't help themselves.'

'She's right, Lally.' Rupert says. 'Try to help those sort of lazy good-for-nothings and just see where it gets you.'

'Miss Howlett did tell me at the Lunts' tennis party the other day that she thought it a crying shame there was only one well for water for the whole of Back Lane, and that's two hundred yards from the nearest cottage.' Con adds her mite.

'Good lord, are they having Board School teachers to tennis parties now?'

'They needed someone to make up the numbers, Rupe. Besides, Miss Howlett's an absolutely topping player.' Con has gone quite pink. 'Keep your hair on, old thing. It's no business of mine who the Lunts invite to their tennis parties. Anyway, the Howlett woman may be a lady for all I know. What I do know is she's a Socialist! Old Briggs at the Four in Hand says she's so red, she practically sleeps with the Red Flag under her pillow, and he don't know what the Board of Governors is coming to.'

'Is it so wicked, then, to be a Socialist?' I ask, helping myself to a honey sandwich. 'Someone has to be, don't they. Who else is there to fight for the poor?'

'Fight?' Rupert lounges back in his chair, shirt open at the neck, tie negligently knotted round his waist, the summer breeze ruffling his hair. But for one fleeting moment, the lazy, laughing, good-natured Rupert I love has gone, to be replaced by another Rupert – a Rupert almost venomous in his conviction of the rightness of his views. Did I imagine the hint of menace in his voice when, with half-closed eyes squinting into the sun, he stubs out his cigarette and drawls: 'But not you, Lally old thing, not you. Best leave all that sort of bunkum to the Ma Pankhursts of this world, doncha know, eh? I votes we waste no more time on the inhabitants of the local village slum, deserving though they may be, or Miss School Ma'am Howlett, worthy though she may be; it's a damned dull subject. I votes we have a quick round of croquet before it's time to change for dinner. Come on, now, any takers?'

A moment later, arms round my waist, hands over mine on the croquet malet, laughing like a schoolboy, he's teaching me his masterstroke. 'We'll beat em yet, Lally Morgan, those harpies, no one's ever been known to resist this particular shot.' And I am laughing too, no end, that other Rupert forgotten.

Except he isn't forgotten, is he, or I wouldn't be writing about him.

18th August Rupe made eighty-five runs at the cricket match, but all the same, the village won.

'Three cheers for the Mosbury Gladiators, stout fellows one and all.'

'And a hearty cheer for you too, sir, and the other young gentlemen. And there never was a better match, nor played in a better spirit, like.' The two captains, Rupe and young Sparkes from the village, solemnly shake hands. 'The refreshment tent, I think, Sparkes – we've earned it, eh?'

'We have indeed, sir, we have indeed.' The Mosbury Boys Brigade Band strikes up 'Hail and Conquering Heroes Come', and two ragged boys in trousers tied with string and no boots fight each other for a piece of gingerbread that's fallen off the cake stall. And why, oh why, did I suddenly think of Julian?

But I enjoyed the dance at Sir George's. Yes, Sir George Rigby, that self-same wicked landlord. Alas, a charming old buffer in a velvet smoking-jacket, with the innocent eyes of a child. 'D'yer ride, Miss Morgan? We've a capital little mare, mouth as soft as velvet, eatin' her head off in the stables with nothin' to do. Come over and try her, if you'd care to, don't stand on ceremony.'

The house is beautiful, I'll grant; mellow stone and polished floors smelling of beeswax; clipped yews and mullioned windows; ancestors everywhere. No Lady Rigby, she died years ago, but a son who never comes home.

Waiting outside the bathroom (very spartan and the only one, Sir G. obviously don't approve of washin') I overheard the following.

First Lady: 'It looks as if the Morgan girl has snaffled young Rupert Eagon. Poor Mildred Grafton, she'll be so disappointed, she had such hopes for Edith.'

Second Lady: 'He hasn't come up to scratch yet, dear, or I would have heard. Does anyone know about the girl?'

But I heard no more, their voices being drowned in the echoing gush of Sir G.'s antediluvian plumbing. But what cheek! Will he? Won't he? Do I? Don't I? What would Pa advise? Oh, but with Rupe's arms round me in the waltz, how could I say anything but yes?

21st August It's happened. It had to, really, did it not? Rupe has proposed!! But . . . but . . . I haven't accepted – not yet. You will, though, Lally Morgan, you will, you won't be able to stop yourself.

'I'll give you my answer tomorrow' (today now) 'six o'clock in the summer house,' I told him, making time. 'Right ho, old thing,' he said, giving my arm a squeeze, 'I'll try to be patient, but its d--d hard waiting.'

Now for the proposal. Did he go down on his knees, promise eternal love, all that sort of rot? Well, er, no, but my goodness, he kissed me; not properly, of course – being a lady, I'm not supposed to know about that – but in a wholly delicious way all the same.

It happened like this. Rupe and I had been ordered by Mrs E. to drive to Axminster station to collect the fish for dinner: salmon sent by a chum of Mr E.'s and due to arrive on the 3.30 train from town. 'Take the motor, my dears,' shouts Mrs E., 'Cranfield says it goes like a bird now he's put the new cylinder in.'

'Humph,' says Rupe, 'what sort of bird, I wonder? I do rather wish the governor hadn't sent Cranfield on that motor mechanics course, it seems to have gone to his head. However,' and he looks at me, 'I'm sure I don't mind if the machine breaks down. That is, if Lally don't.'

'Cook says she must have the fish by six,' yells Mrs E., 'perhaps you had better take the dog-cart.'

But of course, we took the motor.

It was on the return journey, the hamper of salmon safely strapped on the back, that the thing happened. We'd been bowling along quite merrily, not talking much, you couldn't, the engine made such a noise. 'The ruddy thing's out of the ark,' Rupe said while we were on the platform waiting for the train, 'the Governor won't invest in a new one. It's all right for him, he never drives in it, he don't approve of the internal combustion engine.'

Anyway, as I've said, we were bowling along at our usual snail's pace when, having reached a straight section of the road, R. took it into his head to try and make the machine go a little faster (as he rightly said, at the rate we were travelling we might as well have had some 'damned fellow walking in front with a flag'). So, settling down into his seat he boldly pressed whatever it is that makes motors go faster, and to our mutual surprise and with an almighty roar, it did.

For a few dizzying, exhilarating moments we tore down the road at absolutely breakneck speed, me clutching my hat and shrieking, with the dust rising in clouds about us. But alas it couldn't last. Quite suddenly, with a series of loud explosions and the most fearsome smell of burning, the motor came to a juddering halt, practically throwing me out of my seat, and gave up the ghost.

'Jump clear!' yells Rupe. 'She might explode at any moment! I'll murder that old fool Cranfield.' But she didn't explode, poor old thing. She merely smoked and fizzled for a moment or two, gave a sort of long-drawn-out groan, and slowly sank down on her haunches in the road. Then silence, broken only by a blackbird calling in the hedge and the faraway clop clop of the carrier's cart we had passed further back on the road.

'She's like a poor, broken-down old cab horse.' I felt quite sad. 'I wonder if there's a happy hunting ground for dead motors like there is for dogs and horses.'

'Oh Lally *darling*,' Rupe, hatless, his face splattered with mud, 'I do so adore you and you do talk such fearful rubbish.' After that we were kissing, and I am pulling him down beside me in the tangled grass at the roadside, my hat rolling about somewhere in the ditch. 'I don't talk rubbish,' I managed to say between kisses. 'Marry me, Lally, please. I love you so very much. From the first moment I saw you, I think, at young Wolf's birthday party all those years ago.'

'I'll have to think,' I said, tickling his nose with a moon daisy. 'But do you love me, Lally?' he said plaintively. 'You'll say I'm a d--d conceited beggar, but truly I thought you felt the same.'

'I do, of course I do. It's just, well, I need a little time.'

'If it's my prospects your worryin' about – '

'Of course not, you ass – '

'They're pretty good, though I says it myself. The business is doing well, expandin' all the time, and I'll be a director next year. Think, my darling, we could have the dearest little house in town, buy a motor of our own; you'd become a famous hostess – what fun we'd have!' Then we were kissing again and it might, ahem, might have developed into something a little bit more than kissing if the carrier cart hadn't rumbled into sight. Rupe leaps to his feet. 'Afternoon, Thompson' (R. is one of those annoying people who never forget anyone's name) 'see what a fix we are in! I'd be no end grateful if you could help me move this d--d machine out of the fairway, and then give Miss Morgan and me a lift to the village. We have to get this blessed salmon back in time for m'mother's dinner party.'

And so now I lie back on the over-stuffed ottoman in my over-stuffed bedroom (Mr E. pronounces all ladies should rest for an hour after luncheon, it helps their 'nerves'), wearing my elegant new dressing-gown with the blue bows and the lace purchased by Granny from Selfridges especially for The Visit ('supposing there was a fire, dear, you must look your best') and biting the end of my pen, wondering what my answer will be.

A dear little house in town all my own; darling Rupe, laughing, teasing, making love – proper love. At this point I shut my eyes and try to think of R.'s naked body. But damn it, all I can see is Julian's skinny one, the mole on his shoulder, the little puckered scar across his back where Mr Wolf had whipped him . . .

23rd August 'Welcome to the family, my dear, Mrs Eagon and myself are quite delighted; this is splendid news.' Kisses all round 'midst tears and laughter'. *And* I'm happy, truly I am – not a doubt in sight.

'Lally, dearest, may I say one thing before you give me your answer?' Rupe said last evening in the summer house. 'I've been thinkin' a bit and wonderin' you might be worried that when we were married I would want you to give up your welfare work and . . . and all that sort of thing. But I wouldn't, of course I wouldn't; I'd be a cad if I did, knowin' how important it is to you. Was that what was worryin' you, why you couldn't give me an answer yesterday?'

'A little,' I say, looking down at the floor. Then he surprises me. 'I could have kicked myself the other day,' he says, taking my hand and looking deep, 'when I tried to cut you off about those wretched cottagers in Back Lane – conceited, thoughtless ass that I am. I thought I'd lost you then, did you know that?'

Of course he'd won then, horse, foot and guns. 'I'd like to marry you most awfully, dear Rupe,' I say, 'if you still want me to.'

27th August   Ladysmith Villas, Bigbury

Sweetness and light and Walter Lark forgotten! Rupe and I stroll arm in arm along the promenade, acknowledging, right regally, the nods and bows of Mother's acquaintances. Last night, a little flushed, fingering the buttons on her blouse, the brandy bottle peeping out from behind the silver-framed photograph of Pa, Mother says: 'Well, Alice, he's more than you deserve, that young man, but the devil always did look after his own.'

'It seems so,' I say, putting the brandy bottle back in the cupboard all ostentatious-like. 'Whatever would we do without the dear old devil . . .'

'Oh Lally, how ripping!' says Suki, jumping up and down. 'May I be a bridesmaid?' And Bob, dear old Bob, so pleased and happy, is to be best man. The engagement's not public yet, although everyone seems to know; it's to be announced in the New Year, and I return to Granny's in September.

And under the walls of the old fort, the scent of honey and wild thyme on the air, and the sound of lazy gulls crying above the grey-green sea, Rupe and I lie tangled in the long grass.

'Don't, Lally darling, don't, you rouse things in a chap you can't possibly understand.'

But I do, darling Rupe, oh but I do.

1st October   58 Ilchester Crescent

Being engaged is restricting, but on the whole enjoyable. Rupe and I are so happy. I have no doubts now, none whatever. Yesterday he actually came to one of our meetings in Whitechapel. The old dears thought he was quite wonderful; I even heard him telling Mrs Prendergast he thought some of the Suffragettes were 'damned plucky', though he 'drew the line at breaking windows'.

*21st October   We are to be married next June. Suki, Mary, Rosa and Con to be bridesmaids, and Bob best man. The honeymoon at Lake Como – what utter bliss!

No time to write more, so *much* to be done.

27th December   Bengers

What a splendid Christmas. Even Mother showed signs of being a human being after all! She giggled in charades and was seen kissing Mr E. under the mistletoe. But a bad outbreak of diphtheria in the village – three deaths. Con and I, with the help of Miss Howlett (who incidentally is an absolute Trojan), did what we could to help, which wasn't much, but between us we did manage to organise things a little.

'Our charming angels of mercy', simpers the Rev Harbutt like the ass he is (he's referring to Con and me, he don't hold with Miss Howlett). Truly that man is enough to put the Angel Gabriel himself off religion; he squats on the village like an oily sponge, sucking away at its lifeblood. 'Old Harbutt ain't the best, I grant you,' says Rupe, 'distant cousin of the Rigbys, that's how he got the living, but he ain't that bad.'

Our engagement is to be announced on New Year's Eve – the Eagons are giving a party in Onslow Square and it will be in *The Times* the following morning. So, Miss Morgan, the die is cast and that's an end on't. Shall I destroy this diary? I think I must. If anyone found it – Rupe??

Back to town in the morning. We must start my trousseau, Granny says.

1st January, 1908   Ilchester Crescent – 6 a.m.

My last entry. A pukka engaged lady must not keep secrets from her intended, that would never do.

I've danced all night, but it's cold in my bedroom now, the fire a heap of stone-cold ashes. Outside, the street is dark and wet with freezing rain; a sodden paper-chain, blown by a sudden gust of icy wind, inches along the gutter like some brightly-coloured snake; light shines on to the area steps; in the basement the servants are already up.

This time next year I shall have been Mrs Rupert Eagon for six whole months. And what will this Mrs Rupert Eagon be like, I wonder? Will she be happy in her dear little house in town, driving her motor, going about her welfare work (just enough to keep the filly happy, we don't want her gettin' her hands dirty or catchin' one of those nasty diseases the poor seem so prone to), giving smart little dinner parties? Of course she will; how could she possibly not be?

And Mr Rupert Eagon, will he be happy too? As happy as he swears he will, with his short-tempered, red-haired wife who argues all the time and who has been made love to by Another? Oh my! What an absurd question – of course he will.

'Lal, you're so *lucky*,' says Suki.

'A real White Man, old Rupe,' says Bob.

'More than you deserve,' says Mother.

And Granny? 'Don't wish for too much, Lally dear,' says Granny. 'Marriage is a wonderful institution, and Rupert is a fine young man, head over ears in love. However, he will want from you certain things, certain responses, that in the beginning you may find hard to give. Bear with him, dear child, bear with him. He cannot help himself and, believe me, you will soon become accustomed to it. Always remember that to meet his desires, no matter how painful or strange these may seem at first, with love and trust and understanding, is the only way to a truly fruitful marriage.'

'I understand, dear Granny,' I say, wide-eyed with innocence, 'I understand.'

'Don't worry about your hymen being broken,' says Mary, 'lots of girls have their hymen broken before marriage – riding, playing games, all that sort of thing.' Until Mary told me, I did not know I had one. But there was blood on the couch in that little room above the café in the boulevard de Clichy, was there not? And pain too. But how much better to have one's hymen broken in that way than playing hockey.

So much, so much has happened this year. And tomorrow my poor old diary will be consigned to the boiler in the basement. Will that make me forget the things I must forget? I hope so; I do hope so.

PART IV

Pettishly I banged shut the battered exercise book – only half filled, they came thicker in those days. Typical of Lally to leave one like that, in mid-air; I was a middle-aged voyeur turned time traveller, deprived of his oats.

What on earth did happen on her wedding night? Did Rupe, on discovering his wife's non-existent maidenhead, angrily toss her unbloodied nightdress out of the bedroom window to the gawping masses waiting beneath? Of course not. Like the sensible chap he surely was, he no doubt accepted his good fortune in finding a girl of his own class who appeared to have been born knowing all about sex. Kept quiet about the fact to the chaps at his club, of course, but that was another matter. But he wasn't as sensible as all that, though, was he? After all, Lally did run away from him, and what's more, with my grandfather – a doubtful runner, one would have thought, from the outset. And the next exercise book was dated three years later – July 1911. Damn!

I finished my whisky – realising with a shock that I'd consumed at least a third of a bottle, three times my normal nightly ration – and peered owlishly at the faint pencil scribble just discernible on the last few pages of the book.

rose bowl – Aunty Dolly – letter
silver epergne (with fawn and elephant) ugh! – Cousin Gladys
R.'s cuff-links – change
tickets Haymarket – 'Getting Married'
hats???
R.'s navel is like an archangel's – will he sprout wings?
telephone, stamps, parcel for Pol – 1s 6d

And that was all. What exactly is an archangel's navel like? After that I went to bed.

Next day there was an obituary in the *Guardian* – yet another surprise.

Mrs Flynn laboured tirelessly throughout her long life for the welfare of the community. She was an active member of the Labour Party for many years, and although she never herself stood as a parliamentary candidate, she was a close friend and adviser of many prominent Labour politicians during the inter-war years. She was awarded the MBE in 1948 for her war-time work in the rehabilitation of bombed-out families, and also for her struggle to improve conditions in refugee camps on the continent in the immediate post-war years.

'Quite a remarkable old girl in her way,' was Peter Davenport's comment at lunch. I thought I was the one who could always be relied upon to produce the appropriate cliché.

Back home, another letter from Marcus, this one to announce his arrival in England the following week. He had an interview for some academic post. 'Won't bore you with the details, suffice it to say that my love affair with the U.S. is over. Whether I can take the U.K. is another matter, but have decided to give it a try. All news when I see you. Will ring from the airport . . .' So that solved that problem.

But one solved, another arose. Just as Warren and I – Warren now back from his course – were sitting down to supper that evening, the phone rang. A siren voice at the other end: 'David Wolf? I believe you and my Dad have had a little get-together. I'm Fiona Maplethorpe, by the way.'

'I would hardly call it that – '

'Well, anyway, from what Daddy said a good time was had by all, and of course I'm tremendously excited about the news.'

'News? I'm sorry, Miss Maplethorpe, I haven't the slightest idea what you're talking about.'

'Oh come on! Don't be such a dog in the manger. Daddy says Lally Flynn left you her diaries. My boss has empowered me to talk money – how soon can we meet?'

Oh Christ!

I looked wildly round the room, seeking inspiration, encountered Warren's interested face, travelled further and saw the open Gladstone bag, cast down on the sofa where I'd left it the night before. 'I'm sorry you've a wasted call, Miss Maplethorpe. Your father was obviously labouring under a misapprehension. Mrs Flynn left only two notebooks and I have already carried out her instructions, namely, to destroy them. I'm sorry I can't help you further. Goodnight.' Something I couldn't quite catch came down the line, I think it was 'Shit', then she hung up.

Warren helped himself to some more salad and refilled our glasses. He was obviously waiting for me to speak, but when I didn't he ventured: 'You sure gave that lady the brush-off. If it isn't a rude question, Dave, what *is* all that stuff over there? Has a client left you their memoirs and the Sunday nasties are after them?'

'In a way,' I said, draining my glass. Then I told him – I had to tell someone.

And in the end we didn't get to bed until 3 a.m., by which time we'd managed between us to consume a large proportion of Warren's duty-free bottle of Courvoisier. It turned out that he too had heard of my grandfather; indeed, he appeared to be no mean authority on the subject. This didn't surprise me really, I was getting used to being the odd one out.

'Well, of course I've heard of the guy,' he said. 'Ju Wolf is pretty well known back home; in his day he was one of vaudeville's all-time greats. The pity was he died before the talkies came in, so they never got his act on film. He did do a bit of work with Chaplin, but that was mime. There's also a rumour he made a couple of records, but no one seems to know where they are. Read any book on American vaudeville and there's sure to be a story about Wolf. They're mostly apocryphal, I guess; to have done all the things they say he did while he was in the States, the guy would have had to be there twenty years instead of the two he was, but he certainly succeeded in making the headlines fairly frequently.

'However, all that sort of stuff, I suppose, is fairly routine show biz – they were most of them wild guys in those days. What makes Wolf so mind-blowing, wherein lay his genius, I guess, was the way he only had to be in a place for twenty-four hours – any place, any country, he was a brilliant linguist – before he managed to pick up exactly how that place ticked; the politics, how people talked, went about their business, made love, the whole damn lot, dirt and all, and somehow managed to epitomise it in his act. I guess you know he wrote all his own material? There were certain famous set-pieces, but the rest of his act he simply changed to suit his audience – forty years – alas, before the tape recorder. Fortunately a certain millionaire by the name of Johnson P. Wyatt – '

'Old Pills,' I interrupted, glad at last to know something he didn't. 'A very good friend of Wolf's,' Warren, ignoring my interruption and well into his stride, carried smoothly on, 'who from the beginning recognised Wolf's genius and employed a shorthand writer to sit in the theatre and get some of the stuff down. It was the recent publication of this material, until now locked up in the Wyatt family archives, that's triggered off so much interest in Wolf. I have to come clean and confess that's how I know so much. It was all in the *New York Times* a few months back, just before I left home.'

'You say he was only in America for two years?'

'I think so, but I can look it up.' I closed my eyes: 'Don't tell me there's a "Definitive Life"?' He shook his head. 'Not yet, but it won't be long before there is. A lot of kids in the States have taken Wolf up as some kind of folk hero.'

Warren poured two more brandies with a hand that was slightly unsteady. 'D'ya know, Dave, I still can't get it into my head you're the guy's grandson. It's like you suddenly came out with Groucho Marx is your uncle, or Chaplin changed your diapers. I mean, Dave Wolf, respected lawyer, embodiment of Brit phlegm and all that stuff, beavering away in the respectable Georgian city of Bath. It just – '

'Did he ever go back – to the States, I mean – after those two years?'

'Only once, as far as I know, after World War One. But it was a disaster. He was really into drinking by then and, I don't know, the climate was wrong, I guess. Anyway, he was booed off the stage in a couple of places, and in the end practically had to be deported. I've seen some of the newspapers of that time – real nasty, as only New York papers know how.'

'Let's go to bed,' I said, 'I've to be in court at ten tomorrow morning.'

And so back to Lally again. Lally Eagon now, in her dear little house in town, with her handsome husband and adorable son; party-giver, party-goer, from ballrooms in Park Lane to studios in Chelsea; trips to Henley, Hurlingham, Ascot; bugs in Bermondsey, Women's Rights in Paddington, bicycling in Battersea . . . What frightful fun, what absolutely topping, ripping fun . . .

PART V

'What do you do, Eagon, if you have a boil that's about to burst?' Edwina, last night at the Burrells' studio party (so uncomfortable, everyone sitting on the floor, not nearly enough to drink and having to listen to Bobo Darlington on the piano). We'd been playing Eddy's favourite game of soul-searching.

'Lance it,' I suggest, wondering what comes next.

'Exactly so,' she says, 'let the poison out. And that, my dear, is what you must do.'

'Poison, Eddy, what can you mean? There's no poison in little me. I admit to getting annoyed when Mrs Minns over-cooks the beef, or Nanny complains about the smallness of the nursery, or Rupe goes on about the Suffragettes – '

'Don't be trivial, Eagon, you know perfectly well what I mean.' Eddy puts her hand on my forehead. 'There's turmoil there, I can feel it. My advice is, write it all down, it helps no end, you know. Just random jottings, no need to write a book. If that fails, take a lover.'

Then up comes Binky Burrell, all rattling earrings and orange beads. 'Come on, you two, come and meet our new young man. He's a poet, my dears, and Leonard says quite brilliant.'

Actually, underneath the breast-beating and the bandeau. Eddy is fairly sound; one does tend to listen to her advice. So, random jottings it shall be. Who wants a lover???

This morning my husband referred to me as a bitch. Perhaps he was right, but at the time it made me rather angry. It was, as usual, after he had (as they say) taken me. That now is the time for our quarrels – has it always been? How useless of me not to be able to remember. Anyway, he slept last night in his dressing-room – 'too damned hot to share a bed' – but came to me early in the morning.

I did my best and so did he, but my mind wandered and then my left leg got trapped underneath his body and it hurt so I had to pull it free, and of course this upset him. He rolled over on his back, collapsed and angry. 'It's only when you want it, my love, isn't it? And then you behave like some damned prostitute.'

'That's not fair,' I say, sitting up, that familiar, sinking feeling in my tummy, 'I always do my best – '

'Do your best! And what in Hades does that mean? You're my wife, not a performing monkey!'

'One could, I think, be forgiven for thinking otherwise.' This came out before I could stop myself. 'Will you never understand I'm a human being first and a wife second? You can rant and bully as much as you please, you won't change that.'

Rupe swung himself out of bed and stumped over to the dressing-table, where he picked up one of my silver-backed hairbrushes. For a moment I thought he was going to beat me with it, but he merely used it to brush his hair; the sense of anti-climax was, need I say, familiar. 'I'm not goin' to argue with you, you little bitch, so you may as well climb down off your damned soap-box. And I'll be dining at the club tonight – but then you wouldn't be interested in that.'

He left me after that, and I cried into the bedclothes until my throat was sore and my eyes ached. Then I lay on my back looking at the ceiling, the early morning sun seeping through the cracks in the curtains, listening to the waking up sounds of London and feeling wretched – my half-roused body tingling with a desire no longer shared, it seemed, either by my mind or my soul.

Nanny has just brought in little Ned. He's crawling round my bedroom floor; well, not exactly crawling, swimming really; his stout pink arms encased in flannel (if I've told that woman once, I've told her a hundred times not to put too many clothes on the child) pushing out manfully across the carpet. His soft, downy hair is the colour of bright corn and he's wholly beautiful. A true Eagon, says Rupe proudly, and I hope he's right; to go through life unaware of the dark side of the moon would be a splendid thing.

In a moment I will pick Ned up, a bulging, pulsating parcel of soft flesh, muslin and flannelette, strung about with tapes and ribbons and tiny bows, smelling faintly of milk, Pears soap and urine. And I will plonk him down on my bed in front of my open jewel case and watch his blue eyes squint with an almost insane excitement as he plunges his fat hands into the mound of brightly-coloured beads. And I will call him my 'petit Roi de Soleil' and fasten a gold chain around his neck and load bracelets on his tiny wrists, and he and I will laugh and shout and sing together until . . . a starched head pokes itself round the door: 'Come along, young man, we mustn't tire your Mummy', and purple with frustration, he is carried screaming from my presence.

'I think I should like to look after Ned myself,' I said to Rupe, 'he loves Nanny better than me.'

'Don't be an ass, old girl, you'd never have the patience. Besides, all boys love their nannies best – I did myself, until I grew up.'

'But I don't want that. It's so absurd; there I am at the Mission, teaching girls how to bath their babies, and if I so much as poke my head round the bathroom door when Ned's having his, Nanny's up in arms. 'We're a little fractious this evening, madam, we're having trouble with our toothypegs, better leave us be.' This made Rupe giggle, though he pretended it didn't. Ever since his father died last year, he's been standing on his dignity. 'Don't make fun of the servants, old thing, you know I don't like it.'

Only a few weeks, then Cornwall. We've been lent a house near Falmouth for September – Nanny, Ned and me, and darling Pol and her two to help out. Rupe is to be there for two weeks in the middle. How I wish I felt more excited . . .

14th July Yesterday morning at the Mission Mrs Prendergast claimed (did I or did I not detect a certain amount of relish?) that Ellie Noakes had stolen ten shillings from the cash-box; Ellie was not there to defend herself, it being her day off. As a result Mrs P. and I had words – I refused to believe her allegations and asked where was her proof.

'I've worked among these people for thirty years,' says Mrs P. very straight, the wings on her hat standing out like horns, and a bright red spot on either cheek. 'I think I can safely claim to know their ways better than you do, dear. When it comes down to bedrock, not one of them can be trusted, not even our dear Ellie.'

'Mrs Prendergast,' I say through clenched teeth (I confess I felt like hitting her), 'just in case you have forgotten, these people, as you call them, are ordinary human beings the same as you or me; you speak of them, if I may say so, as though they were apes. The only difference between us is that they endure conditions which should never be tolerated in a so-called civilized country, and we do not. What is more, I would trust Ellie Noakes with my life, and my child's.'

'I do not wish to discuss the matter any further,' says Mrs P., rapidly sorting through a pile of babies' bonnets. 'There is a great deal to be done this morning and I for one would prefer to get on with it. Naturally, I will not call in the police until tomorrow when, as I am sure will be the case, the girl does not report for duty.'

'You won't call the police at all, if I have anything to do with it,' I mutter under my breath, and not another word was exchanged between us, except in the line of duty, until just before it was time to shut up shop. I was locking the door to the stores cupboard when in rushes Miss Henniker, the new helper in the soup kitchen, all bosom and breathlessness.

'Mrs Prendergast, whatever will you think of me, but it's been such a day! So hot, and the meat crawling with maggots first thing, so we couldn't start the soup until gone eleven. I had to send Benjie Cribbins down to the market for some more, and he's such an unreliable boy and took an absolute age, so we were late opening and the queue was miles long. Then Effie fainted while serving the soup, and Dr Thomas (thank the Lord he happened to be there) said she'd started to miscarry. We'd no idea the girl was expecting and didn't have any towels, and some of the younger women were cat-calling – you know, the ones from Rivers Buildings whose husbands are out on strike – '

'Say what you have to say, Henniker, I've no time for gossip,' barks Mrs P. 'No, no, of course you haven't,' Henniker, scarlet-faced, grease all over her skirt, blood in her fingernails, stands there looking like a stricken sheep.

'Well, get on with it, girl, have you something to tell me or not?'

'A message from Ellie Noakes, actually. She asked me last thing last night to tell you and it went clean out of my head until now, what with the meat and everything – '

'Well?'

'She asked me to tell you she borrowed ten shillings from the cash-box. An emergency call for Dr Thomas; he needed some supplies from the chemist urgently. One of the O'Leary children – leg mangled under a coster's cart in Brick Lane.

Ellie said she'd bring the receipt in with her in the morning.'

'Thank you, Henniker. Another time, perhaps you could remember to pass on messages as soon as you receive them, or at least leave a note if no one is here. We are just as hard-pressed as you are, you know, and co-operation is so important.'

But I didn't crow. Suddenly I felt sorry for Mrs P., battling all her life against a tide of poverty and misery that always seemed about to engulf her but never quite did. Surely she could be forgiven for a little human jealousy – and there's no doubt she's jealous of Ellie.

'Come home and dine with us, Letitia,' I said, greatly daring, as we locked up, 'I'm sorry I spoke out of turn this morning.' Unbending, Mrs P. looked straight ahead of her. 'I'm afraid I have far too much to do,' she said, and gave one of her jeering laughs. 'Goodnight to you.' And off she marched up the alley, head high, not looking to right nor left, her button boots picking their way through rotting cabbage stalks, dung and bits of greasy paper, and followed by the inevitable retinue of ragged boys impudently mimicking her jerky stride; an elderly Pied Piper pursued by river rats.

I stood there under the sooty archway, inhaling the sweet, pungent smell of unwashed humanity mixed with bad drains, a dead cat reeking in the gutter at my feet. And as I watched her retreating figure until it disappeared round the corner, I felt such despair and hopelessness as I had not experienced since I'd watched helpless while Pa's body was carried out of the house in St Wilfred's Square all those years ago. I wanted to cry, but couldn't, and stood there in the hot sun staring vacantly at a little girl in a faded pink pinafore seated on a doorstep a few yards up the street, an even smaller boy – no doubt her brother – struggling about on her knee. I don't know how long I stood there, but gradually, in spite of myself, I began to wonder what the little girl was up to. Then it dawned on me; she was picking nits out of the child's hair. The boy, pink-faced with annoyance, scowling dreadfully and wriggling like a young minnow on a line, suddenly could stand his sister's ministrations no longer, and reached up in a vain attempt to dislodge the hand from his head. But the girl would have none of it and cuffed him smartly over the ear. 'Keep still, will yer, yer little perisher. I'm gettin' them bugs out of yer 'ead if it kills yer.'

And suddenly, absurdly, I felt better. There was something so indomitable, so brave, in the child's determination to do right by her brother, and the boy's own fierce little spirit, quite undimmed by the fearful squalor that surrounded him. Square-jawed and grim, clad only in an ancient, ragged jersey several sizes too large for him, he looked ahead and endured.

I watched fascinated, until suddenly he became aware that he and his tormentor had an audience. Slowly his head turned round to look; our eyes met for a full minute before he decided what to make of me. Then, ignoring his sister's admonitions to 'keep still, will yer', he stretched out a skinny arm. 'Lidy,' he shouted, all life in his hoarse, cockney voice, 'pre-y lidy.'

I was still smiling when Miss Henniker pounded up behind me at the bus stop. 'Mrs Eagon, so glad I caught you. I'm afraid the Prendergast was in a most frightful wax about my not giving her Ellie's message, but it's been such an awful day.' She looked, poor girl, near to tears. 'Everyone calls me Lally,' I said. 'Are you in a hurry, or should we stop at a tea shop on the way home? I often do, it helps me to readjust. I sometimes find the contrast between Sun Lane and Bayswater just a little indigestible. And there's such a nice tea shop opened in Victoria Street, where I change buses.'

'Oh Mrs . . . Lally, what an absolutely splendid idea, I could die for a cup of tea! I know the place you mean, I only live round the corner, in Warwick Square. It would help no end to have a chat with a chum before getting home. I was worrying like anything over what Mother will say about the state I'm in. She doesn't approve of me working in the soup kitchen. And what with all that blood at lunchtime – I didn't know there would be so much blood with a miscarriage; it was quite awful, really, and on top of the maggots – '

'Do you two ladies want to catch this 'ere bus or don't you? We do 'ave a timetable to keep, in case you didn't know, and there's others waiting.'

'Oh goodness, I am most fearfully sorry. I didn't realise . . .' Henniker's round, red face, glistening with sweat and tears, gazed tragically up at the equally red-faced bus conductor. His rodent-like visage split into a thin smile. 'Keep yer 'air on, dearie – it ain't the end of the bloomin' world, not yet it ain't, but just get a move on, will yer.'

20th July   To the Eton and Harrow match. All that light blue and dark blue and flannelled fools at the wicket. Rosa and Mrs Eagon were in our party. Rosa whispered to me she'd had a letter at last from Con, who is apparently expecting. 'Herbert – I refuse to call the man Herbie, it's really too much to ask – has a job as a bank clerk. Manchester is rather awful, but their room is quite nice, if a little cramped, and they've discovered a tennis court in the park round the corner where they can play tennis in the evening.'

'But Ros, if Con's expecting, one room in Manchester, Herbie out all day and tennis in the evening is surely not enough?'

'She should have thought of that before she ran off,' says Rosa, putting on her sulky look. 'What on earth she saw in that little pipsqueak I simply cannot imagine, apart from the fact that he's a good tennis-player. And whatever anyone says, I still think it was the shock of them marrying like that that brought on Papa's stroke.'

'The doctor said not.' I was beginning to feel annoyed and forgot to whisper. 'And whatever you may think, Con should not be left to have her baby alone in the middle of Manchester with only Herbert Potter to look after her.'

'Quiet there, if you please, Saxby-Gore's about to bowl.' Heads turn, Rosa scowls, and I feel like screaming. Who won the match? D'you know, I don't care.

While we were undressing last night (one in the morning and both of us having drunk quite a considerable amount of fizz during the course of the oh-so-long evening) I suggested we had Con to live with us until after her baby is born. 'Playing lady bountiful to m'sister Con and little Herbie Potter now, are we?'

'If that's how you choose to describe it. She's your sister, after all, and one room in Manchester is hardly – '

'Hasn't the wretched fella any parents? Those sort of people usually have the most enormous families.'

'You know damn well he has! Mr Potter senior came to see you after your father died.' Rupe made a face and slowly pulled the studs out of his dress shirt. 'Don't remind me – it's an episode I'd prefer to forget.'

'You're a conceited, self-satisfied snob, Rupert Eagon, and a bore into the bargain. I would – '

'Don't you dare speak to me like that!' And for the first time in our married life, Rupe struck me: only a slap across the face, it didn't hurt much, but suddenly, without warning and with appalling clarity, I saw Mrs Wolf. Mrs Wolf as she was the night of Pa's death, her dark hair falling round her shoulders, her poor hands scrabbling at the crumbling wall, the long, trailing skirt of her white dress entangled in the strands of ivy. Crying out as she fell – down, down, down on to the stones. Mr Wolf, his cigar glowing in the darkness, watching, smiling, waiting . . .

'If you ever do that to me again,' I heard my own voice as cold as a splinter of ice, 'I shall leave you – do you hear me? – I shall leave you. Now get out.' He came towards me then, arms outstretched, so much hurt and pain in his eyes. 'Lally, darling, don't talk like that – please. I can't bear it. I'm a beastly cad, I should never have – reminded you – your Pa . . .' And suddenly he was in my arms and we were both crying and apologising, horrified at the spectre we had in our stupid childishness invoked. Later we made love, and it was sweeter than it had been for a long time, though I cried afterwards, feeling the salt tears on my cheeks as Rupe, one arm across my breasts, slept the sleep of a contented child.

22nd July The problem of Con not solved. Perhaps Rupe is right, our house is too small, and he and Con do row. I've written to her suggesting I visit – if they can find me a quiet hotel nearby. At least I could see for myself what life for her is like. R. (reluctantly) agrees to the trip. 'Only two days, mind, and no wanderin' about in the slums.' I agree, meek-like. I don't want to spoil our new-found happiness any more than he does. It is at best a frail and fragile thing.

24th July 'Dearest Lally, how absolutely splendid of you!' writes Con. 'We've found you just the hotel. The Glen Lymmon, only ten minutes walk away, family, temperance, and ever so clean and respectable. Guests, so Herbie informs me, are elderly widows and superior commercial travellers. Will that suit? I do hope so. How I long to see you. We will meet you off the ten-thirty from town.'

26th July   The Glen Lymmon Hotel, Manchester

I didn't believe two people could be so ridiculously happy! There they were, hand in hand; Herbie's bowler tipped rakishly over one eye, neat as ninepence in his dark suit and celluloid collar; Con, hair like a bird's nest, a toque of surpassing ugliness plonked down on top; their joy in each other shining like a beacon in the noisy, sooty cavern of Manchester's London Road station.

'Lally dear, isn't this the most frightful place? Are you dead from the journey? Herbie will see to your bags.'

'Ripping of you to come, Mrs Eagon. Con could do with some company other than yours truly, she – '

'Get *on* with it, dearest. If we don't hurry we'll never get a cab.'

The one room is actually two; in a quiet suburban street and close to a small, not unpleasant park. The landlady is distinctly grim, but undoubtedly respectable, the furnishings strictly of the seaside boarding-house variety, but perfectly comfortable. Con (of course) has acquired a dog, a sort of terrier who goes by the name of Pan.

On our arrival we took tea, brought by Mrs Bloxham, who eyed me up and down with some suspicion but finally gave me her seal of approval by enquiring if I had any nippers myself. After she'd gone, the happy couple fell about with laughter; they do this all the time. Surely Rupe and I didn't when we were first married?

And the Glen Lymmon Hotel? Well, perhaps a trifle grim too, but Manchester is a pretty grim place. Several layers of lace curtains cover the windows and there's a perpetual smell of cooking cabbage, but the staff are affable enough, and a gent in a decidedly bright check suit and the biggest watch-chain I've ever clapped eyes on (one of the superior commercial travellers?) winked at me as I waited for the Potters to collect me this evening. We dined out and had such a jolly time.

Now I am writing at the rickety little desk in my dark little bedroom. I don't feel tired, there is only an odd sense of excitement. Is this because for almost the first time since I married, I'm alone? For three blessed days I've ceased to be Mrs Rupert Eagon and am Miss Lally Morgan again, waiting, waiting, waiting for an adventure . . .

27th July   I must have second sight! I have had an adventure, and I have to admit that it has disturbed me more than somewhat.

This morning at breakfast the gent in the check suit gave me his newspaper. 'Nice to have something to read over your kipper,' he shouted, laughing heartily, 'and I've no more use for it.' I thanked him as prettily as I knew how, glad to have something to look at other than the elderly widows, turned a page and received a near mortal shock.

'"This obscene entertainment is an insult to our city"; "Mr Julian Wolf and his confederates should be drummed out of town"; "disgusting, sacrilegious, unpatriotic." These are some of the critical comments that have already been made on the decidedly odd entertainment "An Evening with Julian Wolf" which opened last night at the Little Theatre in Oak Street. Julian Wolf . . .' But it shouldn't be a shock, not such a shock. Sooner or later Julian would have come to England. We'd read from time to time of his success in America, but he never wrote, and after my marriage he seemed so far away. Now he was in the same town!

Later: 'A childhood friend, Rupe and I both knew him,' I told Con, 'it was his mother who – '

'But Lally, how thrilling! Of course we must go and see his show. Julian Wolf is quite famous, isn't he. How killing if the theatre is raided by the police while we're there!' Killing indeed.

And so we went, after dining at the Midland, paid for (amidst protest) by me. And??? He was incredible, brilliant, better than I could have imagined possible. I wanted to cry and to take the barracking idiots seated round us by the scruff of their bulging red necks and hurl them into the street. Herbie spluttered with laughter like a bubbling tea-kettle throughout, and Con sat, eyes wide in surprise at the daring of it all, loving every minute.

At the end the audience split into factions – for and against – clapping and bravos mingling with catcalls and boos in equal proportions. The three of us stood up and clapped and cheered like mad; Herbie threw his hat in the air, and the man in front of us turned round and shouted: 'As to you, sir, you should be ashamed of yourself, bringing ladies to such disgraceful entertainment.'

'Muttonhead!' yelled Herbie, now thoroughly overexcited. It was then, my heart beating much too fast, that I whispered in Con's ear: 'Shall we go round and see him? We'll have to be careful, there may be police outside the theatre – '

'Oh Lally, yes, yes *please*.'

So there we stood, the three of us, in the bleak, carpetless passageway backstage where we'd been dumped by a harassed stage-doorman, slightly dishevelled from battling our way through the excited crowds outside, and feeling suddenly a little foolish.

'Perhaps we shouldn't wait. Mr Wolf will be tired – so unkind, all those people.'

'We'll have to wait a little longer, dear,' said Herbie, 'we shan't get a cab until some of this brouhaha dies down.'

'I could write him a note instead, leave it with the doorman,' I said, 'if you'd rather not wait – '

'For the Lord's sake, Bert, stop jawin' and get us a cab. There must surely be some sort of civilized watering-hole in this confounded town. If I have to face that damned woman's Welsh rarebit again tonight, I swear I'll not be responsible for the consequences.' Julian's voice, slightly hoarse; the familiar public school drawl, yet carrying with it an unfamiliar actorish, faintly foreign intonation. A voice that made my soul tingle with new life, a voice I thought I had forgotten.

I stepped forward under the dim, spluttering gas lamp and faced him. 'Congratulations, Mr Wolf, we thought your performance quite splendid.' For one dreadful moment I was afraid he was going to run from me, as he had run from me that afternoon in the boulevard St Michel; in another world, another life . . .

'Lally, Lally Morgan! God help me, I thought you were a ghost.' And then our arms were round each other, and I could feel the wetness of tears; his or mine, I'll never know.

And after that? Well, there were the introductions, every one talking at once, jostling each other in the narrow, stifling passage.

'Cab's out front. Best go quick, lad, and put thy coat and cap on, there's a right mob waiting round the back.' The stage-doorkeeper, even more harassed. 'Stout fellow, you think of everything. But I wonder if I shouldn't face my tormentors – so ignominious to be smuggled out the front. I might as well be one of those anarchist fellows. Disappointin', really, I hoped for something better. Did I not tell you, Bert, that Albion is invariably perfidious – '

'For heaven's sake, man, hurry. I told you you should never have put that bit in about the City Fathers.' Bert was looking as harassed as the door-keeper, and the rest of us were giggling helplessly.

Julian pulled his cap down over his eyes; it made him look like a demented Sherlock Holmes. 'Very well, then, if it must be ignominy let us at least drown our sorrows at supper at the Midland. One thing about all this hullabaloo, it does bring in the dibs.' Then, seizing me by the arm: 'D'you know, Lally, the last time you and me ran away together was when I threw one of m'father's walking sticks through a window in Kensington Palace – you dared me to, you witch, and then denied all knowledge of it.'

And oh, what an evening! The only person who didn't appear to be enjoying it was Bert, who turned out to be Julian's business manager. 'Afraid they just won't take another performance, Ju. Too much commotion – difficult times, strikes and all that. Mr Wise wants to see me first thing in the morning; cancel the booking, I shouldn't wonder.'

'Oh, Mr Wolf, what a dreadful shame. How horribly unfair!'

'Can't expect life to be fair, Mrs Potter. The Lord didn't make the world according to public school rules, you know, but thank you all the same. And may I say here and now that Mr Herbert Potter is a very lucky man indeed – quite bowls me over to find old Eagon has such a splendid sister.'

Julian walked with me back to my hotel after we'd dropped the Potters. Quite improper, of course, but somehow it didn't seem to matter. It was a warm night, the roses sweet-smelling in the sooty, suburban gardens, the sound of our footsteps echoing in the deserted street. 'So you married old Eagon, then. I'm not surprised, he's a good fellow under all the side. I remember when we were at school – '

146

'And you, are you married?' I'd no desire to talk about Rupe. 'Yes, as a matter of fact.' He cleared his throat and rattled his stick along the iron railings of someone's front garden. 'Sweet little thing, Florrie, met her on the beach at Boulogne; got talking and one thing led to another – '

'She's in England?'

'Yes, we've rooms in Ebury Street. That's why I decided to come back, try my luck over here. We've a boy, you see, Florrie don't want him brought up abroad; she don't like foreigners.'

'What was she doing in France then?' I knew my voice sounded waspish, but couldn't help it. To be so brilliant, famous everywhere but England, then to marry a girl called Florrie who didn't like foreigners! Julian gave his quick, sideways glance. 'Parents took her. Father on a week's holiday, wanted to see what the Frogs were like. Said he'd never go again.'

'And your boy?'

'Sidney – Florrie would call him that. Stout little chap, six months old.'

'You and your wife must dine with us,' I said, feeling like someone in a play. 'Might be difficult. Florrie, you see, she's not too good in company. Likes a quiet sort of life; never should have married her, really.'

'Oh Ju, you are such an *ass* – you always were.' And then we're kissing and the world – Rupe, Florrie, little Sidney, Ned, everything – is blotted out in the timeless wonder of it.

It's Ju who pulls away. 'You're a monstrous girl, Lally Morgan, why can't you obey the rules?'

'Rules are made to be broken, I thought you of all people would know that.'

The Glen Lymmon Hotel loomed up, a solitary lamp illuminating the dank laurel bush at the gate. Ju fumbled in his pocket and pulled out a crumpled visiting card. 'Perhaps you'd like to call when you return to town. We don't get many visitors, Florrie and me.' I took the card. It's been a lovely evening, I'm sorry the audience behaved so stupidly, it must be sad not to have your talent appreciated. Your performance was wonderful, truly it was.'

'*Merci, madame, mille fois.*' He took my hand and kissed it.

'But sometimes I enjoy the battle, I think. Do you still have the lucky cat?' And the silence between us was so charged that I could have cried out. 'I have him,' I said, 'goodnight.'

'*Au revoir, ma chèrie – à bientôt.*'

'Goodnight, madam,' says the sleepy clerk at the desk, 'I trust you had a pleasant evening . . .'

31st July   3 Wyndham Gardens
I did not see Julian again. He telephoned me the next morning: Mr Wise had cancelled their booking at the Little Theatre and they were leaving Manchester on the afternoon train. They would continue the tour, however, in the hope (forlorn) that their reputation for trouble had not gone before them. 'Bert says to play safe, but it don't come easy.' No, I don't suppose it would.

Con is to come to Cornwall with us! I suggested and Herbie insisted. 'You must have fresh air, dearest, you must, you look so peaky. And while you are away I'll move heaven and earth to get my pa to lend us the ready for a house somewhere on the edge of town. Up on the moors, perhaps. I could buy a bicycle . . .'

Rupe was glad to see me – I think. Refused to discuss the Potters, but gave his consent to Con coming to Cornwall. He did evince a flicker of interest at the news of Julian: 'Extraordinary fellow, always was. And by God, he could sometimes hit the nail slap bang on the head. I remember his imitation of his governor – bad form, of course, but absolutely uncanny – quite gave one the creeps.'

'I shall ask them to dine,' I say, cool-like, 'if you have no objection.'

'I've no objection,' he says, 'why should I? Fellow don't eat with his knife as far as I remember; no knowing what the wife's like, though.'

10th August   Called on Florrie Wolf in Ebury Street. I shouldn't say this (let alone write it) but it's hard to find what Julian sees in her. Pretty brown hair and good skin, that's about all one can say. She has the air of a person who, believing she's purchased a chicken, returns home to discover that she's landed a peacock instead.

She evinced a most unflattering lack of interest in yours truly. 'Your husband and I were childhood playmates, Mrs

Wolf,' I said in my best Mrs-Rupert-Eagon manner.

'Fancy,' she said. 'Perhaps you'd like to step inside and have a cup of tea.'

'It must be so exciting to have a husband on the stage,' I said. 'Yes,' she said, 'very.'

Down among the teacups she unbent a little. We talked of Reigate (her parents' home) and what a convenient and pleasant place it is (is it?) And how if only Julian managed to make a little money from his English tour (I gather, although she didn't say so, that the money he made in America has all been spent), Father had suggested they buy one of the new villas going up in Reigate. Very stylish, Father said, with a porch, three beds and a garden, not to mention a conservatory.

'But, Mrs Wolf,' I said, 'would it not be rather impractical to have a house in Surrey when your husband spends so much of his time abroad?' Florrie patted her hair and popped another lump of sugar in her tea. 'He likes a home to come back to,' she said. And suddenly I saw again the suffocating opulence of No 4 St Wilfred's Square, the feeling of tragedy impending, the sense of desolation; then the bare, shabby little room above the café in the boulevard de Clichy, the little room where we had made love; and I knew she was right. Poor Julian.

'May I see your boy?' I said. 'I have one myself – Edward. He was one year old on Coronation Day.'

15th August   A letter from Julian!

(Platform 2, Wolverhampton Station)
Sunday

Lally –

We return to town with our tails between our legs. The inhabitants of these foggy islands don't much care for me, I'm afraid. And here we sit, old Bert and I, disconsolate upon a pile of fish boxes, waiting for a train that never comes.

Florrie writes you've called and asked us to dine. She seems uncommon keen to go. So, for that matter, am I. Welsh rarebit and black pudding are playing hell with my gastric juices. I trust, *madame*, you have a good cook.

Incidentally, Bert has been approached by a group of

149

Socialists – Bloomsbury and Earls Court with a dash of the Webbs and Welwyn Garden City thrown in – frightfully avant-garde, doncha know (Bert don't hold with such people, but as he rightly says, we ain't got much choice) who had got wind of me being a chum of Eddy Gordon Craig. They want me to 'do a season' at the Companions Theatre in Soho. Holes in the roof and rats in the dressing-rooms, no doubt, but I'm not one to complain.

Lally, I can't tell you how good it was to see you t'other night. Truth, to tell, I was feeling a little down. I know all that about a prophet being not without honour save in his own backyard, but I have to confess that Watch Committees lusting for blood, not to speak of City Fathers breathing hellfire and preachers preaching eternal damnation, was not quite what I had hoped for – after all, I only aim to please. Then, suddenly, joyfully, there's my splendid Lally! Red hair on fire, those wonderful, frightening, glorious eyes – eyes a fellow could drown in if he ain't careful – looming up in the lamplight. Oh, what a miraculous sight!

Mon dieu – I do believe the d--d train arrives at last. The stationmaster is rubbing his eyes and stretching; some coves are walking up and down a bit, and another elderly cove is sauntering over to a mail truck. The passengers are showing some signs of excitement too, longing to get away, no doubt. Can't blame 'em, Wolverhampton's a place once seen, never revisited. It comes as no surprise to hear the late Sir Henry Irving died here.

See you, dear Mrs Eagon (and your esteemed spouse) à Thursday.

Julian

20th August What maggot of insanity possessed me to ask Julian and Florrie to dine? How could it have been anything but the miserable failure it was? If Bob had come it might have helped, but perhaps not, the thing was doomed from the start. I invited Bob and his fiancé, Miss Emily Inchcape (the banking family, my dear, Bob is always so sensible) but Bob declined. 'Sorry, old girl, but I just don't fancy having anything to do with that family. It's not the fellow's fault – but there it is, I'd rather not. Besides, by all accounts he moves in a pretty fast set, if his doings in New York are anything to go by, and Emmie's been brought up strict. Sorry and all that, old thing.'

'How d'you find England, Wolf, after all those years in exile?'

'Pretty unspeakable, Eagon, if you must know.'

'Oh really? I'm surprised you bothered to return, then.'

'Had to, m'wife don't like foreigners and wanted the boy to be brought up in England. You don't like foreigners, do you, my dear?' Florrie (in a most unbecoming raspberry-pink) looked as though she were going to be sick. 'Not reely, they . . . they're so foreign.' Ju's eyes, void of expression, met mine. Rupe looked down at Florrie as though she were some rare type of insect and in a voice that made me want to hit him, said: 'Exactly so, couldn't have put it better myself. Shall we go in to dinner?'

And it went on like that.

After dinner (interminable), the four of us grouped in various attitudes of embarrassment round the coffee tray. I poked away more or less at random at my embroidery – I had to be doing something or I swear I should have screamed – and Rupe lounged against the mantlepiece, a small boy intent on mischief.

'Saw your governor the other day, Wolf. Seemed in splendid shape, I thought. I believe he's married again.' The silence stretched from here to Alaska. I heard a taxi drive up to the house next door; the sound of well-bred voices, the cabby's growl, 'Thank you kindly, governor', a door slam. Ju's voice at last, icy, on his dignity, taking up Rupe's challenge.

'I'm not unaware of your kindness in asking my wife and myself to dine at your house, Eagon, but I have to tell you that I do not care to have that particular gentleman's name mentioned in my presence.'

'Oh come on, man, there's no need to – '

'Have you taken leave of your senses, Rupert?' My hands shook so, I plunged the needle into my finger; a few scarlet drops of blood dripped on to the bright colours of the embroidery.

'I think it is time we went home, Mrs Eagon. Little Sidney –

151

Mrs Soames is minding him, but she likes to retire early,' Florrie, trembling, rises to her feet. 'Of course! Let me take you upstairs to collect your wrap.' Gratefully, I too jump to my feet.

Later, much later, Rupe knocks on my bedroom door. 'Look here, I'm frightfully sorry, old thing. I ruined your dinner party, didn't I. But you have to admit they are the most frightful pair! I mean, one knew Wolf, of course, when we were children, but quite honestly – now! Togged up like some counter-jumper. And Mrs Wolf!! Of course, if you like dining with the housemaid. I personally – '

'How dare you speak like that about my friends, you stupid, rotten, conceited cad!' Rage, simmering for hours, erupted, and I went for him tooth and claw. Taken by surprise (he'd been drinking heavily ever since the Wolfs' departure) Rupe fell backwards, hitting his head against the door, then slumped to the ground where he lay, his eyes closed, breathing heavily. I knelt beside him, blind rage slowly dying, replaced by shame and a sort of dreadful sadness. Gently I put my hand on his forehead, and he opened his eyes. 'If you ever do that to me again, you little vixen, I'll beat the daylights out of you.'

'Get out. Get out of my bedroom, d'you hear me.' He scrambled heavily to his feet, his collar undone, blood dripping from a scratch over his eyebrow. 'And don't you ever invite that damned Jew-boy or his ghastly little wife to my house again – do you hear.'

And that was the end of the dinner party.

Oh Pa, what shall I do? What shall I do??

21st August Rupe and I not speaking. I go about like an automaton, trying not to think. Thankfully, life is busy; much illness at the Mission, the hot weather I suppose – and packing up the house in preparation for Cornwall. Dear Con is to travel down with us; how glad I am she is coming.

Today at the Mission, Mrs Phelps brought in a girl whose ribs had been broken by her husband pushing her downstairs. Mrs Phelps said: 'He don't 'alf carry on, that Alf Johnson, when 'e's 'ad a drink or two. Ever so sorry 'e is now at what 'e done.'

'A little down today, Eagon?' Mrs P. sticks a mug of

scalding tea into my hand. 'You mustn't let these things upset you. I've told you before, these people are children, they don't understand what they're doing. That girl, she'll be as right as a trivet in a couple of days, nor will she bear the slightest grudge against her husband, believe you me.' And I, like an idiot, burst into tears.

'Come on now, dear, this is not like you. How fortunate you are to be going off to Cornwall – plenty of fresh air and sun is just what you need.'

'It's what everyone needs, but most don't get – that's what's wrong . . .'

And I wrote a note to Ju. I shouldn't have, but I did. I said I was sorry the dinner party had been such a failure – Rupe was not himself. Perhaps I could call at Ebury Street one day next week? But the truth is that Rupe was jealous, insanely, stupidly jealous. But how could he be – how could he *know*?

22nd August And Ju's reply to my note.

Ebury Street – late

Lally, I must see you – I must. Meet me *please* very, very soon. Write c/o The Companions Theatre, Monks Passage, Soho – Ebury Street no go.

I think I love you.

Ju

22rd August I want to destroy J.'s letter; I want to, but I can't. It's madness, I know, but all the same I wrote back – to meet at the tea shop in Victoria Street, four-thirty tomorrow. If he doesn't come, then so be it.

Rupe spoke today at breakfast. Looking at a point on the wall somewhere above my left shoulder, he said: 'By the way, I've had an invitation to shoot at Tubby Prescott's – second week in September – he's gettin' up a houseparty. If I go, it would mean missin' Cornwall. Should you mind?'

No, Rupe, I shouldn't mind.

24th August Today – over scones and tea and little chocolate buns – Ju told me he's fallen in love with me. It was raining outside in Victoria Street; inside, the smell of wet mackintoshes and damp bodies. 'I want you, Lally, more than I've ever wanted anything in my life. I can't sleep, can't work – '

'But when,' I asked, 'when did it start?'

'What does it matter? I've always loved you, I think, since

we were children. But it was when I say you the other night; for the first time you were a woman, no longer a child. Oh Lord, this sounds such fustian! I ain't used to it, you see. I've never fallen for anyone before.'

'Florrie?'

'No, not Florrie.'

'But Ju, I'm married, I've a son, I – '

'Eagon knew, though, didn't he? Eagon knew you cared, that's why he behaved like a damned scoundrel – '

'He only mentioned your father, he – '

'You defendin' him, then?'

But in the end I said I did care, of course I did. I always have – I know that now.

Out in the street we held hands. The rain had stopped, leaving the pavements wet and slippery. On the corner of Buckingham Gate, newsboys shouted of the latest murder: 'orrible murder in Stepney, woman in bath; read all about it; 'orrible murder . . .' Starlings were circling black in the evening sky, calling high above the sound of the grinding traffic. 'I must catch my bus . . .'

'Lally, darling, don't go – there are hotels – come with me – just for an hour – people do, you know.' In sudden helpless fury I slap his face. 'I'm not a prostitute! How can you suggest such a thing! Is that all you think of me – is it? It happened before, didn't it – in Paris?'

'I'll see you to your bus.' His face shut, closed against me.

'Ju, I'm sorry – '

'It doesn't matter, doubtless I deserved it, I usually do.'

26th August But of course that wasn't the end of it. How can you halt a raging storm by standing in its path and ordering it to stop? I wrote and Ju wrote and I wrote again, and little Ned has a tummy upset and we dine at the Mayers tonight and I can't eat and Rupe never speaks and . . . Oh God!

Companions Theatre – Saturday

Darling – please, please, please come to me this afternoon – 3 Cheyne Studios, Chelsea. Cecil G. is away and says we can meet there. Of course he doesn't know your name, so there's nothing to worry about. I'll wait all afternoon. If you don't come, I think I shall die.

Ju

28th August   And what am I to do now? After this afternoon with Ju, how could I, how can I, face Rupe – coming to my bed – loving me? Even the thought makes me shiver. And yet, too, I still love him, certainly wish him no harm. But then I love Ju so much, much more. How bitter and unjust is life.

As we lay together this afternoon, Ju and me, the life draining out of us, letting the waves of love wash over our bodies, two sleepy children stranded one endless summer afternoon on a sunny beach of total happiness – I knew with a sadness that in an odd way was part of my happiness, that I should never feel quite this way again. It was not possible, human beings being what they are and the world being what it is. But that I had experienced such happiness and peace with and in another should make me eternally grateful. I tried to explain a little of this to Ju. He only smiled and gently pinched my nipples between his finger and thumb. 'You're awfully like your Pa, you know. Always wantin' to explain the inexplicable, wantin' to set the world to rights. Sometimes these things are best just left alone.'

Later, when we had dressed and were making tea in Cecil's tiny kitchen – dark and full of black beetles – I asked about Ju's father. Did he still hate him so very much? He was quiet for quite a long time, while he heated the teapot and arranged two cups on a tray, his movements quick and neat – tidy.

'He wrote, you know, when I was in the States. He must have read of me in some newspaper or other. Wasn't it time we buried the hatchet? Proud of me – only son – he was sure "dear Rachel" and I would hit it off, gettin' old. The vile mealy-mouthed hypocrisy of the man! I wrote back saying I could never forgive him for what he did to Mother and as far as I was concerned I had no father. I didn't hear from him again. Sometimes I hate him, sometimes not. I acted up a bit when Eagon mentioned him t'other evening because he had no right to, and I knew the fellow wanted to pick a fight, and old Wolf's never been one to hold back on such occasions. But my Aunt Lotty – she lives now at No 4, has done for years, m'father made the lease over to her, she always keeps in touch; she's told me things about Mother I never knew before. Not defendin' Father, you understand, no decent person could do that, and Aunt Lotty's a decent old stick, but explainin'. She told me Mother had always been odd. She had these fits from when she was quite a young girl, that's why the family let her marry Father. No, not what you're thinkin', epilepsy or somethin' like that, not that. It was . . . well, she would – oh Lord, this is difficult to explain – '

'I'm not a child, Ju. I work in the East End, I've seen things.' He smiled, a slanting, sideways smile. 'I always forget what a know-all you are. Very well, I'll say it straight. In certain moods – somethin' to do with the moon, Aunt Lotty says, but I can't believe that – my mother would take it into her head to go after men; any man who happened to cross her path. Soon after her eighteenth birthday her father found her lying with the stable boy, thought he'd better marry her off quick before something else happened. And there was Father, rich, besotted, said he wanted to marry her come what may. That he was Jewish and a swine didn't matter, all that mattered was that he was willin'.'

'And the "fits" continued?'

'They continued. Father beat her black and blue, but it made no difference.'

'And my Pa?' There was another long pause. Ju appeared to be studying the antics of two sparrows balanced precariously on a straying branch of creeper outside the small, grimy kitchen window. At last: 'Your Pa was different. She loved him, you see.'

'Oh Ju . . .' Then we were loving one another again, down on the hard kitchen floor, down among the black beetles, crying, laughing, forgetting.

29th August It was the same today, only better; except it couldn't be better. Afterwards I told Ju about Cornwall. 'Let me come, I can take a room nearby, the show don't open until October.'

'No.'

'But why not? Think of it, Lally, rocks and sand and sea – no one to bother us – '

'Ju, don't. Please don't. It's best we part for a while. Everything's such a muddle; I seem to live from hour to hour; I must have rest. And what about Florrie and little Sidney, they've done no one any harm, you can't – '

'Eagon done you any harm, then? I tell you, Lally, life *is*

156

unfair. You must take joy when and where you can, not turn away when it's offered. Besides, Florrie talks of goin' back to Reigate to her parents. She says London's no good for little Sid, and I'm never at home.'

'Does she guess?' Ju lit a cheroot; he was seated cross-legged on the divan in the studio, wearing one of Cecil's arab robes. 'Florrie don't believe in adultery – '

'But that's absurd, she must know it exists – '

'She knows it exists, but in her book it's something that only bad people get up to, "not the class of person Mother and Father would fancy meeting".' The take-off of Florrie was so accurate it was painful; to my shame it made me giggle. 'If you ever mimic me, Julian Wolf, I swear I'll kill you.'

We kissed goodbye under the mulberry tree in the studio garden. Such a lovely little garden, once part of Sir Thomas More's country estate in Chelsea. I think I shall always remember the scent of summer jasmine wet from rain, scattered white petals on the grass, the sound of a blackbird singing in the crab apple tree growing in the next door garden, the hoot of a tug on the slow-moving river, the feeling of pain mixed with joy. 'Don't come to Cornwall, my darling, I'll write, I promise.'

6th September Trenant House, Dog Creek, Falmouth
But of course, letters aren't enough. From Ju:

Ebury Street – Tuesday
My darling – I *must* come, I must. Every day, every hour without you is wasted. Last night I walked the streets and watched the sun come up over the river. Home to bed then in these stifling rooms, but couldn't sleep; when I did it was to dream of you.

F. and the boy have gone to Reigate. And I, cad that I am, am thankful for it. I could give them nothing. I've done a little work, but not much. Write to me, Lally, you must, one letter is not enough – let me come – please – please.

12th September Cornwall
The sun suddenly emerges from behind the racing clouds, turning the muddy water of the creek to a brilliant blue-green. Little Ned, arms outstretched, totters unsteadily across the rough grass towards me; Pol's children play their wild noisy games amongst the dark green trees that reach right down to

the water; the long, low white house sleeps in the sun, its magnolia-covered walls alive with bees. Mother, seated in a long chair on the terrace, is shelling peas for dinner, Con beside her knitting; Pol shakes a duster out of an upstairs window, and I, who should be the centre of all this, sit alone in the shadows, longing only not to be here.

I think I cannot bear it any longer. I shall wire to Ju. He could come – just for a day – surely; get a bed in Truro. No harm in that, it wouldn't be giving in. Con and Mother can take the children for their promised picnic on Saturday. I'll cry off, say I'm ill, they'll be gone all day.

16th September 'Lally, dear, you're not *enceinte*, are you? How ripping if you were, we could both be sick together.'

'No, just a little unwell, that's all. I don't think I could manage two hours in a boat and all that sun. And for the Lord's sake, Con, don't give Mother ideas, you know what she's like.'

'You overdo it, Lal, that's what it is. All that work at the Mission and all those parties.'

'You unwell, Miss Lally? First I've heard of it.' Pol looks at me sharp-like, she knows something.

They went at last, the heavy old rowing-boat laden to the gunwales with picnic hampers, rugs and cushions, buckets and spades, shouting children and arguing adults. 'Goodbye, goodbye, have a lovely day', I stand on the tiny jetty trying to look frail, aware only of an immense, rising tide of excitement.

There's no one left here now but me; the silence is blessed and complete. Debbie, the girl from the village, has gone home for the day, and cook has gone on the picnic. Quite soon now I too will have gone, bicycling along the narrow rutted lane that leads to the village a mile away beyond the creek. The lane is a dank green tunnel, its steep banks alive with red campion, purple vetch and huge, succulent pennywort, and they say that on a sunny day, if you stand quite still and watch carefully, you may see the quivering, deadly shape of an adder slide quickly through the lacy fronds of bracken that border its dusty, broken surface. But I shan't watch for adders, or pick the ragged wildflowers, or even listen to the birdsong. I shall have another purpose in mind: I

158

shall be on my way to meet the midday carrier cart from Truro; I shall be on my way to meet Julian.

17th September And he came! Hatless, his poor tired face haggard, bits of straw adhering to his smart London suit, his boots all dusty – Oh Julian!

'What a pair of miseries we look. I'd give my life for a pint of ale.'

'And for me?'

'*Ca va sans dire*,' he said, holding my hand very tight.

We hired a pony and trap from the butcher, and after lunch – bread and cheese in the tiny bar parlour of the pub (bright-coloured birds petrified under glass, yellow notices of long-gone fat stock sales, a clock on the mantlepiece shaped like St Paul's Cathedral, a jar of bulrushes) – drove up into the woods behind the village. And we made our love in a grassy clearing ringed by foxgloves, while the fat old pony munched grass and the summer flies hummed in the bracken.

'Would you leave him, Lally – come away with me? We can't go on like this.'

'I don't know. How can I know?'

'But you ain't happy with him, couldn't be, he's not your sort.'

'Don't be an idiot, you don't know that. He's a good man and he loves me. People don't just up and leave their husbands, not people like us.'

'But you weren't happy. I could see. That evening at the Midland in Manchester, you were like someone suddenly come alive. The kind of life I lead, that's for you too, not penned up in stuffy Bayswater, giving charmin' little dinners to old Eagon's boring City friends.'

'I have friends of my own – writers, painters – Rupe lets me, he's a good man, he's – '

'So you won't, then?'

'Florrie, what about Florrie?' He rolled over on his back and squinted up at the brilliant blue sky. 'I told you, she's gone, gone to live with her parents.'

'But I thought just for a rest, to – '

'I asked her to go.'

'Ju, how could you? She loved you – and what about your boy?'

159

'Don't be sentimental, Lal. It wasn't cruel, it was sense. She ain't happy in London, she don't like my friends, don't understand my work, don't like me all that much. It's better this way, honest it is. She'll marry again, and it will be the right man next time.'

'You're ruthless, Ju, as ruthless as your father.'

'Had to be.' But nothing was arranged, nothing planned; how could it be?

'Come again tomorrow, Lally, please.'

'Don't be absurd. It's not possible, you know it's not. Go back to London, Ju, I'll write, I promise.' Then we were in one another's arms, not caring who saw us, not caring about anything.

'Sorry to intrude, sir, but be time to leave, we're due in Truro by seven o'clock.'

'You must make up your mind, Lal, you must. I can't stand much more . . .'

I watched the carrier cart until it was out of sight, then empty of every emotion, my head aching from long hours in the sun, I collected my bicycle and rode home.

Morning service today in the tiny village church. I wore a veil – God help me, I hope no one recognised me. Everyone fractious from their day at the sea. 'It was such a splendid day, Lally dear, such a shame you couldn't come.'

20th September 'How lucky you are, Alice, to have so much post. Dear Rupert always so attentive. How he must miss you.' Mother's eyes are sharp and suspicious; she knows quite well my letters are not from Rupe. 'Rupe has only written once, Mother, surely you can recognise his writing. This is from Mary Wentworth.'

'How silly of me – of course. She's in London again, then? I thought her people moved to Oxford last year.'

'You've checked the postmark?'

'Are you accusing me of prying, Alice?'

'Don't be absurd, Mother, I'm not accusing you of anything, simply remarking on your powers of observation.' Mother tosses her head and flounces out of the breakfast-room. Con and I look at one another and burst out laughing. Thank God for Con.

Meanwhile I write and J. writes and it is only ten days until our return to London.

22nd September A wire from Rupe. He's coming until Monday – hiring a motor in Truro. Oh God!

23rd September Rupe: 'Lally darling, I'm a cad and a bounder, can you ever forgive me? Couldn't shoot a single bird at Tubby's, missin' you so much. Look here, shall we get tickets for that fellow Wolf's show? It opens next month, so I hear. Spoke to that friend of yours, Binky Burrell, the other night. She said all her set were goin' – she'd get tickets if we liked.'

Oh Rupe!

After dinner we took the boat out, Rupe and me. Twilight, but still warm: rooks rustling sleepily in the overhanging trees, fireflies, swooping swallows, the splash and ripple of a flight of wild duck skimming the water, the harsh croak of the old heron from the reeds on the other side of the creek.

We hardly speak, just now and again Rupe points out something. 'Look there, Lally, a kingfisher – by the clump of trees. Quick, d'you see him. There he goes . . .'

Out in the middle, Rupe rests the oars, allowing the boat to drift with the tide, and lights a cheroot to keep away the midges. 'It's all right between us now, old thing, say it's all right.' I trail my hand in the water and watch the smoke from the chimneys of the house slowly curling up into the trees behind it. 'Don't let's talk now, Rupe, it's so beautiful out here.'

Oh, coward that I am.

24th September 'By the way, bumped into old Mr Wentworth last week – up in town for a funeral – said Mary had gone off to Italy with a gaggle of schoolmarms, taken a villa in Florence for a month.' Mother's eyes meet mine across the breakfast table. 'How nice for her. No doubt she will be sending Lally a postcard, they've always been such chums.'

25th September Rupe has gone. Last night he made love to me. I escaped the other nights, I said it was my monthly, but last night I was sick of lies and – God in heaven – he is my husband. But it was no good, how could it be? Afterwards, we lay side by side not speaking.

'Rupe.' I took his hand, 'Rupe, are you all right?' Gently he removed my hand and turned over on his side. 'Best get some sleep, my dear, early start for town in the morning.'

27th September And so we go home – home? Tears and goodbyes; Ben the boatman, Debbie, promises to come another summer, another year. Con sad, but longing for Herbie. Herbie has found the promised villa on the edge of town. 'A brand new suburb,' he writes, 'gardens, shops and trams right to the centre of Manchester. It's only a three-up-and-downer, but there's a monkey puzzle tree at the back. It's ours, and it's a start.'

28th September Pol dropped her bombshell this evening while we were hunting for her Bella's teddy. The child swore she'd taken him down to the jetty yesterday to watch the ducks, and he's not been seen by mortal eye since. 'I shall have to stay, Mrs Eagon,' she said in her forthright little voice, 'I cannot possibly leave Cornwall without teddy.'

It was as we were wandering aimlessly along the path at the edge of the creek, peering now and again into the under-growth in the vain hope that teddy had been thrown under the trees there by a forgetful owner, that Pol suddenly stopped and took my arm. 'Sit down a minute, Miss Lally, I must say what I have to say now, we'll be gone tomorrow and then it will be too late.'

'Of course, Pol, say anything you like, you're my friend, you know that.' So we sat down side by side on a grassy patch at the edge of the water, and I felt fear curling in my stomach.

'Miss Lally, forgive me, but you and Mr Rupert – things aren't right between you?'

'What makes you say that, Pol?' Pol sat quite still, looking out across the creek, green fronds of bracken brushing the skirt of her pink cotton dress; the air around us was alive with buzzing insects. 'You know how you were all ragging me about old Ben's nephew taking me for a drink the other evening?'

'Yes,' I said, knowing what was to come.

'Well, we went to the Gull Inn in the village, like I told you.'

'Yes.'

'Well, the landlord, we got talking like, and he said as how when we was on the picnic that Saturday, you'd come to the village and met a red-headed gentleman off the carrier cart from Truro – a city gentleman, he said, and . . . and how the two of you'd hired a trap from Bob Treginnis and gone up into the woods. Miss Lally, don't take on, I never was one to repeat gossip, but you had to know.'

'If it came to it, Pol, that Mr Rupert and I parted, would you stay my friend – would you?'

'It's that Julian, ain't it? When you spoke of him the other day, I knew. It was him you met?' I nodded. What was the use of denying it?

'Miss Lally, dear, he won't bring you no happiness, he couldn't, not if he tried ever so. Blokes like him don't. He and his family are trouble, they always were, you should know that.'

'You haven't answered my question, Pol. Would you stick by me? No one else will.' Pol picked up a stone and threw it angrily far out across the water. 'You know the answer to that, Miss Lally. We're friends, ain't we, you and me, always have been, always will be, but it ain't half a bleeding shame.'

'Mrs Eagon, Ma! I've found him, I've found him! Pan had hidden him in the pantry behind the flour bin, the wicked dog. Teddy's ever so angry.' I squeezed Pol's hand, I couldn't speak. Far out on a mud bank, a cormorant was quietly fishing, a crowd of squealing gulls flew above us over the trees towards the open sea. I bent my head so that the sharp-eyed little girl clutching her battered teddy should not see that I was crying.

2nd October   3 Wyndham Gardens

'I wish you didn't look so seedy, Lally. You'll come, won't you, when little Robert is born?'

'Don't be absurd, Con, I'm as fit as a flea, always am, and how, may I ask, do you know little Robert will be a boy?'

'He will, we know he will, that's all.' Two beaming faces out of the train window. 'Goodbye, goodbye, see you very soon.' Herbie has been promoted in his job already; Potter senior has come up trumps 'now a nipper's on the way'.

Oh lucky, lucky Con.

'Meet you at the Albert Gate, three o'clock,' Ju writes, 'I love you, love you, love you.'

4th October   'If you would rather not come to Julian's show tomorrow, Rupe, I'm sure Binky can get rid of your ticket. She said – '

'Not intellectual enough, am I, eh?'

'Oh, don't be so absurd. It's just . . . well, it's not your sort of thing.'

'You've been seein' Wolf, haven't you? He's been writin' too.'

'We've met once or twice, the Burrells have taken him up; why shouldn't I? As to writing – '

'Don't lie to me, Lally, you're no damned good at it. That's one of the reasons why I loved you.'

Loved? 'Rupe, surely we – '

'I must go, I've a meeting at ten. And you can tell your precious Binky Burrell she ain't havin' my ticket. I'm comin' tomorrow night if it's the last thing I do.'

5th October 3 a.m. I think perhaps this may be the last entry in this diary. In the future there will be no need, surely, for secrets. Because tonight I have made up my mind.

This afternoon at Ebury Street, Ju white with nerves, drinking far too much: 'I can't go on tonight, Lal, I *can't*. Not with that fellow in the audience, not – '

'Don't be such a coward, Ju, of course you can. I tell you what, I'll bring our lucky cat to the theatre, he's not had an outing for such a long time, you'll be all right then.'

'Perhaps.'

We dined early with the Burrells in Russell Square. 'So pleased you could come, Rupert, we see far too little of you. So intriguing you and Lally knew Mr Wolf when you were children. It does add a certain piquancy to the occasion, don't you agree? Chums of mine who saw him in New York say he's quite quite brilliant.'

I eat nothing; Rupe drinks. The theatre, when we get there, is shabby, drafty, down-at-heel.

'A somewhat mixed audience, I fear, and no bar. Often wondered why these Socialist shindigs have to be so frightfully uncomfortable.'

'It's not a Socialist shindig, Granville, as you know perfectly well. Mr Wolf is a great artist, the shame of it is he's not recognised in his own country.'

'Thought you said the fellow was German.'

'Oh shut up, G. and organise the seating: I want to sit next to Lally and blow the sexes being wrong.'

We're three rows back, better than being in front, but still too near for comfort. The auditorium is filling up. In the stalls, several people I know; they nod and smile; I smile back, nonchalantly waving my programme, inwardly quaking. What will they think of him? Do they really know what they are letting themselves in for? Binky points out Mr Bernard Shaw, there's a rumour Miss Ellen Terry is in the audience but no one can see her. The plebs (as Granville so charmingly describes them) occupy the balcony and gallery, there is no dress circle. A scruffy-looking lot, from what I can see, and some of them out for trouble. In the orchestra pit a young man in a celluloid dicky thumps out Viennese waltzes and extracts from *Flora Dora*. I find myself wishing it were ragtime, or even something from the Russian Ballet – wouldn't that have been more suitable?

'Amateur night at the Band of Hope, eh? No doubt the vicar will come on at any minute to push the hat round.' Rupe, silent for several minutes, suddenly breaks his silence in a voice both loud and deliberately offensive. Several people in our vicinity titter and someone shouts, 'Hear, hear!'

'Rupe, you didn't have to come. Please, please don't spoil it. Can't you see I'm sick with nerves?' Rupe smiles, his eyes glittering, angry. 'Sorry m'dear, I keep forgettin'.'

'Forgetting – forgetting what?' But already the house is darkening, the lights on the stage go up, and there is Ju.

I knew at once he'd been drinking heavily; there was a reckless, jeering quality in his act that had not been there in Manchester. Like a lion-tamer cocking a snook at danger, only a swagger-stick between himself and certain death, he deliberately provoked the audience to the very limits of their endurance. Then, as snarling they prepared to spring, with a flutter of eyelashes, a shrug of the shoulders, he would become a woman, down-trodden, helpless, begging for their mercy – he only aimed to please. And baffled, fascinated in spite of themselves, they would subside, muttering, biding their time – waiting their chance to put an end once and for all to the unsufferable, unforgivable arrogance of this foreigner (that half the time he talked with an English public school accent somehow made it worse) who dared to poke his prying fingers into their

165

souls, and say things that never should be said save guiltily, secretly, behind closed doors.

For a while I became lost in the sheer brilliance of it: the taunting, pleading, wildly funny creature on the stage, part man, part woman, part god, was not Julian, not my Ju, the man I loved, had lain with, laughed with, the man I had sat with this very afternoon and soothed as though he were a frightened child. He was someone else, a stranger never before encountered.

Then something happened; for one brief instant Ju's eyes met mine in recognition over the footlights, and in that instant I knew with absolute certainty there was a bond between us so strong that no matter what happened in the future, it could not break. I knew, too, that the battle was over and he had won. With the realisation came sadness, and despite the pandemonium now raging round me, a sense of loneliness and isolation. I wanted to cry, but couldn't, and just sat still on my hard seat, waiting for the performance to end and, in an odd way, for my life to begin.

'Come on, we're goin' home.' Rupe's arm was roughly dragging me to my feet, heads were turning. 'I refuse to endure one more minute of this obscene rubbish, or see you makin' a further fool of yourself. Say you feel ill – I don't give a damn what you say – but you're comin' home with me – now!'

And what could I do but go?

As, heads bent, we pushed our way along the row, Ju faltered for a second and then, to my agony, stopped dead in his act and, lifting an imperious arm, with a single gesture commanded the audience to silence; they obeyed, such was his power over them when he chose to use it. So it was with the entire theatre's eyes upon us that we stumbled up the aisle and out through the exit door at the end; the noise of the door closing behind us reverberated through the silence like the crack of doom. Once on the other side, Rupe seized my hand and half dragged me down the passage towards the entrance. But not before I heard Ju's mocking voice, obviously commenting on our abrupt departure – followed by laughter and a burst of spontaneous applause. Like all artists, he had no compunction in using whatever situation came to hand to further his creation.

We journeyed home in an aged hansom, apparently the only form of transport available at that time of the evening, Rupe and I, side by side locked in our prison of misunderstanding. Rupe was silent, isolated in his sense of outrage, glaring out of the cab window; I sat with my eyes closed, head resting against the dusty squabs, feeling a weariness akin to death.

It was as we were passing Marble Arch, the gold-brown of the trees in Hyde Park softly glowing in the light from the lamps strung out along the Bayswater Road, the grassy paths beneath them empty now of people, mysterious and faintly sinister in the half-dark, that I knew suddenly and with an appalling clarity that our marriage, Rupe's and mine, was over, and that I loved Julian Wolf more than my husband, my home, even my child. I also knew that never, for as long as I lived, would I be anyone's possession – man or woman, it didn't matter. I would give as much as there was in me to give, or as much as my conscience told me to give, but never again should what I had to offer be snatched from me by another as though it were his right. I had no desire to exercise such power over others, neither should they over me. I would leave Rupe and all he stood for; I would leave him now because of Julian, but had Julian not come back, or had he never existed, in the end I should have left Rupe just the same. With this realisation I was once again overwhelmed by the same feelings of sadness and isolation that I had experienced in the theatre. Why could I not be like other women? Why did I have to be me – why?

As the cab turned into Wyndham Gardens, I put my hand on Rupe's arm. 'Rupe, I'm sorry, so sorry.' Angrily he shook it off. 'I don't want apologies, just get out of my sight, that's all I ask – get out of my sight.'

So here I sit at my window, watching the night sky, waiting . . . wondering . . . trying to see into the future, trying not to think of little Ned . . .

6th October   Russell Square

At the Burrells'. Yesterday I left Wyndham Gardens. So simple, just to pack a bag, write a note and change your whole life. Not so easy to forget the people you have left behind. Rupe will never forgive me, I know that.

Ju stayed here last night – the first we ever spent together. When, I wonder, will be our last? His show continues to the end of the week, but each night is a battle. The critics who stayed at least recognise his talent – the ones who didn't scream filth and obscenity, like their chums in the provinces.

We leave for Paris on Sunday. Binky so kind: 'How brave, Lally, to sacrifice so much for love;' Granville wary, polite as always, but wanting me to go. A foretaste of things to come? *Saturday – late* Goodbye, England. I wonder when I shall see you again. No word from Rupe . . .

PART VI

Well, I knew that was going to happen, didn't I? But it was quite a thing to have done in the year of grace 1911, all the same.

'Personally, I feel sorry for poor little Florrie,' said Philippa. We were taking Merry for her customary walk on Poor Man's Down. I had, inevitably, shown Philippa the diaries, I couldn't help myself; I was, I regret to say, becoming obsessed with the whole thing.

'Nonsense, she wasn't poor little Florrie at all. The trouble with you is, you regard all this as though it were some damned soap opera on TV; you seem to forget the people involved are my relatives. As a matter of fact, I remember my Grandma Hen rather well. She was small, completely square, chewed cough sweets all the time and taught me to play snap. I agree with Lally, I simply cannot understand what got into my grandfather. Of all the girls he could have bumped into on that beach at Boulogne, why choose her?'

'Just as well he did,' said Philippa tiresomely, 'or you wouldn't be here now, would you?' Philippa's like that, she was like that when she was my secretary years ago, before she married the unspeakable Arthur. She used to claim (against overwhelming evidence to the contrary and the opinion of those far better qualified to judge, i.e. my wife Amy) that I was a romantic manqué, whose flights of fancy it was necessary to depress every now and again before, as she put it, 'disappointment set in and there were tears before bedtime'. In the end she was the one who was disappointed, she married Arthur. Actually, we'd only met up again recently; on her marriage to Arthur she'd moved away from Bath, only returning after the break-up. We'd bumped into each other buying fish in the market, I hadn't seen her for ten years. 'How's Arthur,' I said. 'Gone,' she said, 'and good riddance. How's Amy?'

'Gone too, as a matter of fact.' And on the strength of that we had lunch together.

And now I found myself looking at the way her dark hair, tinged not unbecomingly with grey, had turned into little ringlets in the damp air, and admiring the graceful way she bent down and picked a cowslip to add to the bunch of wild flowers she carried. Suddenly I knew Lally would have liked her, though why that should have mattered beats me. 'Don't waste your tears on Grandma Hen,' I said, putting the panting Merry on her lead, 'what about poor old Rupe?'

Then, a couple of days before Marcus was due to arrive, I had a phone call one morning at the office. 'A Mr Mathew Parsons' secretary wants to speak to you, Mr Wolf,' Phoebe sounded bored and appeared to be chewing something, 'is he a new client?'

'Not *the* Mathew Parsons?'

'I wouldn't know, Mr Wolf, shall I put her through?'

Do they teach the young nothing these days? Mathew Parsons, OM, one of the Grand Old Men of literature. Could it be him? Surely not.

It was.

'Mr Parsons would like to arrange a meeting, Mr Wolf. He's staying with friends in Bath until Thursday.' A hushed female voice with a pronounced Oxford accent; she might have been referring to God. 'Number 14 Sheldon Place, six o'clock tomorrow evening, if that's all right for you.'

'Yes, that would be absolutely fine. May I ask why?'

'It's about your grandfather, Mr Wolf. Mr Parsons was a great admirer of his, you know.'

Him too?

'My dear fellow, this is truly an exciting moment for me; your esteemed grandparent was one of the idols of my boyhood.' Incredibly old, incredibly alive, the figure in the wheelchair whizzed across the elegant Aubusson carpet, one hand outstretched – Mathew Parsons in the flesh. His face was familiar from a hundred photographs; there was a bust too, wasn't there, in the Tate, by Epstein or Hepworth? No, it must have been Epstein, Hepworth didn't do that sort of thing.

I had arrived at the august portals of No 14 Sheldon Place dead on time, and been ushered into the study by a formidable lady who looked me up and down as though I'd come to sell brushes. Feeling suitably awed, I took Mathew Parsons' hand, then stood there goggling, unable to think of a damned thing to say. It was, after all, rather like meeting a ghost; one always has this absurd notion that people as famous as Mathew Parsons aren't real; it comes as a shock to discover they are.

172

'I'm afraid I'm not much like him, sir,' I managed at last, and followed that up with an inane giggle. 'You have the look, dear boy, you have the look; there's no mistaking the stable. Come, sit you down and Agatha will get you a cocktail.'

But before we settled down to what Mr Parsons referred to as serious drinking, I did manage to pull myself together sufficiently to ask him how he had come across me, and why now. Had he, perhaps, heard of Lally Flynn's death?

'No, no, nothing like that,' he said cheerfully, 'mere coincidence. No, I had a letter the other day from some woman calling herself Fiona Maplethorpe – Agatha tells me she's one of these television personalities. Never heard of her myself, but then I wouldn't; I don't watch the box except for cricket, and that's scarcely worth seeing nowadays. Anyway, this Fiona Maplethorpe said she was gathering material for some sort of documentary in aid of Ju Wolf's centenary; she'd ferreted out a piece I'd done on him years ago, and had I anything to add. I was just about to put the thing in the wastepaper basket – can't abide these instant TV histories, never let them do one on me – when my eye caught the postscript. Was I aware that Wolf's mistress, Lally Eagon, had died recently in Bath, and that his grandson, David Wolf, who practised as a solicitor in the self-same city, had been left her diaries? Well, I didn't care a fig for the diaries, but I suddenly had a desire to see Ju's grandson, don't ask me why, the old get these sudden fancies. Then Agatha informs me I'm booked for a visit to Polly and Dick Reresby-Dawson' (Sir Richard and Lady Reresby-Dawson were more or less the uncrowned king and queen of what Bathonians like to call the 'Bath élite'; it is said people have committed murder to get an invitation to one of their Georgian soirées; they were, needless to say, way above my touch) 'and so here I am. And do you know, I'm very glad I came; I nearly didn't. I always find Dick R-D. a bit of a stuffed shirt and Polly talks too much. But seeing you brings those times with Ju back, and by God they were good times – great times . . . Come on, drink up, boy, your grandfather would have finished the bottle by now and been on to the next.'

God, he was a fascinating old devil! That session with him (and session it was, I could barely stand by the time it was

173

over) I shall remember to the end of my days, and I left the place feeling about a foot taller than when I came in; Mathew Parsons was that sort of person.

And he had known Lally. 'A beauty, of course, and those eyes, but rather frightening to a boy such as I was then. The very first time I met her, she ordered me to get some lotion or other for my acne, and recommended a cold bath every morning! Absolutely nutty about Ju, of course, even I could see that.' Parsons' first meeting with my grandfather had apparently been during his ill-fated tour of the provinces in 1911: aged fourteen, he had braved parental wrath to see Wolf when he came to Bradford, Parsons' home town.

'I shall never forget that evening, never; when the performance was finished, my only desire was to sit through it all over again. So many of the things my generation were thinking then, feeling, had an inkling of, Ju Wolf put into words – and made you laugh until you cried while he was doing it. I wanted to rush on to the stage, kiss his hand, shout. I didn't, of course, that would have been too un-English, and I was very English in those days, but I wanted to. I did, however, have the nerve to go backstage afterwards. I remember it so well: being ushered into the shabby little dressing-room, barely more than a cupboard, by the aged stage-doorkeeper; Ju lying back in a chair, his feet on the table, his collar undone, red hair damp with sweat. He'd a glass of whisky in his hand and he looked utterly spent. I stammered out my appreciation of his performance and how he was the first person I had encountered who thought as I did (I was a conceited young bugger in those days, as no doubt you've guessed), and Ju, puffing away at his cigarette, looked at me in silence. Then, to my considerable chagrin, he burst out laughing. "Ain't you got a governor, boy?" I nodded glumly. "Well, if he's anything like mine was, he'll have the hide off you for this night's work. Be off home with you before I'm arrested for child-stealing." Considerably abashed, and I have to admit, near to tears, I apologised for troubling him (I was a well brought-up lad) and made for the door. Then just as I reached it he called after me: "Care for buns and lemonade?" Misery turning into ecstasy, I nodded. "Four o'clock tomorrow afternoon, outside the station? We'll go for a spin in my motor, then if you know of a decent tea shop – "'

'"Oh yes, please, sir, thank you, sir." The bliss of it; I remember the feeling to this day. It wasn't until long afterwards I discovered that the motor wasn't his, he'd hired it especially, just to take me for a ride.'

After that first meeting, it became imperative to the young Parsons to see Wolf again – Wolf had by this time returned to London and was preparing for his stint in the Companions Theatre. To this end he somehow managed to persuade his parents to let him spend his summer holidays with a devoted maiden aunt in Clapham. The Parsons family was large, Mathew the eldest of eight, so no doubt they were quite glad to see the back of him for a few weeks; he must have been a rather unnerving child. Anyway, the doting aunt, after much cajoling and, as he put it, 'the odd white lie', was induced to let him spend his time hanging about the Companions Theatre, acting as a sort of unpaid body servant and acolyte to my grandfather.

'My main job was to keep him supplied with drink,' Parsons said. 'There was a public house just round the corner from the theatre, I remember, the Nag's Head, where I would be sent to collect what he referred to as his medicine. Of course, he drank too much even then; killed him in the end, so they said. But the best times were when he'd try out new material for his act, using me as his guinea pig. This would always be late at night, in the room behind the stage at the theatre. (The Companions was demolished donkey's years ago, soon after the Great War. Last time I saw it, it was a Chinese restaurant; the Lord knows what it is now.) My chief memory of that room is that it smelled of gas and mutton stew. I seem to remember they used it as a soup kitchen in the mornings. Some old harridan was supposed to clean the place, but it was always ankle-deep in dust and there were cockroaches everywhere. Anyway, there we'd be; Ju, glass balanced on the ledge beside him, hair on end and collar undone as usual, going through his act; and me, tears pouring down my face, begging him to stop, the pain of laughing becoming more than I could bear. Then in would come Bertie Dugdale, opera cloak round his shoulders, topper on the back of his head – Dugdale was Wolf's manager, good chap, killed at the second battle of Ypres in 1915. "Time the boy went home, Ju. Come

175

now, let him go, there's a good fellow." And still aching with laughter, protesting, I would be packed into a cab and sent back to Clapham.'

'Mathew, it's nearly seven o'clock,' Agatha's head round the study door, 'just time for a nap before the Hilliards arrive at eight. I'm sure Mr Wolf will understand – '

'Go away, woman, can't you see I'm busy?' Agatha's head disappeared, but her voice could be heard outside in the hall. 'I think we'd better leave him for a little while longer, Sir Richard, he's in one of his moods.' Mr Parsons winked and poured us each another cocktail. I began to feel like a character in a film.

'Of course I was jealous of Mrs Eagon – Lally – I suppose that was inevitable. Didn't mind "our Florrie", though, Ju's wife. Homely little thing, used to bring me sandwiches, I remember, and once sewed a button on my jacket. Ju was always very respectful to her; he used to hide the drink when she came down to the theatre. "For the Lord's sake, boy, get that damned booze out of sight, rumour has it my better half is on her way," he'd hiss out of the corner of his mouth, and trying unsuccessfully to control my giggles, I'd dash round collecting up every bottle in sight.'

Mr Parsons smiled, his eyes far away. 'Do you know, young man, looking back, those few weeks in London in the summer of 1911 were some of the happiest I ever spent. Your grandfather had the gift – and in ninety odd years I can tell you here and now I haven't come across it very often – of being able to make people happy just by his very existence. The Lord knows, his was a tragic life and his great talent cruelly, wilfully wasted, but he was not a tragic man.'

'Did you see him afterwards, sir, after he and Lally Eagon went away together?' There was a pause, Mr Parsons still seemed lost in that cloudless summer of long ago when he was a boy and all the world was young. 'Only once,' he said at last. 'Met him in Paris not long after the war. It wasn't a success. I was a pretty self-opinionated young prig in those days. Most of my friends had been killed, and all I wanted to do was to forget the war and everything connected with it. My own part in it had been pretty ignominious. No heroics for me. Weak eyesight, they said, so spent my war drilling elderly bank managers on Salisbury Plain and checking stores in some benighted ammunitions depot somewhere in East Anglia. And with my generation, d'you see, if you hadn't been in the trenches you simply didn't belong to the club. No one blamed you for it – I mean, no one who had been there, and was still alive to tell the tale, and there were precious few of them – you just didn't belong and that was that. D'you understand what I mean?' I nodded. I didn't really but knew it had been so.

'Well, because of this – the guilt, I suppose – I set out to knock the whole thing – wasted lives, sacrifice of a generation, all that. A cliché now, but new then. I thought Ju Wolf would agree, he of all people – make a joke of it, show the capitalist war profiteers for what they were . . . but he didn't. He simply sat there, in that dreary little café he'd insisted we meet in, drinking away and saying damn all. I'd thought we'd make a night of it, but in the end, God help me, I pretended I'd forgotten another engagement. I just wanted to get away. It was only later I heard that when we met, the poor devil had only just been released from hospital – shell-shock, and his lungs damaged by gas. Bumped into Bertie Dugdale's younger brother, Jack, at some party in London – he told me.'

It was then I realised I had never known, never even wondered whether my grandfather had been in the Great War. Certainly no one had ever told me he had. One always knew that Grandpa Hen had been, he seldom allowed one to forget it. 'When I was in the trenches, young fellow-me-lad . . .' had become a sort of family joke. But Grandfather Wolf. . . ? And where was Lally?

'When you met in Paris, was Lally Eagon with my grand-father?' Mathew Parsons shook his head. 'No, he was living with some tart or other – Fifi, or Gigi. He told me she was big and soft and kept him warm at nights. Telling me about her was the only time he showed a flash of the old Ju Wolf of pre-war days. I didn't ask him what had happened to Mrs Eagon, thought it might upset him.' We were both of us silent for a while. I don't know whether it was the cocktails or what, but sadness and ghosts were certainly in the air.

The spell was broken by a ring at the front door bell and the rush of feet on marble floors; the Hilliards had arrived to dine. I rose somewhat unsteadily to my feet. 'I can't tell you what a privilege it has been to meet you, sir, and I do hope I haven't taken up too much of your time.'

Mathew Parsons smiled his singularly sweet smile. 'The privilege is mine, dear boy, sorry it couldn't have been longer. By the way, I wouldn't let that TV harpie get hold of those diaries if I were you. Leave em in peace – eh?' For a long moment we looked at one another, the ninety-year-old poet in his wheelchair and the middle-aged solicitor in his dark suit and respectable tie, and something – what the hell it was I don't know, but it was something all right – passed between us. And suddenly it wasn't Mathew Parsons OM, the celebrated man of letters, I saw before me, but the passionate, idealistic, hero-worshipping youth he once had been. And he saw – I'm convinced of this – not me, but my grandfather, Ju Wolf.

'God, this country doesn't get any better, does it? Paddington looked as if it was scheduled for demolition and the train was so packed I had to stand all the way down. How are you, Dad?' My son Marcus in a black leather jacket, lean, hungry-looking, a pair of fashionably-shaped dark glasses perched on top of his head. And he'd already managed to get my back up. I know Paddington's a tip, but I don't like visiting Americans to tell me so. 'Fine thanks, had a good trip over?' He shrugged and fumbled for his ticket. 'Pretty bloody.'

'Hardly worth coming.' I couldn't stop myself.

'Still the same old Dad.' He gave me the quick, sideways look I knew so well. A look – and it came to me with a thrill of excitement – directly inherited from his celebrated great-grandfather. Suddenly I wanted to laugh, God knows why. I didn't, of course. I squeezed him on the shoulder in the way I'd seen American 'dads' do in countless TV series, and left it at that. Then, as he continued to maintain a rather frigid silence while we were loading up the car, I said placatingly: 'We'll go straight home, shall we, old boy? What you need is a good, stiff drink. I've bought a bottle of Irish in your honour – hope it's still your tipple. I wonder if Merry will remember you, it's all of three years, isn't it, since she saw you last?'

Marcus blinked, and to my surprise (and I have to confess, gratification) looked about to burst into tears. However, after lighting a particularly evil-smelling French cigarette and pushing his dark glasses back down on to his nose, all he said was. What exactly were we celebrating? 'I don't know,' I said as I nosed the car through the tangle of taxis and luggage-laden tourists. 'Life, perhaps. Does the name Ju Wolf mean anything to you?'

And against all the odds, the evening was a success. Warren helped a lot; he and Marcus got on, and even discovered they had mutual acquaintances in the States – the academic world, it seems, is surprisingly small. But it wasn't that, really. It was those others – Ju, Lally, Florrie even – who did the trick. They achieved what had for the last twenty years seemed an impossibility, they brought me and my son, Marcus, together. They were there, I'll swear they were, egging us on from the sidelines. Fanciful stuff, no doubt; Philippa is right, I must be a romantic manqué. But really it did seem so – Marcus felt it too, I know he did. Never, or not since he was in nappies, had we been so relaxed in each other's company. Merry helped too; she remembered him. She's always been a tactful and accommodating animal, that's one of the reasons why I love her.

Initially, as was to be expected, Marcus refused to accept that '*the* Julian Wolf' was his great-grandfather, and claimed, with a hint of the old 'put upon' aggression, that as usual I had got it wrong. But in the end, faced with all the evidence, he was forced to concede that it must indeed be true. He even contributed his own mite to the proceedings by telling us, as we sat down to beef en daube (prepared by me before going to work that morning) how Dad – to whom, as I think I've said before, he was always very close – told him that he had been badly let down by his father. 'Grandpa used to say, making one of his faces – you know, Dad, the one when he disapproved of something' (I did): '"My father was a bad hat, Marcus old man, make no mistake about that. Tried the stage for a while, then buggered off with someone else's wife, leaving your grandmother, with me no more than a nipper, alone in the middle of London".' Marcus's imitation of Dad was so perfect it made me shiver – was he too in the room with us – waiting – watching?

'It's the darndest cover-up job I've ever come across,' Warren said, 'most people would be proud to have a genius like Ju Wolf in the family. "Tried the stage for a while" – my arse!' My son and I looked at one another and laughed, and for the first time I can remember, there was a bond between us.

In the end, drink-slurred and jet-lagged but surprisingly cheerful, Marcus took Lally's early diaries to bed with him. Tomorrow, he announced, being Saturday, he and I would do an organised turn-out of the box-room. Who knew what further riches we should find? It wasn't until I was in the bathroom cleaning my teeth that I realised we'd never once mentioned Amy, or indeed the break-up of his and Barbie's marriage.

In bed I knew at once I was too wound up for sleep, so switching on the bedside light, I reached for volume 4 of Lally's diaries. Tucked into the back were several letters and a newspaper cutting. Recognising a few now familiar names, I decided to tackle these first.

PART VII

From *The Daily News*, Monday 9th November 1914.

City Financier Dies   Foul Play Suspected

Mr Marcus Wolf, the well known City financier, was burned to death in his country mansion near Henley-on-Thames yesterday. It is alleged that Mr Wolf's home was deliberately set on fire by a band of ruffians from the nearby town of Henley, acting under the mistaken impression that Mr Wolf was of German extraction and therefore an enemy of our country.

'This is a most dastardly act. My husband, although born in Germany, came to England as a boy in the seventies of the last century, and has indeed been a British subject for many years', said the heartbroken widow, herself an Englishwoman and proud of it.

An onlooker at the scene told our reporter that there had been some delay in the fire services reaching the mansion, and that because of the high wind that night, the building had been almost gutted by the time they arrived. Our informant also alleged that there had been a certain amount of looting; the late Mr Wolf was a collector of some note – and it was indeed his collection that ultimately caused Mr Wolf to lose his life. For although he and his wife, together with their servants, had managed to escape the blazing building unharmed, Mr Wolf insisted on returning into what had by then become an inferno, for the purpose of retrieving a much-cherished and extremely valuable bronze statuette of, it is thought, the Roman deity, Mithras. In the event, while crossing the entrance hall, a blazing beam from the main staircase collapsed upon the unfortunate gentleman as he tried to make his way to the drawing-room, where the statuette was apparently kept. He was killed instantly; the statuette in question was not recovered.

Mr Wolf, aged sixty-three years, was a well known figure in City circles. He and his wife had already begun preparations for turning their beautiful home into a hospital for wounded officers for the duration of the war, and Mr Wolf was chairman of a recently formed committee set up to assist in the welfare of Belgian refugees. He leaves one son.

J.D. Wolf, Esq   Bourne, Symons and
Hotel Regent   Anstruther
Paris   Packhams Chambers,
                                        London, E.C.
                                        3rd December, 1914

Dear Mr Wolf,

Further to our communication of the 15th last, in which
we informed you of the demise of your father, Mr Marcus
David Wolf. We now regret to have to inform you that
despite Mr Wolf having left provision for you in his Will
dated 8th June 1910, preliminary investigation into his
financial affairs now suggests that after sundry outstanding
debts are paid and mortgages redeemed, the estate will
hold insufficient funds to honour the before-mentioned
financial provision for yourself. We understand that your
late father sustained serious financial losses at the outbreak
of hostilities with Germany, and that in addition he had
invested a considerable amount of capital in his art collection, the bulk of which, as you are no doubt aware, was
destroyed in the late conflagration. Regrettably, it appears
that the major proportion of this collection was uninsured.

We will write in more detail once Probate has been
granted, but must, however, reiterate that we cannot hold
out any hope that once debts have been paid, there will be
any monies accruing to your good self.

We remain etc

                                        The Butts Cottage
                                        Little Slowcombe
                                        21st December 1914

My Dearest Lally,

I can hardly write for crying. What a goose I am, but I
cannot bear to part with my darling Herbie. Yes, the fool
has enlisted! He came home from work last evening looking sheepish and said he'd just 'popped in' at the recruiting
office. Oh Lally, I could have died! 'But darling,' I
moaned, 'it will all be over in a month or two, why not wait
just a little longer and see what happens?' 'You're talking
bunkum, old girl, and you know it,' he says with one of his
looks. 'I can't let other chaps go out there and die, while I

184

stay home snug as a bug in a rug, minding my own business and reaping the benefits, now can I?' Put like that, what could one say? In any case I'm no good at arguing. He goes on New Year's Day, and all he can say is, Aren't I pleased to hear he was passed A1 fit!! There's nothing to be done with the man, truly there isn't. He wants me and the children to go and live for the time being with Mama and Rosa at Bengers. But can I bear it? I suppose I may have to. Rosa writes she is joining the VADs and Rupe is commissioned into some fearfully grand regiment or other (I can't remember which) – of course, James is in already. They've taken nearly all the horses at Bengers for military duties, and ploughed up the tennis lawn for potatoes. Oh, this hateful, hateful war.

Lally dear, how are you – and of course, dear Julian? Are you coming home? How I long to see you. Little Robert is two now, and has never yet seen his Aunt Lally. As to your namesake – we call her Ally not to be confused with Lally – she sleeps and smiles and eats her dinner and sleeps again, and that completes her repertoire, apart from a few other things I don't care to mention!

How dreadful about Julian's father. I know he was a horrid man, but such a death! War seems to bring out the best and worst in people.

Herbie sends his love – he says next time he sees you he'll be a real 'officer boy', the idiot.

All love, dearest,

Con

ON ACTIVE SERVICE

22 Febry '15

My dear Lally,

Excuse the state of the pencil, the point has just broken and I have nothing to sharpen it with and no more pencils. Very many thanks indeed for the socks *and* the tobacco *and* the books – you're a Trojan, my dear, you really are. Things, I'm glad to say, are fairly quiet here at the moment, but there are rumours we may go up the line soon. Meanwhile it rains.

You say you are worried about Ju. I've been worried about Ju ever since I saved him from more or less certain death at the hands of a gang of cut-throats in a back alley in Berlin in that far off year of 07! Ju, ipso facto, is a person one worries about, and I can't tell you the relief it was when you appeared on the scene and one was able to abnegate some of the responsibility. Does that sound selfish? It's not meant to be. You say his father's death cut him up more than he likes to admit, and because of this he is drinking more than ever. Well, I hold no brief for Wolf senior, but neither do I hold any brief for the cads who caused his death. Witch-hunting of that order makes one ashamed for one's fellow countrymen. What can I suggest? I know your views about the War, my dear, and respect them, although I cannot agree with them. If Ju's are the same – and the last time I saw him they certainly were – why don't you both go to the States for a while? Pills Wyatt would jump at the chance to have you and could, I'm sure, get really good bookings for Ju. Paris is no place for either of you at the moment. Sooner or later Ju is going to shoot his mouth off about the War once too often, and they'll string him up – you know what the Frogs are like. And you, my dear, are not exactly the soul of reticence so far as your own views are concerned!

You say audiences are falling off and Ju's contract is not to be renewed beyond the summer. I'm afraid this is inevitable. What audiences want now – and this goes for French as well as English audiences, probably the Hun too – is 'jelly-bellied Flag waving', as Kipling so aptly puts it, and that is what they will get. No theatrical impresario is going to risk Ju. Wait until the advent of the brave new world they promise us after the War, then he'll come into his own – you'll see. My advice is, therefore, to get the idiot out to the States where, in an odd way, I think he's always belonged, spiritually anyway, and there await events. Sorry not to be of more help, my dear, it must be a worrying time for you. Give my love to the dear old boy, and tell him from his erstwhile manager to lay off the d--d booze!

Hope to see you both before too long. Let me know if

you decide to take my advice and I will drop a line to Pills.

Yrs affctly

Bertie

PS My brother Jack, on forty-eight hours leave from his ship, took the liberty of going to his local public house wearing mufti, and was promptly handed a white feather! *C'est la guerre*!

HMS Lightning,
c/o G.P.O. London
21st April 1915

My dear Wolf,

It is with very great regret I have to inform you that my brother Bertie has been killed in action. His Colonel says he acquitted himself as one would have expected, most gallantly, and mercifully he would have been killed instantly.

I know what tremendous chums you and my brother were, and realise this news will come as a terrible blow. Please do call on me if you need any help in the future. I know Bertie would have wanted this. I believe that shortly before he died he was in the throes of negotiating a contract for you in the United States. I have taken it upon myself to write to Mr Wyatt and inform him of Bertie's death – no doubt he will be in touch with you.

I doubt whether we will meet before your departure for New York, but let us hope, God willing, we will do so again in happier times.

Please give my regards to Mrs Eagon.

Yours sincerely
Jack Dugdale

Bengers
20th July 1915

Dearest Lally,

It is selfish of me, I know, but I am so happy you and Julian are returning to England at last. Whitesgreen – what an odd-named village, but Glebe Cottage sounds splendid. What awfully kind people the Dugdales must be, but then Bertie was one of the best, wasn't he? Do you remember when we first met him? In that awful old theatre in Manchester, and dining afterwards at the Midland – how we laughed. I can't believe it's only three years ago – before the war already seems another world, doesn't it?

Dearest, I find it hard to imagine you and Julian leading the simple life, but lots of fresh air and exercise will, I'm sure, help him to get strong again. Can me and my brood come and visit?

Herbie is due to go to France any moment. The fool says he loves the army! I have to admit he looks very well on it and eats like a horse when he's home on leave. Bengers is a hospital now, we had our first patients a week ago. Some are survivors from Ypres – I thought of dear Bertie and wanted to cry. Mama, me and the children, plus old Nanny and one maid, are boxed up in the chauffeur's cottage – *very* trying for all concerned! Rosa is VADing at St Thomas's Hospital in London and hoping to get out to France. I help in the wards here when I can, so we are all very busy.

Oh my dearest, I cannot help thinking you and Julian are doing the right thing in coming home. Somehow at this sad time, I feel it is right for us all to stick together. Please write *as soon as* you reach Glebe Cottage. I must be the first to hear what it is like!

All my love to you both,
Con

PS   Rupe's battalion left for France ten days ago. We have had one letter saying they are billeted in an 'extremely smelly town' and being bitten to death by mosquitoes!

58 Ilchester Crescent
31st Jly 1915

Dearest Child,

Yr letter just received. Of course, dear, I understand your companion's and your own desire to return to your country in time of war, it is only right that you should wish to do so. However, I cannot help but feel that under the circumstances it would have been better to have stuck to your original plan of going to the United States. Romantic gestures are all very well in their way, but sometimes it is better to let the head rule the heart – as by now I am sure you have come to realise. What very kind people the

Dugdales must be to let you have one of their cottages – so tragic about their boy. I confess I cannot see you out amongst the vegetables, dear, but despite the discomfort it will be a healthy life at least, and you have been racketing about on the continent for far too long. I enclose a small cheque, which will, I hope, smooth your way a little – it is a big leap from a comfortable hotel in Paris to an uncomfortable cottage in the wilds of Wiltshire.

I am afraid I shall be holidaying in Scotland with some old friends for the few days you are in town. Perhaps this is for the best. My views remained unchanged on the decision you made to leave your husband, and although I shall always be pleased to see you – indeed, have missed you sorely these last years – I would not wish to entertain your companion in my house.

You ask for family news. Your mother, I am sorry to say, still refuses to have your name mentioned in her presence. However, she is well and busy, indeed appears to have taken on a new lease of life (despite the fuss she made at the time) since Suki departed to breed horses with that extraordinary woman at Epsom. Bob and dear Emily spent his last leave with me here in town. We had such a jolly time together and went to several shows. I was quite exhausted when they left, not being used to such gadding about. Bob is thinner and perhaps a little quieter, but still the same dear Bob. He thinks he may be quite close to Rupert when he goes out to France next month. As to little Ned, Nurse brings him to tea here every Monday. He is such a fine boy, dear, full of mischief as all boys should be, but loves to be read stories and is quite a cool hand at snap. He is to attend a dame school in October, which I think will benefit him greatly; he needs the companionship of other children. Rupert's Aunt Louisa is a very good sort of woman in her way, and it was most sporting of her to agree to help bring up Ned, but in a year or so, without some much-needed discipline, he will have her completely under his thumb; not a desirable state of affairs. As to schools, the boy is down for Eton, his father's old house, but his preparatory school has not yet been decided upon.

And as to your old Granny, she is sunk deep in committee work – quite literally up to her eyes in bandages! How she wishes she still had her oh-so-capable secretary to set things straight!

Dear child, I must stop now – so many things to do. Please believe me when I say that all my thoughts and prayers go with you in this difficult time.

Your loving
Granny

Haycock House
Westbury
31st August 1915

My dear Lally and Julian,

Welcome to Glebe Cottage! Milly insisted we should come over and, as she put it, add a few finishing touches to the place before you arrived.

Before I forget, Mrs Taylor, 1 Church Cottages, has an extra key and pronounces she is willing to come and 'do' for you, if you so wish. Milly says Mrs Taylor is most reliable and hard-working. Milk and eggs from the farm down the road, and the butcher and grocer call twice weekly.

By the by, you are known as 'Mr and Mrs Wolf' – country people are slow to turn to modern ways of thinking and both Milly and I consider it best. We will be over next week to see how you go on – leave you in peace for a few days to settle in.

With all good wishes
Yrs very sincerely
Richard Dugdale

Friday, 1st October 1915   Glebe Cottage, Whitesgreen
'Now there will be no need for secrets,' I wrote in my diary that last night at Wyndham Gardens. But I was wrong; no one person can ever entirely bare their soul to another, I know that now. So here I sit on the broken-down armchair by the open kitchen window, the stew for dinner bubbling on the range, the only sounds the tick of the clock on the mantelpiece and an occasional crow from Mr Creed's farmyard cock, once again writing my diary.

We have been here a month now, and have had such

happiness. What a glorious September! Day after day of brave, blue skies and sun, and cold, bright, starry nights. Mushrooms in the fields, blackberries in the hedges, Michaelmas daisies in the gardens, the smell of woodsmoke at dusk when Ju and I come in from digging our patch. Only the shiver of wind in the copse above the house to break the silence, and the bleat of sheep up on the downs; or the song of larks and the hum of a late September bee.

Did those frightening, exhilarating, heart-breaking, vaga-bond years ever really happen? I almost begin to wonder. They seem like a dream – the reality here, now, with Ju, the two of us together in this lovely place. Hard to believe that only a few short weeks ago we were in Paris, jammed into two stifling rooms in the Hotel Regent, with the smell of cats and cooking coming up from the courtyard below – Ju drinking, money dwindling, debts rising, and me feeling that no matter how hard I tried, I could never catch up, never be in step. War hysteria was everywhere. 'Your husband's part Boche, isn't he, Mrs Wolf? For your own sake, my dear, I wouldn't let the other girls know' – Mrs Brindley-Jones, typing supervisor at the Embassy, smiling her thin smile, her little pebble eyes alight with malice. I had to swallow my anger because we needed the money, and returned home to find Ju in a drunken stupor when he should have been on his way to the theatre. The audience, that ghastly Saturday night, hissed Ju off the stage: his white, furious face afterwards; how dare they – how bloody dare they? Plans: we'll do this – do that – go here – go there. What about New York? Of course, why didn't we think of that before? Old Pills is sure to come up trumps. Goodbye, goodbye, everyone, we'll be back when this stupid war is over.

Packing; Ju drinking less, cheerful, busy. 'Don't forget our lucky cat, Lal, we'll need him in the States.' Then, that bright, sunny afternoon, when it seemed at last all our problems were about to be solved; 'Let's go shopping in the rue de Rivoli and buy old Pills a present from Gay Paree – somethin really classy – '

'A letter for you, Mr Wolf, just this minute arrived.'

'Oh God, oh my God. Bert's dead, Lal, he's dead.'

Much later, Ju's head in my lap. 'Can't let old Bert die for nothin', it wouldn't seem right.' And I'm too tired to try and bridge the gulf between us; the madness, it seems, must go on.

So here we are, the prodigals returned. Perhaps, after all, what we have done is right. Certainly the gods, if gods there be, seem to think so. They've seen fit to reward us with such joy in each other as no two human beings have a right to expect.

Is there something lacking in me that, despite the joy, I know this is only a resting time for both of us? For myself, a time to let our child grow in peace inside me, and to take stock, although I already know, and have known for a long time (the knowledge itself a kind of treason) that I could not now return to that other life. To be the mistress of a 'vaga-bond player', helpmeet to genius, suits me little better than being Mrs Rupert Eagon, the doyenne of upper-middle-class hostesses. And yet, God help me, I love Ju more than life itself. 'You're a difficult hap'orth, imp,' Pa said, 'there's two of you, and neither of 'em bad. When you grow up, I wonder which one will win.' And the answer to that is, neither – not yet, at any rate.

And as for Ju, Glebe Cottage is a place where he can rest and become strong again, a place where he can slough off the ravages caused by drink and the way he has chosen to live these last ten years. He is not doing this for me, I hasten to add, nor even for his unborn child. He is doing it so that he may join those others in this stupid, senseless, murderous war. 'Young Wolf's a good 'un, but his governor . . .' Rupe said at that birthday party long ago. And despite everything that has happened since, a piece of Ju has always wanted to re-enter that world again – that safe, privileged, arrogant, incestuous world of decent, cricket-playing, public school chaps, that world his mother so desperately wanted him to be part of. And now, because that self-same world in its infinite insanity is suddenly, inexplicably, suicidally, hell-bent on sacrificing the best of its youth to the tarnished, profit-hungry god of patriotism, Ju's chance has come. If he cannot live with those same, decent, public school chaps, he is only too wel-come to die with them. Oh Lord, don't let me feel bitter, but I do, I do, I do.

And now Miss Lally, you can damn well climb down off your soap-box and walk down to the farm and collect our daily quart of milk. 'Another lovely day, then, Mrs Wolf,' says Mrs Greenwell. 'Yes, isn't it, and do you think we could have some more eggs – we seem to get through them so quickly.' And Mrs Greenwell will smile indulgently, averting her eyes from my already swelling stomach. 'Husband keeping well?'

And tonight, after supper cooked by me – I'm getting quite good at it, truly I am – I will sit on Ju's knee by the fire in our stuffy, little front parlour, the brass oil lamp – the only one there is ¬ on the rickety table beside us, and Ju will read out loud from Grossmith's *Diary of a Nobody* until we cry with laughter and he has to stop. And then . . . upstairs to the big, sagging, lumpy brass bed that creaks every time you move.

'Ju, it's freezing – the sheets feel all clammy and cold – get in quickly and make me warm.'

And he does; oh God, he does . . .

9th October   A letter from Bob! What a surprise. He will be at Trowbridge for a few days next week; can he come over? Is all forgiven? It must be, I suppose. I wonder if Granny did a little persuading? Ju seems quite excited and talks of ordering a chicken from Mr Creed for lunch. Suddenly I wonder if he is missing masculine company. But Bob? Surely they have little in common now.

Today the baby moved! I felt it, and rushed straight out into the garden to tell Ju, and he knelt down there and then, on the wet grass, his ear against my tummy, and said he could hear its heartbeat. Already we love this child so much. Is it because of those other two, the little boys we left behind us, that we lavish so much love on one as yet unborn?

14th October   It rained today, and Bob came. How odd it was to see him after so long. We heard him coming before we saw him, splashing through the puddles in the lane on his big, bumbling army motorbike. 'Bless my soul, this is worse than the trenches – talk about the back of beyond!' Then I'm in his arms, rain trickling down my neck. 'You've grown a moustache, oh Bob, it's beautiful!'

'Not bad, old thing, not bad. Keeps me warm of nights.' Then Bob and Ju are shaking hands. 'Hullo, Wolf, it's been a long time.'

In the kitchen, we stand about looking at one another, suddenly, absurdly, shy. 'Let's get that mackintosh cape off you, Morgan, we can't have you drippin' water all over Lally's kitchen floor.'

'I've brought a couple of bottles . . . thought they might be acceptable . . .'

And lunch *was* a success, it really was. The chicken done to a turn, one of Mrs Taylor's perfect apple pies (I'm not yet up to making pastry) and Bob's wine, a bit rough, but good. Was it the wine that made things go wrong? (Ju and I have not touched alcohol since we came here.) Well, not wrong exactly, but not so right as before. Halfway through the meal, Ju said something – I can't even remember what it was, but suddenly there was a silence. It was as though a bad fairy had crept into the room and waved her wand, causing a blanket of quite inexplicable tension to descend on all three of us. It was Bob – dear Bob, it wasn't until I saw him again that I realised how much I had missed him – who broke the spell (if spell it was) by making some stupid joke; we all burst out laughing, and the bad fairy, her cloak wrapped over her face, returned whence she came.

But somehow after that things weren't quite the same. Ju took Bob into the parlour after we had finished the meal, having produced, with the flourish of a conjurer conjuring a white rabbit from his waistcoat pocket, a bottle of brandy from a cupboard in the dresser. 'Bought especially in your honour, Morgan, Lall and I have taken the pledge.'

'Have you, by Jove. Must be something the matter with my eyesight, I could have sworn I saw – '

'Now then, young Morgan, none of your lip!' And they were laughing and scuffling like two schoolboys. But later, when I joined them in the parlour, they were sitting like two old men on either side of the fire, the brandy bottle between them, and I realised with a shock how drawn and sad Bob's face had become underneath the absurd, bristling moustache, and knew at once they were talking of the war.

'Can I be godfather, sis?' Bob said as he kissed me good-bye. It was the only time he mentioned the baby. 'Of course, you can, you ass – who else?'

We watched him mount his cumbersome machine – the rain

had cleared by now. A big, beefy young man, wearing goggles, a long brightly-coloured muffler ('a present from Mother's knitting circle,' he'd told us earlier, 'a trifle on the bright side, but handy on the bike'.) Then, in a roar of exhaust, he was away, bumping down the track, stones and mud spraying up around him.

'Goodbye, goodbye – see you soon . . .' At the gate he waved, his scarf flying out in the wind, then disappeared from view. But you could hear the motorbike engine for a long time after he had gone, right down into the valley.

Ju squeezed my hand, then walked quickly back into the kitchen and poured himself another brandy. 'Bob says if I want to, he's pretty sure he can pull a few strings and get me a commission. Better than foot-slogging in the poor bloody infantry, eh?' He looked like a small boy frightened he was going to be ticked off.

Oh Ju.

25th October   'But you said we'd wait until the baby is born – you *said* so.'

'If I don't go soon the war'll be over.'

'Are you mad? Of course it won't be over; it won't be over until they've killed the lot of you. In a few months time you'll have no choice anyway; once the Military Service Act comes in, they'll make you. Unless you've drunk yourself into the ground by then.'

'Shut up, will you, you little bitch – ' The brandy stung my eyes and dripped down the front of my blouse. 'Lally, darling, I'm sorry, I'm so sorry, I didn't mean it, I didn't mean anything – I love you . . . I love you . . .'

And so it goes on. Ever since Bob's visit. Bob's not to blame, he was just the catalyst. Ju must be *doing*. Now he's well, he's like a bird in a cage beating its wings against the bars, clawing at anyone who tries to stop him.

6th November   Yesterday was a happy day. Are there so few now? We went on an expedition to Bath. Lunch with some 'artistic' friends of the Dugdales (only artistic people are prepared to meet us, it seems). But it was fun all the same. We window-shopped and wandered up and down the steep streets, marvelling like a pair of greenhorns at the Georgian splendour of the tall, soot-blackened houses. The Bradberrys quite charming, with a 'greenery yallery' drawing-room, ever so *fin de siècle*, and a Belgian refugee cook. After lunch (superb) Mr B. showed Ju some extremely rude drawings he had in a folder in his studio. 'Not for Nanny's eyes,' Ju said – he's taken to calling me Nanny lately. I try not to let this annoy me, but it does, oh it does, and he knows it.

Home late, trudging up the dark lane laden with parcels, Ju shouting out a stupid song we heard the soldiers singing on Bath station while we waited for the train:

> Oh Ma, put the cat out tonight,
> Put the cat out tonight,
> Put the cat out tonight.
> Oh Ma, put the cat out tonight
> For we won't be home till the morning.

What the owls thought I cannot imagine.

20th November   Con is coming for Christmas! 'Much disapproval from all at Bengers,' she writes, 'so disloyal to dearest Rupert. But I don't care, I must get away no matter what, and how I long to see you both.' We've ordered a goose from the farm and Mrs Taylor is making a Christmas pudding.

Ju has started drinking again, not much, but enough. He goes down to the Drover's Arms in the village most evenings now: his excuse, he's studying the local dialect. Last night he came back late and did an impromptu performance. Of course it was marvellous, and in the laughter I forgot all my grouches and grumbles. But today I feel sick and ill, dragging my heavy body about the house, my back aching. Outside, I hear the sound of Ju chopping wood, a robin has perched itself on top of the pump in the yard, Mr Creed says there will be snow . . .

1st December   A letter arrived today from Rupe. I wrote to him last summer, begging him to divorce me, but had given up hope of a reply. He won't divorce me – did I really think he would? 'I happen to believe that marriage vows are sacred,' he writes, with all the old, familiar pomposity, 'and not to be broken, and the sooner you learn that in this life you cannot simply turn your back on your responsibilities because something more interesting has turned up, the better. You are not a child, Lally my dear, despite the fact that you frequently behave like one.' And so on. I shan't show the letter to Ju, it

will only make him angry. Florrie (as usual) is more accommodating. Mr Pope, her father, has been busy for some time
on her behalf, and divorce proceedings for desertion are well
under way. 'The boy is thriving,' writes Mr Pope, who sounds
surprisingly enlightened, 'and my daughter bearing up as well
as can be expected under the circumstances prevailing. All
the best for Christmas and the New Year, and let us hope this
dreadful war will soon be over and our brave lads back home
with their loved ones once again.' No such kind thoughts from
Rupe! Did I expect any? I suppose not. And yet . . .

27th December Christmas is over, and how splendid it has
been! At the very last moment we had a wire from Con:
'Rejoice, rejoice. Herbie has Xmas leave. Please may he
come. Con.' Of course we wired back yes, and oh what fun we
all had.

There they were, at three o'clock on Christmas Eve, the
entire Potter family coming up the lane in the station fly,
packed tight as sardines. Rob in a bright red hat: 'Happy
Christmas, Aunt Lally. We've been on a train – will Father
Christmas come on a train?' Little Ally, my namesake,
sleeping like an angel in her bassinet; Pan the terrier barking;
Con shrieking: 'Herbie, darling, I'm sure we should have got
out and walked up the hill, that poor, old horse.' And Herbie
himself, gently smiling, his tired eyes blinking like an owl
suddenly dragged into the daylight: 'Calm down, ducky, for
the Lord's sake.'

It's both morbid and absurd, but I have a feeling there will
never again be such a happy Christmas, such laughter, such
fun, such busyness. Con, an ancient apron we found in a
cupboard tied round her middle, vainly tried to cope with the
goose. 'Oh Lally, what shall we *do* with all this dreadful fat?'
The pudding fell on the floor while we struggled to extract it
from the saucepan, and Pan ran off with half the sausages.
But in the end, despite the mishaps, the meal was the best any
of us had ever tasted. Afterwards, with the children safely
tucked up in bed, Ju got out his old gramophone (Con had
brought with her a stack of the latest ragtime records) and we
danced and danced until we dropped.

On Boxing Day the four of us walked for miles over the
frozen downs, baby Ally safely ensconced with Mrs Taylor in

her cottage, Robby, well wrapped up, riding on his father's shoulders. Did we talk of the war? I don't think so; we didn't need to, it was there, round the corner just out of sight, waiting for us all. Meanwhile, we forgot it, and perhaps our happiness was all the sweeter because we knew it could not last.

Then suddenly the holiday was over and it was time for them to go. Ju and I went down to the station to wave goodbye, walking slowly home up the long hill to the cottage through the gathering dusk, our arms round each other.

1st January 1916 Bob is dead – I cannot write more now. What, anyway, is there left to write?

10th January So cold. Ju and I seem to row all the time. Oh God, what has happened to us? Since we heard of Bob's death, he's been drinking more than ever. Last night he went out and didn't come back until the early hours.

Dr Musgrove called this morning. He says I must rest. 'Give the babe a chance, my dear, and no more gadding about.' He seems a nice man, though, and capable. I'm to send for the midwife as soon as the pains start, and she will telephone him. So all that, it appears, is taken care of.

Granny has sent another cheque: 'To buy baby clothes, dear, you never were much of a knitter.' I don't deserve Granny. I don't deserve anything.

28th January Ju has had an invitation to entertain the troops at Warminster. He's so excited. 'Help me get it right, Lal, mustn't tread on anyone's toes. Just simple stuff, nothin' political.' So here we are, hammering out his act, and for a little while, at least, we are happy.

31st January Ju's concert a great success. He was away for the night, home on the lunchtime train the following day, flushed with happiness. 'They loved it, Lal, they really did. I dined in the officers' mess, grand set of fellows, not in the least starchy – '

'Why don't you go now, then, and be done with it? That's what you really want to do, isn't it – get away.'

'Don't be an ass, Lal, I promised I'd stay until the baby was born, I wouldn't leave you . . .'

But later he slams out of the house, and I sit by the fire feeling ashamed. Where is that brave, strong, sensible Lally

Morgan now? She who was going to put the world to rights, live her own life according to her own lofty ideals. Where indeed?

6th February Ju has gone to London for an interview at the War Office. It seems the last thing Bob did before he was killed was to pull the promised strings.

'You'll be all right, Lal,' eyes pleading, trying not to look excited, 'I'll only be gone a couple of days, the baby's not due for two weeks. I can't miss this chance. And old Jack's in town on leave – you don't grudge me a night out, do you?' And I stand there like a lump of stone, trying not to cry. Lord help me, what has happened to that wild, daring romance of ours? But it is I who feel ashamed.

He left yesterday morning, looking so smart in his best suit, wobbling down the lane on Mr Taylor's bone-shaker bicycle. 'You'll fall for me, Lal, all over again, once you see me in uniform.'

And today it snowed. I fell asleep before the fire, my sewing on my lap, and woke to find the world outside turned white. Did I never find the silence here oppressive?

7th February *After breakfast* No more snow, but the frost so harsh this morning that the windows were ice-covered on the inside. I brought the bedding down from upstairs and slept on the floor by the kitchen range. It was so warm and comfortable, but I awoke, shivering, in the early hours. It was when I dragged myself up to revive the dying fire that I felt the first onslaught of pain. I clung to the dresser, teeth clenched, wondering what I should do. Then, after a moment, the pain died away and to my relief did not return. I crept back to my improvised bed and slept again almost immediately.

Later A wire from Ju: he is staying another night in town. And the water in the pump is frozen. I asked the telegraph boy to drop a note in on Mrs Warren, the midwife. I think I'm beginning to feel just a little frightened. More pain since I fell over on the ice in the yard, getting coal. Ju brought in several scuttlefuls before he left, but I have used so much.

Later still Mrs Warren is here. 'There, there, my love, you won't feel a thing, don't you fret.' But the pains are worse than I ever could have imagined, the fire in the bedroom smokes and there is hardly any water. Oh, how I wish Pa were

199

here to hold my hand. I can hear his voice: 'Come on, imp, where's that famous grit of yours?' I can't write any more now –

12th February Ju has gone to the village to ring Dr Musgrove. Outside the snow is beginning to thaw. The bedroom fire no longer smokes but glows comfortably, invitingly, but I feel cold, cold with fear. Soon Ju will return and bring me my tea. Downstairs I hear movement and a faint, gurgling cry, followed by Mrs Taylor's soft voice: 'There, there, my precious, Daddy will be back in a trice and bring you some nice medicine to make you better – you see.' And I am afraid, more afraid even than when Pa died. Perhaps writing will make me unafraid.

After lunch, when they thought I was asleep, Mrs Taylor put her head round the bedroom door and whispered: 'Best get doctor, Mr Wolf, nothing to worry about but . . . best get him.' And I saw my fear mirrored in Ju's face. When he had gone, I buried my own in the pillow and cried. Afterwards I tried to sleep, but my mind wouldn't rest and kept returning to that other evening, the evening our daughter, Julia, was born – Ju standing by my bed, his face white, snow on his boots, eyes red-rimmed with tiredness, blinking in the unaccustomed light.

'Lal, forgive me, I couldn't get here sooner. I tried my damndest. Lal, please . . .' And I turn angrily away from him, to find the mocking face of our so-called lucky cat grinning up at me from a fold in my nightdress – the ribbon that held him round my neck must have broken. In sudden fury I pick the thing up and hurl it on the floor. 'Take it, I never want to see it again.' I hear my own voice as though it were another's, shrill, bitter, shaming: 'Nor you, for that matter.' Without a word Ju bends down and picks up the cat, then turns and walks out of the bedroom, his snowy boots leaving a trail of water across the floor.

Later still – or was it the next day already? I can't remember – Mrs Taylor placing my daughter in my arms. 'Best get little one christened, Mrs Wolf – soon as may be. Safer that way. I could pop in at vicarage on my way home, when Mr Wolf gets back.'

'What do you mean, best get her christened? Is my

daughter going to die – is that what you're saying? Mr Wolf and I don't believe in God, anyway, we – ' Mrs Taylor does not blink or look shocked or . . . anything. She merely puts her hand on my forehead. 'The little one's none too strong, my love, best be on the safe side. I'll call in at vicar's.'

14th February   Julia died last night. Pneumonia, Dr Musgrove said, 'but the wee mite was ailing from the start.'

'Don't you fret, my love,' says Mrs Taylor, 'she's gone to the Lord, that one, I could see it on her face. You can always see it on their faces, those that are chosen. I'll send for Mr Allinson, he do a lovely funeral, especially for the little ones. Helps folks a lot, he does, helps them to bear the pain.'

Ju and I speak only when necessary. It is as though we have lived through some terrible storm and there is nothing left for us to say. But last night, when everything was quiet, I heard him crying in the room below; harsh, racking sobs. And I longed to take him in my arms and try to comfort him, but knew that if I did so, I should only prolong the agony for both of us.

18th February   Today Mrs Dugdale called and brought me a bunch of spring flowers. I can see them as I write; Mrs Taylor has put them in an old, blue honey jar on the windowsill, they look so pretty. What should we do without Mrs Taylor?

In two weeks from now we shall have gone from here. Others will sow the seeds for summer vegetables in the ground we so carefully prepared, will chop the wood and prime the pump and empty the ash from the kitchen range. Other lovers will share the big bed upstairs and laugh and fight and make love, and other, luckier children will be born here as a result of that love-making. And as for us, Ju Wolf and Lally Morgan, we will leave nothing behind us, nothing, that is, but a small headstone in the churchyard; and, perhaps, our youth.

We have been very sensible, Ju and I, in the days since our daughter's funeral, very sensible indeed. And last night we sat down together by the fire and made our very sensible plans. We are to part (what else); not just because Ju is to join the army and I'm to live with Granny in London, but properly, irrevocably. This is not because we no longer love each other, or feel desire for each other – God knows, we do –

but because the sad and shameful fact is that we cannot live with each other. Perhaps neither of us is made for marriage, I don't know. If this is so – and it may well be – the future is lonely indeed. But I know, and so does Ju, that if we try to go on together, we shall end by destroying not only our love, but each other as well. As Wilde said, and how horribly right he was:

> Yet each man kills the thing he loves,
> By each let this be heard,
> Some do it with a bitter look
> Some with a flattering word.
> The coward does it with a kiss,
> The brave man with a sword.

So . . . there we are. Ju goes first, he is to report for duty at Catterick Camp on the 28th, and will leave on the 26th. I shall stay until the 1st March and help Mrs Taylor clear up. There's nothing more to say, except that I feel I am on the edge of a desolation I cannot bear to contemplate and yet am powerless to prevent.

22nd February Farewell visit to the Dugdales – they sent their motor to fetch us. They don't know we are parting, we've told no one but Granny. Mrs D. kissed Ju goodbye. 'Dear Julian. I always knew you would do the right thing. Please God you come home safe.' Is everyone afflicted with this madness, even kind, sensible Mrs Dugdale?

25th February Ju has gone. He must have left early this morning while I was still asleep. Just a scrawled note under a jar of snowdrops on the kitchen table. And I feel nothing but emptiness.

The rest of Lally's diary was blank. But in the bundle of letters at the back, much creased, as though someone had screwed it into a ball and then retrieved it, was a note.

My darling –

I'm a coward, I know, but I couldn't have borne a formal parting – best go now, eh, without any fuss?

My dearest, I shall love you to the day I die, but I'm a rotten, selfish sort of chap in many ways and it's time I let you go. Old Ju must learn to stand on his own two feet again, and you, my love, must go out and set the world to rights – it needs people like you a great deal more than it needs people like me.

There – no more waffling, no more tears – just thank you, my love, for . . . so much.

Ju

PART VIII

And now for the last exercise book. It was late, but I was past sleep. Anyway, there wasn't a lot left of this one, the front cover had gone and with it at least half the pages. As in diary No 4, there was a sheaf of papers pushed into the back – only two letters this time (from Con, and Bertie Dugdale's brother Jack), the rest consisting of a cutting from the Deaths column of *The Times*, several theatre-ticket stubs, a recipe for carrot marmalade, and a postcard of the front at Bognor Regis addressed to 'Dear Mama' and signed 'Your affectionate son Edward.'

> 2 Farm Cottages
> Bengers
> 2nd February 1918

Dearest Lally,

Many thanks for the lovely long letter. How you find the time to write I cannot imagine, with all the work you are doing. One of your speeches was reported in *The Times* on Friday – the one on allowances for soldiers' widows – we were *most* impressed!! You ask for news, dearest, so here we go.

Herbie is getting on quite wonderfully well with his new leg. The idiot says it won't be long before he's back on the tennis court! Thank the Lord, the powers-that-be relented and let him take his convalescence at Bengers. I can't tell you how wonderful it is to have him home again after all those dreadful months of worry and waiting when he was in that horrible hospital in the north. He's been so good and brave. Even Mama has overcome her prejudice at last – I heard her refer to him as 'our dearest Herbie' when the vicar came to tea on Saturday – praise indeed!

We moved into our cottage just before Christmas, and you cannot imagine the bliss, to have a place of our own at last. Robby is quite grown up now and has a pony, and Ally is into everything; she's a wicked little puss, but so funny it's hard to be cross with her. Gerry is going to be like his father – he has his eyes and his smile; we pray that he will have his wonderful, happy temperament too. Rosa is back from France and James is doing something frightfully important in Aldershot. He returns to Bengers from time to time, and remains as pompous as ever. Such a pity he has no wife, I'm sure marriage would do him a power of good.

Dearest, you ask for news of Rupe. So strange you should not know, we thought Louisa would have told you – this silly feud – so absurd. Lally dear, Rupe was very badly wounded last November; a bullet lodged in his skull; no one can understand why he wasn't killed. He had been in hospital in France for several weeks when Rosa saw him; he didn't recognise her – so dreadfully upsetting. Now, he's been brought back to England and is in a hospital near London which specialises in such cases. Of course we get regular reports of him and people visit, but the news is not good. He simply lies there looking at the ceiling. Mama thinks he recognised her, but no one else. The doctors talk of an operation, but the risk is very great. I am sorry, dearest, to have to finish on such a sad note. When will this war end – to think my Ally has never known anything else.

All our fondest love and Herbie says don't work too hard –

Con

H.M.S. Lightning
c/o G.P.O. London
29 Febry '18

My dear Lally,

Much thanks for yr letter. It was good to have news of you again after so long. I don't think we've met since the summer of '16, when we dined together at the Savoy. And still this d--d war goes on!

You ask for news of Julian. Hard to come by, I'm afraid. He doesn't appear to have corresponded much with any of his erstwhile chums. And even the Pater hasn't heard a word for months. I did, however, bump into a chap who'd served in J.'s regiment for a time early in '17; one Bobby Hunt, who used to be on the stage himself in happier times. He told me that, from what little he saw of him, Ju didn't appear to take kindly to discipline (as one would have expected) but the men adored him. Hunt also said that he and Ju had put on an impromptu concert during one of their rest periods behind the lines, which had been a quite spectacular success. Shortly after that Hunt was posted away from the regiment and hadn't seen or heard of J. since. I'm pretty sure his mob were in that ghastly business at Passchendaele, but I'm quite certain the Pater would have heard if anything had happened to him. The Pater has several chums at the War House, and knows a great deal more about what is going on than the likes of me. I'm only sorry I can't be of more help.

Please may I call next time I'm in town? And please give my respects to your most estimable grandmother.

Yrs affctnly
Jack

PS Read yr speech in *The Times* the
      other day – Bravo!!

. . . home late too tired to eat – just bath and bed.

5th March What a solemn young man my son is! Our monthly interviews get harder and harder. Today we discussed, in the most stilted manner imaginable, his clothes list for St David's.

'I must have Cash's name tapes on absolutely everything, Mama,' he announces suddenly. 'How tiresome for poor Miss Chevely to have to sew them all on,' I say brightly, unable to think of anything else, and he looks at me as if I were half-mad.

I longed to ask Miss Chevely if there is any news of Rupe, but somehow couldn't. Those chill, disapproving eyes are altogether too much for me. Granny did ask, however, when I was out of the room. Apparently he's had the operation and they await results. Poor dear Rupe, I dreamed of him last night. So odd – he was laughing like anything and running his hands through my hair.

15th March Why do I continue with this stupid diary? The Lord knows I have enough writing to do as it is. It must be that if I don't I feel I might lose a part of myself for ever: it will simply slip away one night while I'm asleep and not come back, and I won't even know it's gone – at least, not until I'm old and grey and full of regrets. What nonsense! But it's a relief to talk nonsense occasionally, even if only to oneself.

My new secretary – one Miss Muriel Hope-Stanley – is a

most formidable young person. Large, beautiful, clever, with the figure of a goddess, she presides over the office, a modern Britannia minus the helmet. 'Don't you bother about that, Mrs Eagon,' she says with her all-engulfing smile, 'I can run it off on my machine in a jiffy, and by the by, I have made a few notes for your speech tonight – one or two points I thought might be worth making.'

Drat the girl!

This afternoon, listening to Mr Bodkin rumble out his predictably interminable train of platitudes while the rest of us waited with the utmost impatience for him to finish so that we could get on with our work, I was suddenly assailed by a quite irresistible urge to jump on the table and execute – with the requisite abandon – my famous (or as some have claimed, infamous) version of the Dance of the Seven Veils. With Ju a lustful and arthritically energetic Herod and me a giggling and none too agile Salome, as a party piece it always caused a sensation in those dear, dead days before the war. Anyway, once conjured up, this vision so occupied my mind that for several moments I was quite overcome with giggles. My efforts to disguise these as a violent fit of coughing met with such success that Dr Shaw was constrained to lean solicitously across the table, and under cover of his agenda ask me with every appearance of concern whether I was sure I was all right? I nodded manfully, wiping my eyes on my handker-chief, and the juggernaut rolled on. It wasn't until later I realised that moment at the meeting was the first time I have thought of Ju in a happy way since we parted. Before, when I allowed myself to do so at all, it has always been with a dull ache of longing and bitterness; a festering wound that will not heal, hidden away behind bandages. Today it was different; I thought of him with laughter, as he likes to be thought of, so perhaps the wound is healing after all.

But Passchendaele – oh God. I've seen some of the results of that particular picnic. But Ju must be alive, he must be, I would feel it if he weren't.

20th March   And now a visit from Rosa!

'Miss Eagon to see you, Miss Lally,' says Chivers, his face as impassive as a Buddhist monk's. And there she is, looking gaunt and tired, straight as a ramrod in her nurse's uniform, standing by the study window. 'Rosa, my dear, it's been a long time.' I put out a tentative hand; Rosa's arm remains at her side.

'I must make it quite clear, Lally, that I do not visit on my own behalf, or for any social reasons. My sentiments remain the same as on the last occasion we met – I come on behalf of my brother.'

'James? Surely – ?'

'Rupert.' For a long moment we face one another, Rosa and I, the silence between us stretching into infinity. I hear Granny's voice on the telephone next door: 'But my dear Lady Hazel, there just aren't enough beds for the ones we have, let alone . . .'

'I understand,' says Rosa at last, 'that you are aware that Rupert has been severely wounded.' I nod, my legs like cottonwool beneath me. 'You may also know he has recently undergone an operation to counteract the effects of the wound. However, despite improvement, his recovery has not been what was hoped. Nevertheless, he is now able to converse in a limited fashion, and he has partially recovered his memory.' Why, oh why did the woman have to talk like some damned medical text book?

'But –' I opened my mouth to interrupt. Rosa raised an imperious hand. 'Bear with me, if you will. The reason for my visit this morning is that on several occasions recently my brother has expressed a wish to see you. At first we – his doctors and I – considered this to be some sort of aberration on his part, but we now believe otherwise. Indeed, we consider that far from being harmful, a visit from you may in fact be beneficial to his health. Under these circumstances, I take it you would be prepared to do this for him?'

I put my hands in my skirt pockets so she won't see they are trembling. 'If that's what he wishes . . . you say his memory is faulty. . . ?' Rosa gives me a long, cold look, then turns away to study a Rowlandson print of the Pump Room at Bath on the wall behind her. 'He has forgotten everything that you . . . that happened,' she says, 'and I should take it as a kindness if you did not remind him.'

And so the die is cast. I'm to be at the hospital tomorrow afternoon at two-thirty ack emma. All arranged beforehand,

211

of course; they must have known I would go. But oh God, that poor darling Rupe should suffer so.

21st March I went. And feel so angry I should like to dash out here and now and burn down the War Office! Anything, *anything* to shake our stupid, senseless, callous masters out of their obstinate complacency. Those smug gentlemen, with their wing collars and 'grave' faces, who maim and crucify our young men as casually as a party of small boys playing a game of conkers. I thought I was inured by now to the horrors of this dreadful war, but seeing Rupe – my beautiful, golden, smiling, arrogant Rupe – lying there so mangled and so pitiful in that horrible place this afternoon, was almost more than I could bear.

Of course I didn't scream, or shout, or tear my hair, I was as hypocritical as the rest of them. 'Hullo, my darling,' I said, smiling brightly, 'I thought you wouldn't approve of flowers, so I've brought you cigars instead. I hope you'll be allowed to smoke them.' Dr Swanley, an exhausted-looking individual in a crumpled white coat, mimed frantic disapproval from the other side of the bed, but Rupe's head, in its helmet of bandages, moved on the pillow. Slowly, his fingers began to crawl over the sheet towards mine. We waited, holding our breath, for him to speak. We had to wait a long time, but the words came at last and with them the dry ghost of a laugh: 'Hope you got them from Bellamy's . . .'

'Of course,' I said, 'where else?' He didn't speak again, although I'm certain he was aware of my presence. I spent the remainder of my allotted fifteen minutes (Dr Swanley having departed, satisfied, presumably, that I was not the scarlet woman he had no doubt been led to expect) describing in painstaking detail the view out of the window behind Rupe's bed, and when that subject was exhausted, inventing stories about his fellow inmates. I was fast running out of things to say by the time Sister, grim as a mother superior, tapped me smartly on the shoulder and announced my time was up. I lent forward to kiss Rupe's poor, bandaged face, but the woman seized me by the arm quite roughly and pulled me away. For a moment I wanted to hit her. I didn't, of course. Head bent, I meekly followed her down the interminable length of the ward, trying not to look at the pathetic, broken occupants of the beds on either side.

'You can find your own way out, I'm sure,' Sister said when we at last reached the top of the stairs, looking me up and down as though I were a scullery-maid applying for a position at the big house. 'We must hope so,' I replied, giving her look for look. 'Bellevue is certainly not the most salubrious of hospitals to get lost in. By the by, the standard of cleanliness prevailing on the domestic side does leave a certain amount to be desired, don't you agree? Perhaps Matron would like me to put in a word for you with my chairman, Sir Humphrey Jones? He might possibly be able to allocate a few extra cleaning staff. I noticed some unemptied rubbish in my husband's ward; we can't have that now, can we?' I've seldom seen a woman look more flummoxed. She turned brick-red, gobbled a bit like an over-sexed turkey, and with a crack of starched apron and a whiff of carbolic, she turned on her heel and flounced away.

I felt a little better after that, but truth to tell it was a pyrrhic victory. Shall I be summoned again? Will I go if I am? I feel as though I were being torn in half, and there's so much to *do*.

5th April   'Look here, we should like you to visit my brother again – two-thirty on Thursday, if you will.' Rosa on the telephone. 'And perhaps this time you could refrain from upsetting the nursing staff. I'm sure you must appreciate how busy they are.' For a moment. I'm quite speechless with rage. To hell with the stupid, bigoted woman and her stupid, bigoted conventions! Then I see poor Rupe's bandaged face; the slow march of his fingers across the bedclothes. ('May I have the honour of this dance – you do waltz, I take it?' A smiling young god looking down at me. 'Oh yes, yes . . .')

'Yes, Rosa,' I say through clenched teeth. 'I will visit Rupert. But in agreeing to do so, I must make certain things quite clear. First, I will visit him as and when I can most suitably fit the visit in with my many commitments, and second, I will be treated with the common courtesy due to anyone visiting a sick friend or relative in hospital. Do I make myself clear?'

'Only too clear, and if you think – '

'I do not think, I am simply stating my terms. And as I have no more desire to see you than you, I'm sure, have to see me, I will arrange for my secretary to ring the hospital and give them due warning of my arrival, thus eliminating any risk of our visits coinciding. As to Thursday, I cannot possibly be there at two-thirty, but will arrive as soon as possible after four o'clock. Perhaps you would be good enough to warn Dr Swanley of the change in times?' There was a silence. Would she hang up? I could feel the stupid tears of anger beginning to trickle down my nose.

'Very well. But let it be understood that if I find your visits are in any way at all upsetting my brother, they will cease. I hope that I, too, make myself clear.' With a hand that shook ever so slightly, I quietly replaced the receiver. Then picking up the paperweight that stands by the telephone on Granny's desk, I hurled it with all my might into the fireplace.

And I have to admit Rosa keeps her side of the bargain. Dr Swanley and I are now firm friends, and the nurses are courteous and helpful. Only Sister is conspicuous by her absence.

And Rupe? He does progress, only a mite each day, but he does. I find myself down there most evenings now. It's only twenty minutes in the train from London Bridge, and Dr Swanley sends a hospital car to meet me at the station. Yesterday the bandages were removed. Somehow it's worse now you can see the poor, scarred face underneath, with the sight of one eye completely gone and only a very little life left in the other.

This evening he pointed to the dress I was wearing – the blue one with the white collar. 'Pretty,' he said, 'ver . . y pretty.' Oh God.

8th May   Nearly summer. London smells of lilac and lime trees, and the park is full of couples making love. And why not, I say, there's not much else for them to do, is there, but die?

Dined with Dr Swanley last night in a hotel near the hospital. Such a nice, nice man. 'I care for you, Mrs Eagon,' he says over the soup, 'I care for you most awfully.'

Rupe is to be moved to a pukka convalescent home in Hampshire. He will have a room of his own and a personal attendant, Mama Eagon presiding – she's taken a house in the nearby village. He's been seen by a 'top Harley Street man', who pronounces with the smooth and oily relish of his kind that my darling Rupe will never get much better than he is now. This means that at the age of thirty-two he has become like an old man of eighty, with all the indignities attendant on that state: failing memory, eyesight, mind, barely able to creep about with the aid of a stick or a person's arm. Sometimes I feel it's not to be borne, and pray to a God I do not believe in that he should die quickly, with no more fuss and no more pain. Then he suddenly laughs, or points to a flower, or runs a finger through my hair, or even makes a feeble joke, and I feel like a murderess.

I gather from Con that *la famille Eagon* are becoming a mite suspicious of yours truly. They think, she reports, I am after Rupe's money. 'James and I had the most *splendid* row about it when he was down at Bengers the other day. Rosa sided with James, of course, but Mama stuck up for you. "I do not in any way condone Lally's behaviour in the past, but whatever else she may be, the girl is not a gold-digger," she said.'

Bravo Mama Eagon!

1st June   And now I'm allowed to vote – how very gracious our masters are! In an act of celebration, I have joined the Labour Party.

Saw Rupe on Sunday – tea on the lawn at 'Chestnuts' to the coo of wood pigeons and the gentle murmur of upper-crust voices. I think – only think, mind – he's beginning to remember. Would it not be better if he didn't? Surely he has endured enough already.

A letter from Jack D. He's been on 'prolonged' sick leave. ''Flu, would you believe,' he writes. Apparently the medics, after much grave consultation, informed him that four years of war must have lowered his resistance – *quelle surprise*!

20th June   Dined last night with Jack D. at the Savoy Grill. He looks pale and thin – but don't they all. The subject uppermost in both our minds wasn't mentioned until the end of the evening.

'And Ju,' I asked, feeling the usual clammy clutch of apprehension, 'have you any news? He doesn't write, you know.' Jack makes a great business of lighting our cigarettes, then leaves his smoking on the ashtray while he makes little squares on the tablecloth with matches.

'Come on, Jack, tell me . . . please.'

'He was in hospital in France last Christmas,' he says at last, still playing with his matches. 'Got some gas in his lungs, apparently. Then the idiot turned down convalescent leave and went back to his regiment. Now he's in hospital again, somewhere in the south of France, the Pater had a long letter only the other day while I was at home – he hadn't heard for months. Look, Lally, would you like another brandy? Hang on a minute while I attract the waiter's attention – '

'I don't want another brandy, I want to know what has happened to Ju. Why hasn't anyone told me, why – '

'Calm down, old girl. The Pater will be writing, I'm sure he will. It's not that bad, anyway, not bad at all, really. Ju's letter was awfully funny – you know what he's like.'

'But I don't know what he's like, do I, not now? I'm asking you to tell me.' I can hear my voice rising hysterically: several well-bred diners turn well-bred faces in well-bred surprise; people don't have tantrums in the Savoy Grill.

'Come on, old thing,' Jack pats my hand and makes soothing noises, as though I were a horse. 'Calm down.' And (as usual) I feel ashamed of myself for such a display of feeling. 'But why is Ju in hospital again, Jack, why?'

'He had a bit of a breakdown, that's all. "Always said a loony bin was my spiritual home and now I know I'm right," he wrote in his letter to the Pater, the ass.'

That was really all I could get out of him, he plainly didn't want to tell me any more, or perhaps he didn't know. How odd it is, the way the young men in this war maintain such a conspiracy of silence on the subject of their suffering. Will they ever tell, those that survive? I doubt it. However, he did at least give me the address of Ju's hospital somewhere near Arles, apparently a chateau owned by a family he knew before the war. So at least my darling has fallen among friends. Shall I write? No, no, he wouldn't want me to. Oh Ju.

1st July   19 Ladysmith Road

A fortnight's rest at Bigbury. Did I say rest? Mother is far more exhausting than work, Bigbury is bleak and shuttered, and it rains every day. I look at family photos and try not to argue with Mother. At least there's darling Pol round the corner.

I write every day to Rupe. They say he waits each morning

for my letter, and when it comes, insists it be read to him several times over. Oh, but it's hard to think of things to say. I've invented a ghastly family who live next door, and report daily on their doings. Is it Ju's influence that helps me make him laugh?

18th August   Yesterday morning I woke, stark naked, in someone else's bed! And how, may one ask, did that come about, Miss Lally? We . . ll –

Binky Burrell – she's back in town: 'Everyone says the war's nearly over now, and besides I find the country quite suffocating' – gave a party. I arrived late, tired, hungry, and so down that for two pins I'd have jumped into the river. I was met at the door by this young Irishman. 'Well, if it isn't the blessed Queen Maeve herself, come back from the dead,' he says, taking me by the hand and leading me to where the drink is. And somehow it goes on from there. He's a poet and a Fenian and goodness knows what else, but he has lovely Irish blue eyes and black curly hair and he makes me laugh. And when did I last do that, pray?

Well, one thing led to another, and he asked if he could come home with me. I said no, because I lived with my granny. 'You're a liar,' he said. 'I'm not,' I said, and we both fell about laughing. In the end we went to his room in Paddington. I can remember arriving, and the noise of trains, then nothing more. Did we make love? I suppose we must have. Do I feel guilty, or even anything? Not really. But it was nice to laugh a little.

The Irishman's name is Tommy Flynn. I know because he left a note pinned to the pillow. The note, addressed to 'Miss Lally', says: 'Have urgent business in Birmingham – stay as long as you want – there's eggs and bacon in the box under the window and the bathroom is six flights down. You are beautiful as a summer's day in Co Kildare – I wonder if we shall see each other again. Tommy (Flynn if you're interested)
PS   Did you know you talk in your sleep??'

'I trust everything is all right, Miss Lally. Cook and I were worried.'

'I'm sorry, Chivers, I should have telephoned. It was so late I stayed the night at Mrs Burrell's.'

15th September   Saw Ned off to his new school this after-

217

noon. Twenty little shavers in new suits, all on the verge of tears.

'Goodbye, Mama,' says Ned, frowning like a little old man, and shakes me by the hand.

'Goodbye, old Aunty Lou,' he says, flinging his arms round his Aunt Louisa Eagon, 'and don't you dare forget that cake you promised, and remember to take Ruff for his walk every day, and tell Tomkins to make sure Starlight has his bran mash and, and . . .' Aunty Louisa is crying, and so am I, but for different reasons.

Please God let him be happy at St David's and don't, don't let him be bullied.

12th November   2 a.m.   And now it's all over, and I sit by my window listening to the noise in the streets: the people celebrating the end of their madness. Is my heart broken? I wonder. It seems so hard to feel anything any more.

Rupe is getting worse. The doctors say they don't think he will live to see the New Year. And Ju, and Bob, and Bertie, and those millions of others who are gone – what of them?

From *The Times*, 4th January 1919
    EAGON, Rupert John. Peacefully, on 2nd January, after a
    long illness incurred in the service of his country, Captain
    Rupert Eagon, MC, eldest son of the late Mr James Eagon
    and Mrs Eagon of Bengers Court, Axminster, Devonshire.
    No flowers.

The rest, it seems, is silence. No more from Lally on the subject of herself And no more from anybody else either.

I switched off the light and slept.

PART IX

It was the following morning, while looking through Marcus's old school magazine, that I found the letters.

Marcus and I had been working away for a couple of hours or more in the box-room, sorting, stacking, throwing out, exclaiming, even laughing from time to time, last night's camaraderie mercifully still with us. We discovered the magazines tangled up in an old football jersey and some distinctly moth-eaten Christmas decorations, half-in half-out of an ancient cardboard box, one side of which had collapsed with age. For some reason I've always found old school magazines an irresistible read; there's something so safe and dependable about them; one always knows exactly what they're going to say and they never really seem to date – Marcus's and mine are virtually interchangeable. So, feeling it was about time I had a break anyway, I settled myself down on a convenient trunk and prepared to enjoy myself. Deep in a graphic description of Fathers' Match at Gordon House (Marcus's Prep School) circa 1972 ('Wolf senior made a most respectable twenty-four before being clean bowled by Trumpington major') I turned the page, and there they were.

Two envelopes, both old, both covered in brightly-coloured Egyptian stamps, and both addressed to Dad at Grandpa Hen's in Coltswood. One, buff-coloured, official, typewritten; the other a rather sickly blue, stained with what looked like coffee, written in thin, faded ink with a spluttering pen in what surely must be my grandfather's hand. How they came to be there, heaven knows. I suppose they must have dropped out of something else, and someone – Amy probably – tucked them into the school mag for safe-keeping.

'They wanted to be found, Dad,' Marcus claimed later, 'it's a phenomenon most researchers have experienced at one time or another.' Well, I wouldn't know, would I, never having been a researcher, but as I called him over to look I remember my hands were trembling so much they appeared to have a life of their own, and for two pins I would have burst into tears. They were, of course, what we were looking for, and it was after we had read them that I gave the 'lucky cat' to Marcus.

Here they are. First my grandfather's.

My dear old boy,

Yr Christmas letter just received – must have been following me round for months. I've been somewhat on the go lately (should it be, perhaps, on the go somewhat?), but who cares, I am only a little drunk; if I were more drunk I should probably care more. Anyway, the gut-rot I am forced to imbibe in this God-forsaken hole has given me a gyppy tummy and the grey matter is not working as it should (does it ever?).

My dear boy, what questions you ask! You should not, you know. It never pays to ask questions, I found that out myself at a very early age. Accept your mother's tale of me – why not? It will do as well as any other, and truth after all is relative. Your mother's mistake lay in her wanting to marry me. We were married, by the way, all right and tight, in case you have any doubts on that score. And a very queer old occasion it was, if I remember rightly – Paddington Register Office, me with a cold as thick as a treacle sandwich, your mother sick as a duck in a thunderstorm, and your Uncle Horace, the only one of her family to attend (none of mine did) so inebriated that he fell down twice during the ceremony. I told your mother she was making a mistake but she refused to listen; she was *enciente* at the time with you, which no doubt accounts for her insistence. She was a taking little thing, though. Is she still, I wonder? All brown curls and big blue eyes, and a penchant for large hats which, in conjunction with her rather short stature, made her look like an animated mushroom. Now, where was I? The black-assed bastard who passes as a waiter in this hell-hole has just refused to serve me another drink. No matter, I shall take my custom elsewhere.

I met your stepfather once, did you know? He was a major then, very pukka – polished Sam Brown, interestin' pallor and one arm in a sling. I'm not sure he didn't sport a monocle, but I can't be certain. 'Wolf,' he says, all flashing teeth and bristling moustache, 'you're a cad and a bounder.

Go to the devil if you must, but leave your boy with Florrie and me. I'll bring him up as my own, you have my word on that.' It was an offer which, under the circumstances prevailing at the time (come to think of it, they've prevailed ever since) I could not refuse.

My boy, you tell me you are bored at home, that you feel hemmed in by middle-class mediocrity. You are lucky!

Many great men have emerged from such a stable. So you disagree with everything 'the Henshaw philosophy stands for'. This is, of course, your right, but don't throw it away too lightly; the world beyond it is both a heartless and a chilly place. I know, and from a younger age than you are now, I knew. My father was a devil, you see. Rich, I grant you, but a devil for all that, who nightly perpetrated upon my poor defenceless mother such cruelties as eventually to drive her into an asylum and from thence to an early grave. And if I had to choose between my childhood and yours, despite the 'stifling gentility' you claim prevails at No 18 Foxglove Avenue, I know which I would plump for.

So you may – as you so colourfully put it – feel like a cuckoo in a nest of crows (by the way, I don't wish to be pedantic, dear boy, but I'm doubtful as to the correctness of your simile – cuckoos and crows??) and deplore the dullness of your adopted family. So your life lacks the singing and the gold which, with the arrogance of youth, you claim to be your birthright – so be it. If you still feel this way in a year or so when you have finished your studies, by all means go out into the world and prove that you are right. But for the Lord's sake – and I do not speak lightly – wait until then.

I was flattered, indeed I was, I even shed a tear or two as I lay on the bug-ridden palliasse which passes for a bed in the 'hotel' I currently occupy, when I read your wish to 'leave it all' and join me out here. But my dear boy, it wouldn't do, you know; it simply would not do. I've been alone too long to want to care for another. Besides, I'm told if I continue my present way of life I shall be dead within the year, and what would you do then, my son, what would you do then? No, stay safe and warm at No 18 until you are ready to fly and then . . . voila. Fly.

I must finish now. The paper (and ink) is running out, and I have to clear my mind for this evening's 'performance'. Yes, I still perform (that is, when I'm not too drunk to stand).

Write again, my boy, if you have the urge. The fellows at the Café Vespasian, rascals though they are, will always seek me out. If you deem it appropriate, give my regards to your mother and stepfather. You could, perhaps (again, only if the time seems ripe) remind the former of a certain afternoon at Kew amongst the daffodils, when for a moment or two, amidst 'this vale of tears' there was indeed some light.

Yr loving father
J.M. Wolf

Then the other, typewritten on Cairo University writing paper, dated 3rd January 1926.

Dear Mr Wolf,

I greatly regret to inform you that your father, Julian Marcus Wolf, was found dead in his room at the Café Vespasian early yesterday morning. The cause of death diagnosed by the doctor attending was bronchopneumonia.

Your father had not been well for some weeks previous to his death, but had continued to do his twice-nightly performance at the Café Vespasian. I myself saw him last on Christmas Day, when he partook of Christmas dinner with my wife and myself at our house in the suburbs. He was in good spirits, but looked sadly ill and frail. My wife, Marian, endeavoured to persuade him to stay on with us for a few days and take things easy for a little while. But he refused, claiming it was essential he did not miss a performance, or the proprietor of the café would replace him, thereby causing not only the loss of his only source of income, but his lodgings as well. Against such arguments we were powerless, but both my wife and I were loth to let him go.

I met your father early in 1925, when I came out here to teach at the university. I was taken to see him perform one night by a colleague, soon after I arrived. Stunned by the brilliance of his act, I went round to see him afterwards to express my appreciation, and from then on we became firm friends. In the short time I knew him, I came to value your father as both a friend and, in my opinion, a great artist. He was, however, a very private man, and in spite of our many evenings together, sometimes talking far into the night, he never spoke of the circumstances which – though blessed with such great gifts – led him to choose his present way of life. I think he appreciated the fact that I never asked, and for this reason trusted me. He did, however, speak of you, his son in England, and on going through his things after his death, I came across a bundle of your letters (these are being returned to you under separate cover) and by this means obtained your address.

No doubt, you will in due course be officially informed of your father's death through the proper channels, but in Cairo these things take time. I have taken the task upon myself, as one of the last things Julian asked of me was that I should act as an 'unofficial executor' in the event of his death. 'Everything I have goes to the boy,' he said, 'there isn't much, but what there is I should like him to have.' Unfortunately, your father's room was ransacked for anything of value before the doctor arrived, leaving nothing but a few books (which I have taken the liberty of keeping) your letters, and the enclosed lucky charm. I remember the charm well, it always hung on your father's watch-chain. I found it on the floor by his bed. Presumably the scoundrel who stole the watch, in his haste, must have dropped it. Your father always referred to it as his 'lucky cat' and never liked to be without it when on the stage.

May I once more express my very great regret at your father's untimely death; please accept my profound sympathy at your great loss. May I also say that my wife, Marian, and I will always be delighted to offer you our hospitality if you ever feel like spending a few days with us in Cairo.

Yours very sincerely
Edward McFadden

After that, Marcus and I abandoned the box-room and went out to lunch.

PART X

That was a pretty eventful weekend in one way and another. Following a fairly inebriated lunch at the local – I'd consumed more alcohol in the few weeks since I'd first encountered Lally Flynn than I had in the whole of the previous year – Marcus and I arrived home to the sound of the phone ringing.

'I've been trying to get you for hours, where on earth have you been?' Amanda from a call-box, on a bad line. 'In the pub with my son, as it happens,' I shouted, 'I do have a life outside Palmer's Building, you know.'

'You're pissed, I can tell by your voice.'

'You may well be right,' I said, 'we were celebrating the return of my grandfather. What can I do for you?'

'Well, actually,' she said, 'it's him I was ringing about, or indirectly. Cousin Alice is staying at the Francis – she couldn't make the funeral – and wants to see you. Can I bring her round this evening?'

'And who, may one ask, is Cousin Alice? If she's anything like Cousin Jeremy, the answer is no.'

'She isn't, and incidentally, I don't know why you always have to be so rude. Cousin Alice is my Great-Great-Aunt Con's daughter – the Con that married Herbie Potter.'

'Oh well, in that case,' I said, feeling the familiar curl of excitement, 'bring her to dinner.'

I suppose it was inevitable that Amanda and Marcus should fall for one another, anyway Philippa said it was. From the first moment Amanda stuck her head out of the taxi window and yelled at Marcus – who was gawping at the sitting-room window – to come and organise the dogs (two enchanting pugs) while she organised Cousin Alice, one could see how it would be. And at the end of the evening, scorning my suggestion of a mini-cab for the two ladies, he announced that he would drive them home in my car, dropping Cousin Alice off at the Francis and then going on with Amanda and the two dogs – the dogs, not welcome at a three star hotel, were staying at Palmer's Building for the weekend.

Needless to say, he did not return until morning.

Cousin Alice turned out to be a tall, thin, intelligent-looking lady with brown eyes (Herbie's?) and a very determined chin. She had been a GP for years, but had now retired, had never married, and suffered from arthritis. Like her mother before her, she adored dogs. Merry thought she was quite wonderful. Over the chicken Kiev and peach flambé ('How delightfully you cook, Mr Wolf, young men are so clever nowadays; in my day, if a man could do so much as boil an egg he was considered a sissy') she gave her version of Lally.

'My Aunt Lally', she said, 'was a totally splendid person. Mum and Dad adored her, so did we children. When she was young she had red hair just like Amanda, and she used to organise the most marvellous games. When I was a child we lived in a big shabby house with an enormous garden in Dulwich, and one of my earliest memories of Aunty Lally is in that garden. I can see her now, wearing a pale green summer dress and standing under the chestnut tree on the lawn, the sun shining through the branches, catching the lights in her red hair. She was laughing at something Mum had said – that wonderful, husky, infectious laugh. And I remember thinking she was the most beautiful person I had ever seen. But of course it was later, when I grew up, that I really came to know her. I had a room in her flat in Kensington when I was a student at medical school; in fact the place became my second home, really, until after the war when I went into general practice and had a house of my own.

'Number 18 Glenarvon Mansions! Aunty Lally lived there for years – right up until 1960 when she moved to Bath. Everybody who was anybody in the Labour Party, from Ramsay Mac and Nye Bevan to the young Harold Wilson, knew it at some time in their careers. She was a very political animal, my Aunty Lally, and if you stayed at Glenarvon Mansions you were expected to work for the cause. I remember her disapproval when Dad got his knighthood' (so young Herbie Potter had made it, had he, I always thought he would). '"Sir Herbert Potter, my arse," she said, "you're a rat, Herbie Potter, you've sold out to the capitalists".) I remember Hugh Gaitskell at one of her Sunday-night supper parties saying . . .'

And so it went on. Cousin Alice was an amusing and vivid raconteuse; her stories of the famous and not so famous figures in the Labour Movement who had known and loved her Aunt Lally were fascinating. Lally putting up Jarrow marchers, organising arms for Spain, evacuees, bombed-out families in the blitz, extinguishing an incendiary bomb on the roof of her flats after a party, broadcasting to the Free French, celebrating VE Night – stirring stuff indeed. And yet . . . Somehow I felt cheated. I had so looked forward to meeting Con's daughter, but it wasn't all this that I had wanted to hear.

'Your aunt never, er, married again, did she, Dr Potter' I asked, trembling a little at my own audacity, and taking advantage of the small pause occasioned by her bending down to feed one of the pugs a small piece of cheese. 'I mean, after Tommy Flynn. You see, I don't know if Amanda has told you, but I have your aunt's diaries and – '

'Amanda told me, Mr Wolf. She also told me you were asked to burn them'. There was a hint of reprimand in Dr Potter's voice. We were all quiet for a minute; unaccountably, a wisp of tension had entered the proceedings. Eagons versus Wolfs again, Philippa said afterwards, but I don't think it was that.

Dr Potter passed another lump of cheese to the watcher under the table, then wiped her fingers on her paper napkin. We waited. 'If I understand you aright, Mr Wolf, you are asking about my aunt's love-life. She was a beautiful woman, she left her husband to live with another man at a time when people of her class rarely did such things, and you cannot believe she spent the rest of her life devoted to public service. In other words, you want me to "dish the dirt". Is that it?'

Suddenly I was angry. Why on earth did it matter? But it did. 'I've read your aunt's diaries,' I said, trying to keep the emotion out of my voice. 'I held her hand when she was dying. Even in the short time I knew her, I think I came to love her, but she was no saint. I now believe that what happened between her and my grandfather, Julian Wolf, had repercussions – at least, as far as my own family is concerned – that continue to this day. I know a great deal of your aunt's story already: I don't wish to hear "the dirt", Dr Potter, but how that story ended.'

There was another long silence. Philippa said afterwards that she had been about to stage a fainting fit, unable in the heat of the moment to think of any less drastic method of breaking the tension. I remember looking up from my plate and seeing Marcus's eyes, half closed, watching me through the flickering candle flame; he appeared to be laughing. Then at last, proving herself the 'lovely woman' Amanda claimed her to be, Alice Potter gulped down the rest of her wine, looked me straight in the eye and apologised. And after that, as they say, everything went splendidly.

It was during subsequent conversations with her, however – I spent a couple of days at her house on the river in Hammersmith a month or so later, while arranging the winding-up of the lease on No 4 St Wilfred's Square – that she told me what she knew of Lally in the years immediately following Rupe's death. In 1919 Alice was only five years old, so inevitably her knowledge of that time, and of the years leading up to my grandfather's death in Egypt in 1926, was pretty patchy, gleaned mainly from her mother, whose reminiscences in later years had become increasingly muddled. Lally herself rarely spoke of the past; if she did, it was in terms of political statistics rather than her own emotions. But the following is a brief account of the facts as far as Alice Potter knew them.

Not long after the Armistice, Lally became a victim of the terrible influenza that swept Europe immediately after the war. She attended Rupe's funeral in January 1919 (much to the Eagon family's annoyance) but succumbed shortly afterwards. The Eagons had cause for annoyance; Rupe left everything, apart from a trust fund for Ned, to Lally. Their annoyance was compounded by the fact that in the years that followed she spent most of it in forwarding the interests of the Labour Party.

Anyway, after a long illness in which she very nearly died, and was devotedly nursed back to life by Con, she announced that she was going to live in Paris. (This would have been around 1920). Alice said her mother had always been convinced that Lally went to Paris to find Julian; she knew for certain she had received a letter from him; but Lally would never speak of him. She had practically no money: the Eagons contested Rupe's Will, and it was several years before she came into possession of the estate. Her grandmother, Mrs Morgan, refused to back such a hair-brained scheme, and she was still in a pretty weak state both mentally and physically. Despite all this, she went.

She remained in Paris for four years, and apart from a brief note to Con saying she had remarried and would write more fully later, nothing was heard from her during all that time. It is known that Julian left for his ill-fated tour of the States towards the end of 1920, so whether they met again, or even briefly lived together, no one really knows. If they did, it must have been very brief indeed, and if that was the case, why did she not go with him to America?

Then sometime in the autumn of 1924 ('after we'd moved to Dulwich and Dad had been made a manager') Con had a letter from Jack Dugdale saying he had bumped into Lally in a bar in Paris, and in his opinion she was in a pretty bad way. She'd obviously been hitting the bottle, and had become none too choosy about who she woke up with in the mornings. 'He put it more delicately, of course, but Mum knew that was what he meant.' Questioned, Lally had told Jack she'd married an Irish poet by the name of Tommy Flynn in 1922. Apparently she and Flynn had originally met during the war, but had lost touch with one another. Then in 1922 he turned up again at some studio party in Paris. The party lasted three days, and at the end of it Lally and Flynn were married. Not surprisingly, the marriage was not a success and the pair were already separated by the time the poet met his untimely death in the Metro. When Jack found her, Lally was living in a couple of rooms in a pretty slummy area of Montmartre, and scratching some sort of living by typing for an agency.

On being apprised of this news, Con instantly despatched Herbie to Paris to find her and bring her back. 'Mum said she told Dad she'd never speak to him again unless he brought Aunt Lally home with him.' A quite unnecessary threat; Herbie, as usual, came up trumps. 'He could do most things if he set his mind to it, could Dad.'

Back in England, Lally seems to have put the past behind her. After spending several months at Dulwich with the Potters – this was the period when Alice Potter first remembered her – and with the Eagon money now finally hers, she bought the lease of 18 Glenarvon Mansions, and there began her long career in politics and public service. A few years later she also acquired a tumbledown cottage in Devon with an acre of more or less virgin land, and proceeded to turn this into 'the most beautiful garden you ever saw'. Only the most privileged of her friends were allowed to stay at the cottage, 'but she really preferred to be there on her own'. Alice remembered her saying once that the garden was all that was left of her other self. 'If she didn't hang on to that, she might die, and she couldn't let that happen yet, there was too much to do.'

As to my grandfather, apparently Alice had no idea of his existence until she was well on into her twenties. 'You know how people used to cover things up. It all happened so long ago, and only a few old fogies in the London clubs, and of course the Eagon family, remembered. My cousin Ned, never spoke of it. He and his mother didn't get on. Sad, really, he was like her in many ways, certainly just as obstinate. But she always got on very well with his daughter, Amanda's mother – it's often so, isn't it, jump a generation and you get a better understanding. Of course Ned was a rabid Tory, which didn't help, and I don't think he ever forgave Aunt Lally for leaving his father.

'Mum told me about Julian Wolf one Christmas just before the last war. We'd all got a bit tiddly, I remember, including Mum, and she suddenly started talking about this Christmas 1915 they'd all spent together – she and Dad, Aunt Lally, and this man called Julian Wolf – what fun they'd had, and how there'd never been another Christmas quite like it. Naturally I asked a few pertinent questions, and it all came out. Mum always used to say that Ju Wolf was a marvellous person to be with, and he and Aunt Lally were so much in love it almost hurt to see them together.'

'Everyone says what a marvellous person my grandfather was to be with, and yet everyone forgot him,' I said, surprised at the bitterness in my voice – what did I care? Cousin Alice patted me on the shoulder; I might have been ten years old. 'Calm down, David dear, it's all old history now. Aunt Lally went out to Cairo, you know, to see his grave. She read of his death in the newspapers, it must have been awful for her.'

I suppose it must have been.

I think it was during the course of some other conversation with Cousin Alice that I asked her, as delicately as I could –

one had to go carefully with Cousin Alice – whether there had been any successors to Tommy Flynn.

'A few,' she said, 'over the years, but none of them serious. The last one was a Polish officer during World War Two; Boris was an absolute sweetie and incredibly handsome – Poles are, aren't they – I was half in love with him myself, but he had no eyes for anyone but Aunt Lally. When that was over, she announced it had been her swansong. "Never," she said, "will I let myself become one of those dreadful creatures – all face-lifts, dyed hair and long fingernails – who chase after young men half their age. From henceforth I shall remain celibate." And so she did. But of course there were always young around her – until the day she died.' I thought of the crowd outside Palmer's Building, of Kevin, Dwight, Amanda herself, and knew that she was right.

But to return to that weekend, the one where I met Alice Potter for the first time and Marcus met Amanda. I said it was eventful, and it was. It was on that Sunday I asked Philippa if she would marry me.

I had decided I wanted to go back to Whitesgreen now I knew so much more, now I knew why Lally had wanted to be buried there. And it may sound morbid, but I wanted to find that headstone Lally and Ju had left behind 'together with their lost youth'. Philippa just seemed the obvious person to go with me. In spite of our new-found comradeship I didn't really want Marcus; I didn't feel I could take his particular brand of transatlantic humour, or cope with the inevitable emotion – two Wolfs together would be altogether too much.

Sunday turned out to be a most glorious day – air like wine, hedges alive with fresh, young green, early orchids already showing on the downs, the sky a gentle washed-out blue. We lunched at the pub where Lally's funeral 'do' had taken place (curry and chips, but the beer wasn't bad). Enquiries re Glebe Cottage drew a blank, until a village ancient came out with the fact that there had been a Glebe Cottage 'up Skinners Lane, pulled down near thirty year ago' to make way for Glebe Close.

The walk up the hill was the same, though, except that the railway station, and even the track, had disappeared; you could just see the contours of the old line winding through the lush green valley meadows. At the top of the hill we stopped, and stood staring glumly into the mouth of Glebe Close, which turned out to be a nest of bungalows and three-bedroomed semis circa 1960. I have to admit that the shrubs in the gardens were quite spectacular. Incidentally, I've often wondered how plant-breeders manage to achieve that parti-cular shade of toothpaste-pink for the modern flowering cherry, it must have taken them years. However, above the whirr of electric mowers, the revving of motorbikes and the gentle drone of a disc-jockey on Radio Wilts, one could just about – if one listened very carefully – hear the cry of a lark up on the downs behind the estate, and of course there was always the view.

Philippa frowned, and picked a dandelion. 'I think this is all a bit silly,' she said, 'what on earth did you expect to find?'

'I don't know,' I said, 'I've never done this sort of thing before, but now I'm doing it I intend to do it properly.'

'Lovely afternoon – looking for someone?' An elderly man in a blue jockey-cap and a flowery shirt emerged from his spotlessly tidy garage. 'Not really,' I said, 'I think they left years ago.'

'What was their name? I know everyone in the Close, we've lived here since 1963.'

'Wolf,' I said. The man took off his jockey-cap and scratched his bald head, then put the cap back on again. 'No one ever lived here by the name of Wolf,' he said, 'must be another estate. Sorry I can't help you.'

'Now you're just being childish,' Philippa said as we walked back to the car. I began to wish I hadn't brought her.

We had better luck with the vicar. 'Oh yes, Mr Wolf, the grave is still there – in the south-west corner of the old churchyard, just to the left of the yew. Perhaps you didn't know, but Mrs Flynn made a covenant many, many years ago – long before my time – to have the grave kept tidy, and it has been kept tidy ever since. We spoke about it when I took tea with Mrs Flynn shortly before her death. Such a remarkable old lady, I was only sorry she couldn't be buried nearer the other grave, as she wished, but tempus fugit and perforce the modern burials are further down the hill.'

Julia Constance Wolf, born 8th February 1916,
departed this life 13th February of the same year.
And Jesus said: 'Suffer little children to come
unto me, for of such is the Kingdom of God'.

Oddly enough, it was Dad's face I saw as I stood looking down at the small headstone, the patch in front of it neatly mown, listening to the wind in the chestnut trees that towered above the drystone boundary wall. Actually, Dad had been cremated; Mother thought it best. 'When you go, you go,' she used to say, 'and that's the end of it. Anyway, cremation is so much more hygienic.' But I wished suddenly that he'd been buried like his half-sister, with a headstone in a country churchyard. Somewhere where I could come and say I was sorry; sorry for the things I'd said, sorry for those last years – sorry for so much. Because it was Dad, wasn't it (and the knowledge when it came was almost overwhelming), poor old Dad with his bad jokes, his style, his hopelessness, his longing to be loved, Dad who never quite made it, who had been the real victim of Lally and Ju's great romance. Not little Julia, not my grandfather – after all, he'd had had his genius, and came to think of it, a hell of a lot besides; OK, the tragedy was there, but at least he'd had a good run for his money. And certainly not Lally, she'd had more than any of us. But Dad . . .

I could hear myself crying – it was most odd – harsh, grating sobs, as though they were coming from someone else.

'I've found a tap at the back of the porch to fill the vase . . .' Philippa, a bunch of sweet-scented narcissus and blue hyacinth in one hand, a jar of water in the other. The sound of the jar falling on the stone path behind me. 'David. Oh David.'

Driving home through the quiet Wiltshire countryside, the lovely day almost over, and just a faint, residual nip of winter still left in the air as the sun went down, I asked Philippa if she would marry me. She said she'd think about it, but I knew she would, and she did.

And we duly burned the diaries. It was Marcus's idea to make a ceremony of it. He seems to have inherited his great-grandfather's flair for the dramatic, he certainly doesn't get it from me.

237

The lease of No 4 St Wilfred's Square was due to come to an end that October, the Wolf family having held it for eighty-eight of its ninety-nine years. Marcus's idea was that we should celebrate its passing by the four of us – Amanda and Marcus and Philippa and me – spending the night there. 'We'll get some champers in, Dad, and do the thing in style. Then we can burn the diaries in the back garden – it'll be a focal point for the party and sod the Clean Air Act.' It sounded a tempting idea, anyway, the way I felt I'd agree to anything, even one of my son's hair-brained schemes. There would be no new lease on No 4; the whole of that side of the square was due for demolition.

In the event, the whole thing was more of a party than even Marcus had envisaged. It happened to coincide with him and me appearing on a currently fashionable television chat show – much to the fury of Fiona Maplethorpe née Eagon, who happened to work for the other side. Indeed, she rang me to tell me that I had behaved like a schmuck, whatever that is, but it wasn't surprising since my grandfather had quite obviously been one too. Be that as it may, the ordeal went surprisingly smoothly, my son and I parrying our celebrity host's thrusts on the vexed question of our famous relative as best we could, assisted greatly, I might add, by the quantity of gin we had consumed in the hospitality room beforehand.

'Let him make the jokes,' hissed our producer, pointing to our host, 'if you don't, he'll tear you apart', and we were only too glad to obey. What Ju himself would have made of it all, God knows, but I could hazard a guess.

So it was in a slightly drunken, slightly ribald mood that we afterwards repaired for the last time to what Marcus insisted on calling our ancestral home. Philippa had made the big room on the ground floor – the conservatory was long since gone – quite habitable she'd even got hold of some ice for the champagne. Out in the garden my possibly future daughter-in-law, looking like a wood sprite in a long green sweater and short black mini-skirt, rushed about feeding the bonfire with old bits of wood and rotting leaves. I say possibly future daughter-in-law advisedly. Though quite obviously devoted, it was hard to envisage two such volatile individuals as Amanda Fenton-Langley and my son Marcus ever settling down together – but stranger things have happened, I suppose. Earlier that evening, Marcus had given Amanda the 'lucky cat', now hanging from a silver chain round her neck. I couldn't help thinking that this might possibly be a mistake – in my view, the little cat should go on the bonfire with the diaries. But, as usual, I was howled down by the others.

It was well past midnight, the champagne was finished and a hunter's moon was sailing high over the trees of Kensington Gardens, when we consigned Lally Flynn's five notebooks to the flames.

'Well, Dad,' my son peered at me through the smoke of the bonfire, his black hair on end, his eyes mocking, 'there goes twenty grand – doesn't it hurt?' Actually, only two days before I'd been offered even more than that for them, but I hadn't dared tell anyone. We were all silent for a minute, the only sounds the crackling of the flames, the whine of a police siren far away across the park, and the grind of a late-night juggernaut rumbling down Kensington High Street on its way to the West. Beside me, Philippa was stoking the fire, her face grave, intent on what she was doing: with her hair curling round her ears in the way I loved, and wearing a dark red sweater that particularly suited her, she looked, I suddenly realised, quite beautiful.

'No,' I said at last, looking him straight in the eye, 'it doesn't hurt one bit.' Just at that moment, a page of Lally's diary uncurled, was clearly readable by the light of the flames, then crumbled and dissolved into ash.

I do not think Julian was very pleased with his cricket bat (it was Mother's idea). He said he doesn't play games, actually, but it was the thought that counted, and he could see it would be a ripping present for most fellows . . .

BELVA PLAIN

HARVEST

From the bestselling author of *Evergreen* and *Blessings*.

Iris and Theo Stern seemed to have it all: a secure marriage, four attractive children, a beautiful house filled with lovely things as well as the respect that came from Theo's work as one of the country's top surgeons.

But one outsider, Paul Werner, knew better. Watching over them with anguish, he knew of Iris's frustrations, Theo's wandering eye and affections. He saw their eldest son, Steve, bright and sensitive, beginning to rebel against the values and beliefs of his family.

But above all he knew the secret that lay buried at the heart of the Stern's seeming security and happiness. The secret that could destroy everything . . .

'Belva Plain writes with such warmth and compassion about family life that you'll enjoy every minute of this book'   *Annabel*

HODDER AND STOUGHTON PAPERBACKS

JUDITH GLOVER

TIGER LILIES

Two girls, of similar age but at opposite ends of the scale in background, education, looks and temperament.

Flora Dennison and Roseen O'Connor are linked by a secret. A strange and painful secret, powerful enough to bring their lives together again and again from their childhood in Wolverhampton through the tragic romance of the First World War and on into the wild abandon of the Twenties.

Flora, daughter of a prosperous businessman, struggles to retain her respectability and goodness despite the passionate temptation of a married man. In her heart she envies Roseen's daring lack of restraint. Roseen, child of a poor Irish widow, is educated only in the harsh realities of back-to-back poverty. Her red-haired beauty and flamboyant tastes catch all eyes but she yearns for the security of Flora's family life.

As envy turns to wary mutual respect, the two girls' contact with each other's lives will prove the turning point towards a lasting happiness.

HODDER AND STOUGHTON PAPERBACKS

LAURIE COLWIN

GOODBYE, WITHOUT LEAVING

With rock and roll in her soul, Geraldine Coleshares abandoned college to join Ruby Shakely and the Shakettes – as the only white backing singer and to the despair of her respectable parents. Now those heady days are over and the pressure is on to conform. But if she is no longer a Shakette, who is she? With wry irreverence, Laurie Colwin draws a sparkling portrait of a woman learning how to be a wife and mother while staying young at heart.

'Delightful'   *Sabine Durrant in The Times*

'Brings freshness to much-explored ground: how to stick to the guns of one's own identity ... It does a wicked job on New York Jewish society and leaves a pleasant tingle on the palate'
          Christopher Wordsworth in The Guardian

'A stylish comedy of love, restlessness and rock'n'roll'
          Company

'Laurie Colwin writes charmingly about love and marriage without being cloying'   *Today*

HODDER AND STOUGHTON PAPERBACKS

RONA JAFFE

AN AMERICAN LOVE STORY

Sophisticated, compulsive, passionate ... the ultimate love story of our age.

Four very different women, each in love with the same man. He is Clay Bowen, superstar producer, irresistibly seductive, incurably unfaithful.

Real women in the glamorous media world where only success and power are respected, *An American Love Story* is a saga of obsession, betrayal and survival.

LAURA is the prima ballerina he married for show and has driven to the edge of mental collapse.
NINA is the daughter who will risk everything for his love and attention.
SUSAN is the fiercely independent writer for whom he has become a near-fatal addiction.
BAMBI is the deviously ambitious companion of his mid-life crisis years.

'Bowen is one of those men you love to hate'
Sunday Express

'Jaffe is one of the best'   *The Sunday Times*

'A best seller'   *The Observer*

HODDER AND STOUGHTON PAPERBACKS

BRENDA MCBRYDE

HANNAH ROBSON

Hannah was twelve when she watched her mother battle with death in agonising childbirth. That day she swore no man would ever put her through such horror.

Years of thankless toil on her father's bleak Northumbrian hill farm have left her unafraid of hard work. She determines to support herself and never be at the mercy of a man. Setting out alone into the world, she encounters kindness and friendship, but trouble dogs her footsteps. In the bustling commercial life of the port in Newcastle, Hannah's courage and quick intelligence are at last rewarded. But it is only the pain of near-loss that will free her heart to love.

A triumph of a book – about a woman whose sparkle, humour, resilience and passion will not be suppressed.

'*Hannah Robson* is a memorable story of a strong-minded and delightful girl and woman. A book full of a kind of gritty warmth which gave me enormous pleasure from the first page to the last.'   *Rosemary Sutcliff*

'I enjoyed *Hannah Robson*. Hannah *is* unusual, her decision to opt out of lady's maiding and so gain independence was interesting – raised the novel above the normal historical romance.'
     Margaret Forster, Author of Lady's Maid

HODDER AND STOUGHTON PAPERBACKS

MORE TITLES AVAILABLE FROM
HODDER AND STOUGHTON PAPERBACKS

BELVA PLAIN
☐ 54290 4 Harvest   £4.99

JUDITH GLOVER
☐ 55919 5 Tiger Lilies   £4.99

LAURIE COLWIN
☐ 55984 5 Goodbye Without Leaving   £6.99

RONA JAFFE
☐ 55830 X An American Love Story   £4.50

All these books are available at your local bookshop or newsagent, or can be ordered direct from the publisher. Just tick the titles you want and fill in the form below.

Prices and availability subject to change without notice.

Hodder & Stoughton Paperbacks, P.O. Box 11, Falmouth, Cornwall.

Please send cheque or postal order for the value of the book, and add the following for postage and packing:

U.K. – 80p for one book, and 20p for each additional book ordered up to a £2.00 maximum.

B.F.P.O. – 80p for the first book, and 20p for each additional book.

OVERSEAS INCLUDING EIRE – £1.50 for the first book, plus £1.00 for the second book, and 30p for each additional book ordered.

OR Please debit this amount from my Access/Visa Card (delete as appropriate).

Card Number ☐☐☐☐☐☐☐☐☐☐☐☐☐☐☐☐☐☐

Amount £ ....

Expiry Date ....

Signed ....

Name ....

Address ....